Hits and Missives

Books by the same author:

The Ben Trovato Files

Will The Real Ben Trovato Please Stand Up?

Ben Trovato Stirred Not Shaken

Ben Trovato's Guide to Everything

Ben Trovato's Art of Survival

Ben Trovato's (mis)Guide to Golf

On The Run

First published in 2006 by Jacana Media (Pty) Ltd
Reprinted in 2008
10 Orange Street
Sunnyside 2092
Johannesburg
South Africa

ISBN 1-77009-307-9

      978-1-77009-307-2

Set in Trade Gothic 8.5/10.5
Printed by CTP Book Printers, Cape Town
Job No. 000868

See a complete list of Jacana titles at www.jacana.co.za

Hits and Missives The worst of BEN TROVATO

JACANA

ACKNOWLEDGEMENTS

This book would not have been possible were it not for Jacana's resident Irish maverick, Maggie Davey; the hundreds of people who took the time to assist me in my quest for answers and explanations; Harley's that stays open later than any other bottle store and my mother who forced me to read dangerously seditious satire when I was little. Thanks also to Marlene Fryer (aka Attila the Publisher) of Zebra Press for allowing me to cannibalise *Ben Trovato – Stirred Not Shaken*.

INTRODUCTION

I still get people coming up to me in bars and asking, "Why did you do it?" But I have learnt to control my gut instincts. I no longer shout, "It wasn't me!" and take off down the street like a common bag snatcher. These days, I stand my ground and give them the lazy eye. "What do you mean by that?" I ask.

"The letters," they say, pinning me up against the counter. "Why did you send all those letters? Did you have nothing better to do? A lot of your victims are very important people. How dare you waste their time and money? Have you no shame? How do you sleep at night, you dirty rat?"

My immediate reaction is to lash out blindly with fists and feet. But I generally refrain from doing so because my interrogator is invariably a woman and I was raised to believe that it is wrong to strike a woman. I was also raised to believe that it is wrong to abuse alcohol, experiment with drugs, mock the afflicted, drive without a licence and have sex before marriage. It took a while to separate the truth from the lies.

The modern woman is a master crafter of questions. Apparently she is also very busy because she has no time to wait for the answers. These days, when an outraged woman accosts me I slap her smartly on the bum and tell her to sit down so that I may defend myself in an orderly fashion. The bum slap works in much the same way as biting a dog on the ear. It lets them know who is in charge. So, right here, right now, let me answer those questions and put an end to this heinous harassment once and for all.

Why did I send all those letters?

I was walking along the Sea Point promenade one shiny April morning in 2001 when it struck me. It felt like a heat-seeking missile slamming into the back of my head. By the time I picked myself up off the ground, a small crowd had gathered. Not around me, but around the biggest, ugliest seagull I had ever set eyes upon.

Staunching the blood from a gaping wound left by the brute's enormous beak, I expected a little sympathy at the very least. But, no. Everyone was more concerned about the pterodactyl that sprawled unconscious on the paving. After much dark muttering and filthy looks shot in my direction, the crowd fell back as the beast roused itself. It shook its giant head like some kind of winged dog, heaved itself up on to its feet and took off down the promenade like a MiG fighter jet.

The mob shifted restlessly and looked at me with reproachful eyes as I tried to explain what had happened. A man clutching a colostomy bag called me a liar. Another rattled his Zimmer frame. They said I had attacked the bird as it flew by. They said someone had seen me do it.

"Why would I do that?" I asked. "The thing is the size of an ostrich!"

5

A lot of people walk along the Sea Point promenade. Some of them come all the way from landlocked suburbs like Rondebosch and Newlands. These are the relatively harmless ones. But the walkers who live in the area are barking mad and cannot be trusted. These are the ones who wanted to see me locked up for gull abuse.

And that's when I got the idea to approach a taxidermist. Stuff the seagulls. Convert them into paperweights and doorstops. Mount them on the mantelpiece and turn them into conversation pieces. The prospect of making a million bucks a month through novelty gull-related items is what started me on the letters. While waiting for a reply from the taxidermists, I discovered that I also needed to communicate with President Thabo Mbeki at the Union Buildings and Eugene Terreblanche at Rooigrond Prison, both of whom were more a lot more cooperative than the taxidermists. Then it dawned on me that I also had issues with Woolworths, Virgin Active, the Seven-Eleven Corporation, Des and Dawn Lindbergh, the Arthur Murray School of Dancing, Eskom, the Rosicrucians, gay and lesbian organisations, Kentucky Fried Chicken, the Pharmaceutical Society and most of the Cabinet.

From there, it spiralled quickly out of control. Surviving on little more than amphetamines and warm beer, I began demanding answers from world leaders like Saddam Hussein, Tony Blair, Ted Kaczynski, Richard Branson, Bill Gates and Douglas Daft, the man who took the coke out of Coke. At one point, overcome by sheer exhaustion, I passed out for about three months. During that time, my letters fell into enemy hands. The next thing I knew, three volumes of my intensely private correspondence were being prepared for publication. What you have in your hands, then, is an unholy union of *The Ben Trovato Files, Will The Real Ben Trovato Please Stand Up?* and *Ben Trovato – Stirred Not Shaken.*

Did I have nothing better to do?

I play neither rugby nor cricket nor golf. I do not watch sport of any kind on the television. My last attempt at hosting a braai ended with the guests complaining of carcinogenic poisoning and leaving early. My DIY skills are laughable and I struggle to tell one end of a hosepipe from the other. I don't wash my car or tinker with its engine. Nor do I go to church or take the family on picnics. I have no hobbies or interests whatsoever. And I do not have a day job. So, yes. I had nothing better to do. I still don't, come to think of it.

How dare I waste their time?

Look, very few of the people to whom I wrote were forced to put their search for a cure for cancer on hold so they could reply to my letters. I corresponded mainly with criminals, politicians and businessmen. Some of them were all three. And apart from blood, these people had nothing but time on their hands. As for wasting their money, I do believe that it was I who came up short. At a time when I was running critically low on beer money, I was sending out R10 notes to all and sundry. To be fair, a lot of them sent the money back. But enough of them pocketed the cash to force me to drink dangerously cheap red wine on more than one occasion. So, Tony Yengeni, once you get out of jail, I would like my money back. The same goes for the Japanese Embassy, Mick Jagger, the headmaster of Hilton College, Hansie Cronje, Prof SM Bhengu, the Pharmaceutical Society of Namibia, the person who opens President Thabo Mbeki's mail, British Airways, someone at the department of labour, Robert at the Life Extension Institute, Manto Tshabalala-Msimang, Tito Mboweni, the Gay and Lesbian Alliance, the International Missionary Society, Theo Grimbeek, Ndaweni Mahlangu and, wrapping up the roll of dishonour, Lord Jeffrey Archer.

Do I have no shame?

Speaking as a man who is familiar with the vagaries of both marriage and divorce, I can honestly say that I have absolutely no shame left in me at all. But if my life had been different, then, yes, I would be ashamed. Deeply.

How do I sleep at night?

Like most South Africans, pretty damn soundly while there is zopiclone and vodka in the house.

Will that do? Does that answer your questions? Can you leave me in peace, now?

Thank you.

Ben Trovato
Somewhere near the end of 2006

President Thabo Mbeki
Private Bag X1000
Pretoria
0001

Mr Ben Trovato
PO Box 1117
Sea Point
8060

19 March, 2001

Dear President Mbeki,

Firstly, let me congratulate you on your appointment! I know it's a little late, but I wanted to be sure you were the man that the posters said you were. And I must say that you have more than proved yourself. It couldn't have been easy taking over from Mandela, but you have done an admirable job.

I saw on the telly the other night that the awful Terre'Blanche man has at last been put away! Congratulations! What a pity that it is only for six years. I am not much of a Mugabe man myself, but couldn't you have had a word with the judge? I think it's important for our country to have people like that sent away for much longer.

Anyway, I don't want to take up too much of your time. Getting right to the point. I have been watching the news on telly recently, and quite frankly I am appalled by the number of animals being burnt at the stake. I understand they have a disease, but the boffins tell me that humans cannot catch foot and mouth. What I do not understand is why the meat of these poor condemned animals is not sold off in job lots. We have a lot of hungry people in our country. Some of them gather at the robots at the bottom of my street, and most of the time I don't have any food to give them. On my way home, I sometimes have a piece of fruit that Brenda (my wife!) packed for me in the morning. And I give it to them. But they need more. I can see it in their eyes. They want more than bananas, Mr President. And if we could give them platters of cooked meat, they would be very grateful. Especially at election time! There would be no point in telling them that they are eating condemned meat. It's not like we would be tricking them. I simply can't see the point in cooking the stuff, and then chucking it out. Let's feed the people!

Well, Mr President, I hope you have time to think about my suggestion. And if you do get the Nobel Prize, maybe you will invite me to a braaivleis at your house! The department of health can provide the meat.

Yours truly,

Ben Trovato (Mr)

THE PRESIDENCY: REPUBLIC OF SOUTH AFRICA
Private Bag X1000, Pretoria, 0001

Ref: P33-2089

5 April 2001

Mr B Trovato
PO Box 1117
SEA POINT
8060

Dear Mr Trovato

On behalf of the President we thank you for your letter of 19 March 2001.

Your concern for the poorest of the poor is noted and appreciated.

You are quite correct when you state that Foot and Mouth disease does not pose a human threat. However, I have done some research and was informed that the virus of this disease is so threatening and deathly to other animals that it would be extremely unwise to even make an attempt to distribute them for the use of human beings. It will spread like wildfire and within a very short while we will have no animals left. This will lead to an even bigger problem for human beings.

Warm regards

ADMINISTRATIVE SECRETARY

Enquiries: Mrs C Groenewald Tel: (012) 319-1500 Fax: (012) 323-8246

Mr Eugene Terre'Blanche
PO Box 101
Rooigrond Prison
2743

Mr Ben Trovato
PO Box 1117
Sea Point
8060

19 March, 2001

Dear Mr Terre'Blanche

I was watching the news on telly the other night and saw you heading off for a stint in the old chookie. I thought that was very brave of you. A lot of men would have snuck out of the country, much like the terrorists did in the old days. But then, where would you have gone? You wouldn't have liked the English weather, being a man of the sun and the soil yourself. And besides, there's a dreadful case of foot and mouth going around. Somewhere Nordic, perhaps. I've heard that there aren't many darkies in those parts.

That was quite a seeing off you got outside the court! I enjoyed the white lads singing the old anthem. They seemed very well behaved. Which is more than I can say for the natives on the other side. They appeared a little over-excited, to say the least.

I must compliment you on your decision not to arrive at court on your horse. The way the darkies were shouting and stamping was enough to terrify any poor animal.

How are you settling into your new accommodation? I've heard that ever since the communists took over, they no longer separate the prisoners. Does that mean you share your space with thugs from the townships? If that is the case, I suggest that you do whatever you can to get a private room. The last thing you want to do is spend most of your day locked up with dangerous criminals who are unable to grasp the finer points of your political philosophy. But I'm sure I don't need to tell you that.

The main thing is to keep your nose clean. Don't make the same mistake as that pilfering rabble-rouser Boesak. If you want to make a call, use the tickey box inside the prison. Don't buy any stolen goods while you're there. And avoid the sodomites! I don't care what they say about you and Jani Allen. At least it proves that you are not a floppy-wristed nancy boy.

Keep your chin up and your back against the wall!

Yours truly,

....
Ben Trovato (Mr)

PS. Are you likely to be spending any time with our old friend Derby-Lewis and his Polish chum? If so, please send them my regards.

Kooigrand Trust.
5 April 2001.

Geagte Ben,

Dankie vir jou brief. Klaar ek het dit baie geniet. Ek was aangename verras met jou "Humor". Jy is inderdaad skerp.

Ek skryf in Afrikaans, want in Engels sal ek dit nie reg kan laat geskied om jou te bedank en my waardering uit te spreek vir die skitterende opbeurende brief nie.

Toemaar ek sal nie dieselfde foute maak "as that pilfering rabble-rouser Boesak," nie.

Derby-Lewis en Janus is goeie vriende van my, maar ongelukkig het ek geen kontak met hulle nie.

Nogmaals baie dankie vir jou brief Mnr. Trovato.

Groete en Sterkte.

Eugéne

Dear Ben

Thank you for your letter, I really enjoyed it. I was pleasantly surprised by your "Humour". You are indeed very witty.
I am writing in Afrikaans, as I feel in English I would not be able to voice my thanks and appreciation for your brilliant letter of encouragement.
Don't worry I will not make the same mistakes "as that pilfering rabble-rouser Boesak". Derby-Lewis and Janus are both good friends of mine, but unfortunately I do not have any contact with them.

Thanks again for your letter Mr. Trovato.

Best wishes.
Eugéne

Minister Steve Tshwete
Private Bag X463
Pretoria
0001

Mr Ben Trovato
PO Box 1117
Sea Point
8060

21 March, 2001

Dear Mr Tshwete,

I thought it important to let you know that not everybody is howling for your resignation. Some of us out here think you are doing a tremendous job. Far too much is being made of this safety and security business, anyway. I mean, after all, how hard can it be? Keep your doors locked, your eyes peeled and your gun cocked. For the ladies, don't wear short skirts and avoid eye contact. If everyone followed these simple rules, most of the criminals would be out of business!

A word of congratulations on keeping those statistics under wraps. The vultures in the media like to pretend that they are in the word business, but give them a few figures and the next thing you know the country has been put on some of other United Nations list and all the embassies start issuing travel advisories.

I'm curious to know what has become of all the police cars. I remember a time when the streets seemed to be full of vans. Are they all unmarked these days? My brother, Roger, has asked me to find out if you are interested in a free car. He has a 1967 Vauxhall which might be of some use to one of your under-resourced police stations. He says the second gear doesn't work, but if you build up enough speed it's a simple matter of slipping it straight into third. The only problem is that you will have to send one of your men around to collect it. Roger hasn't driven it in nine years, and he has been having a little trouble getting it started. Drop me a note if you think The Green Devil (Roger's name!) can help in the fight against crime, and I'll give you an address.

What's your position on vigilantes? My wife, Brenda, got her purse nicked the other day (her own damn fault for leaving the house), and now she wants to know how we can go about becoming vigilantes. I must say, the idea quite appeals to me. Law-abiding citizens like ourselves are often in the best position to judge whether someone should be punished for something. The Yanks use a jury system made up of ordinary people to put their crooks behind bars. So why shouldn't Brenda round up the neighbours (Ted and Mary Goodfellow) and set up a people's court that can convene on Tuesday afternoons in my lounge. Hang on, Doris comes on Tuesdays. Maybe we can do it on Fridays. The point is that if we are going to get involved, then it's only fair we see a bit of action on the frontline. Do we need anything more than a copy of the Geneva Convention?

Finally, I must complain about your Mr Selebi. Have you had him checked out? Firstly, Jackie is a girl's name. Secondly, he strikes me as a particularly nasty piece of work. He seems to have trouble relating to people. Are you sure that he is even South African? There is something terribly Mediterranean about him. Get your boys to have him followed, and I'm sure you will be surprised at what pops up.

Keep cracking the whip.

Yours truly,

....
Ben Trovato (Mr)

Republic of South Africa

Ministry for Safety and Security

Your Reference:

Reference: 3/2/1(55/2001)

Mr B Trovato
PO Box 1117
SEA POINT
8060

9 April 2001

Dear Mr Trovato

RE - YOUR CORRESPONDENCE REGARDING CRIME

Your letter dated 21 March 2001 regarding the aforesaid refers.

Kindly note that the matter has been referred to the National Commissioner of the South African Police Service for further action. Future enquiries in this regard should be directed to Captain Makena on (012) 339 1567 during office hours. You are reminded that this matter could take approximately 4 to 6 weeks for a thorough investigation to be finalized by the office of the National Commissioner. Kindly quote the reference number provided at the top of this letter when making any enquiry.

Should you feel it necessary to approach the Ministry again in the future regarding this particular matter, you are more than welcome.

Kind regards.

Kissoonduth.

KRISHNEE KISSOONDUTH
ADMINISTRATIVE SECRETARY (DIRECTOR)

Private Bag X463 • Pretoria • 0001 • Tel: (27) (012) 339 2800/1/2/3 • Fax: (27) (012) 339 2819/20 • Email: tshwete@saps.org.za
Please quote our reference number in your correspondence

SUID-AFRIKAANSE POLISIEDIENS  SOUTH AFRICAN POLICE SERVICE

Privaatsak/Private Bag   X241
Posbus/Post Office Box

Verwysing Reference	25/6/2(1474)
Navrae Enquiries	Div Comm Makhubela
Telefoon Telephone	( )
Faksnommer Fax number	(012) 421-8074 (012) 421-8235

THE DIVISIONAL COMMISSIONER
CRIME PREVENTION
HEAD OFFICE
PRETORIA
0001

2001-05-08

Mr B Trovato
P O Box 1117
SEA POINT
8060

Dear Mr Trovato

CRIME

Thank you for your most encouraging letter dated 21 March 2001.

Please convey our sincere appreciation to your brother for his kind offer of a free car which we must unfortunately decline. We do not have a dire need for that particular make and model at this time.

As far as your enquiry regarding vigilantes and peoples court is concerned, may we suggest the Constitution as reading material.

Thank you for your interest.

Yours sincerely

DIVISIONAL COMMISSIONER
DIVISION: CRIME PREVENTION
M W MAKHUBELA

Minister Mangosuthu Buthelezi
Private Bag X741
Pretoria
0001

Mr Ben Trovato
PO Box 1117
Sea Point
8060

21 March, 2001

Dear Mr Buthelezi,

I would like to thank you for getting rid of the Nigerians at the bottom of my street. For the past seven months my wife, Brenda, has been nagging at me to go down and tell them to stop selling drugs. It got so bad that I grabbed an old tennis racquet from the spare room and said, right, I'm going to sort them out. But as soon as she went inside, I nipped through the park and sat in the pub for an hour and a half. I came back out of breath from too many cigarettes and said, there, that will teach them. There was a time that I thought the Nigerians were less trouble than Brenda. But they weren't. Not really.

Anyway, last Tuesday the police came around and sent the scoundrels packing. Now the house is full of pretty young things who come and go at all hours. Brenda is still not happy, so I offered to go and sort them out. But she threatened to leave me. I hope you have more luck understanding women.

I also wanted to congratulate you on your occasional promotion to President. Does this only happen when Thabo is out of the country? What happens if he's not feeling well, or if he just wants to be left alone for a few weeks? Do you still get to step into the breach? What happens if something really awful happens to Thabo? Do you get to fight it out with Zuma, or do we all have to line up again and get our thumbs blackened? Either way we are headed for an all-Zulu Cabinet, which I don't mind at all. Some of my best friends are Zulus. But Brenda feels you chaps need to brush up on the old crime and punishment thing. She feels political discussions should go beyond machete fights at the local market. I've tried to explain that there's a new dynamic at work, but she does the old snort and head toss and walks away. And that's when I feel the Zulu in me coming out!

By the way, whatever happened to that senile old turncoat who stabbed you with the short end of the assegai? Made off with all the documents, if I remember. Issued a few irrational threats and disappeared. Is he still alive? Don't take any nonsense from these ex-patriots. They will never know what it's like to be President, acting or otherwise!

Keep the Home Affairs fires burning!

Yours truly,

....
Ben Trovato (Mr)

PS. Brenda asks why you don't use the name Gatsha any more?

Ministry of Home Affairs

3 April 2001

Mr Ben Trovato
P O Box 1117
SEA POINT
8060

Dear Mr Trovato

I thank you for your letter of the 21st March 2001.

I am pleased that you are finally rid of the pests that bothered you and your family so much.

We have a very difficult task trying to keep out these elements from our country but it is an impossible task since we have a border which is more than 7000 kilometres. These people are destroying our young people with the amount of drug-trafficking they bring into the country. Even today's Cape Times has a front-page story: *"Drugs dealers reveal shocking truths - cocaine city - a Cape Times investigation into hard drug usage in Cape Town"*. All this is really heart-rending for we should not have people who create new problems for us instead of us fighting the scourge of HIV/AIDS.

I only act when both the President and the Deputy President are out of the country. Since 1994, I have acted as President 14 times.

If I were elected as Head of State my Cabinet would have the same face as my Political Party the IFP. I have people of all races in Parliament not just Zulus only.

The person you referred to who fled with my documents is a member of the ruling Party in the KwaZulu Natal Legislature. The wife from whom he was divorced still works for me and is based in Ulundi. The wife he married after he divorced his wife unfortunately died of cancer.

Thanks for your encouraging message.

My warm regards.

Yours sincerely

M G BUTHELEZI, MP
MINISTER OF HOME AFFAIRS

Minister: Private Bag X741
PRETORIA 0001
Tel. (012) 326-8081
Fax. (012) 321-6491

Private Bag X9102
CAPE TOWN 8000
Tel. (021) 461-5818
Fax. (021) 461-2359

Deputy Minister: Private Bag X741
PRETORIA 0001
Tel. (012) 324-3153
Fax. (012) 323-3716

Private Bag X9102
CAPE TOWN 8000
Tel. (021) 45-3456
Fax. (021) 461-4191

BI-574

The Head   Mr Ben Trovato
Pollsmoor Prison   PO Box 1117
Private Bag X4   Sea Point
Tokai   8060
7966

                                           10 May, 2001

Dear Sir,

I was alarmed to read in one of the local papers that there are prison gangs who publicly pride themselves on buggery.

I think they are called the 28s or the 26s, or something. And that they are known for their predilection for bum-rushing other prisoners. Is this true? It must be, if the newspapers are reporting on it.

Quite honesty, I fail to see how any good can come out of your inmates banging each other in the showers. Is this part of the rehabilitation process?

My wife, Brenda, feels it would be better to allow the men to have conjugal visits from their wives. Being a married man myself, I suspect they would get more sex than if they were at home. This way, you would be able to reduce the number of tailgunners emerging from our prisons.

Ever since I read about these hellish goings-on, I haven't felt safe walking in the streets. Brenda is a nervous wreck, and is convinced that one of these degenerates is going to ravage my bottom while I am out buying the paper.

Please tell us that there is nothing to worry about.

Yours truly,

....
Ben Trovato (Mr)

PS. Are there similar goings-on in the women's section of your jail? If so, I would appreciate any photographs your wardens might have snapped. I need these to show my pastor in order for him to pray for their souls.

cc. Minister Ben Skosana
    Ministry of Correctional Services

Department Of Correctional Services

Office of the Area Manager
Private Bag X4
Pollsmoor
Tokai
7966

28 May 2001

Mr Ben Travato
P.O. Box 1117
Sea Point
7966

Dear Sir

Thank you for your letter to The Head, dated 10 May 2001, concerning homosexual behaviour in prisons.

In general, it should be stated that homosexual behaviour in the general population has as many psychodynamic variations as heterosexual behaviour. For example, sometimes the relationship is caring and nurturing, sometimes it is abusive; sometimes it is consensual, sometimes it is forced; sometimes it is bartered for emotional reasons, sometimes for material gain.

In prison, homosexual behaviour can show elements of any of the above, an additionally is effected by the context, in as much as it is in any institutionalized setting, particularly where that institution is single sexed. It must be remembered that the sexual urge in most offenders does not simply disappear at the point of arrest. Its expression as a heterosexual or homosexual act is most often a matter of conscious choice when that choice is available, as is the case in free society. In South African prisons at this point, there is no provision made for conjugal facilities. Furthermore, insufficient funds exist for the creation of such facilities. In cases particularly where prisoners have lengthy prison sentences, normally heterosexual inmates often resort to homosexual acts due to lack of alternative opportunities.

However, the situation in prison may be aggravated since the inmates are mostly residential against their will. This introduces an element of disempowerment. Sex, particularly rape, may play a role in taking power back and by so doing, rebelling against a system which is perceived to be hostile. Feelings of need for empowerment and to express anger may therefore be more highly prevalent in sexuality in prison.

In light of the above, please be assured and please reassure you wife that, for as long as you remain in free society, your private areas should remain as untouched by unwanted attention as they have been up to the point when you read the particular article you mentioned in the local papers. Please also be assured that where sexual activity in prison is seen to take place against the law i.e. where it is non-consensual, appropriate investigations, charges and sanctions are implemented.

Finally, life in prison is never a pleasant experience for inmates or their custodians, although it may always be a learning experience for both. You and your pastors' prayers will therefore always be welcomed by all concerned. It is difficult, though, to understand why photographs of sexual acts may be a prerequisite for such prayers.

I hope the above answers your questions and lays to rest your and your wife's fears. Please feel free to direct any further questions to myself at the above address, or telephone number (021) 700 1145.

Yours sincerely

Hoffman

Ms. S. Hoffman
(Counselling Psychologist)
For : Mr. E. Engelbrecht
(Area Manager)

Ms Geraldine Fraser-Moleketi
Public Service Minister
Private Bag X9148
Cape Town
8000

Mr Ben Trovato
PO Box 1117
Sea Point
8060

10 May, 2001

Dear Minister,

First, let me me say that I think you very attractive for a communist. My wife, Brenda, says that doesn't mean you can get away with it. Most of the time, I have no idea what she is talking about. And I have found it best not to ask.

However, I feel that your good looks are interfering with your ability to deal firmly with freeloading bureaucrats who continue to feed off the bloated carcass of our civil service. Salary increases? You once said: "Get off your fat, lazy butts and then we will talk about money!" With language like that, you've got my vote. But you seem to have gone soft since those heady days.

My biggest concern is that the civil service continues to provide sheltered employment to thousands of beer-bellied moustache-wearing fascists from the Old Order. I need not remind you that these people are not friends of the government. They are slow-moving saboteurs out to cripple the economy. Some start small by stealing the office paper clips. But soon they grow into monsters sewing hatred and chaos with every memo.

Don't go easy on these people. They need to be intimidated and threatened at every turn. Get the NIA to phone in death threats throughout the night. Have someone from the VIP protection unit slash their tyres while they are slumped over their desks waiting for 5pm to roll around. Abduct their pets and terrorise their children if you have to.

I have a balaclava, and I am prepared to use it. My wife, Brenda, has hidden the knives so I might have to borrow one from the Ministry.

The time is ripe for a purge, and I am at your service. Should I visit your offices, or will you mail me my instructions?

Let's get them!

Yours truly,

....
Ben Trovato (Mr)

MINISTRY: PUBLIC SERVICE AND ADMINISTRATION
REPUBLIC OF SOUTH AFRICA
Private Bag X884, Pretoria, 0001, Tel: (012) 314 7911, Fax: (012) 328 6529
Private Bag X9148, Cape Town, 8000, Tel: (021) 465 5491/2/3, Fax: (021) 465 5484

Mr Ben Trovato
PO Box 1117
Sea Point
8060

16 May 2001

Dear Mr Trovato

Your letter dated 10 May 2001 refers.

On behalf of the Minister of Public Service and Administration, Ms
Geraldine Fraser-Moleketi, I acknowledge receipt of your letter
regarding corruption in Government.

The Minister will appreciate it if you could provide any information of
officials which you know are involved in corruption and the Department of
public Service will deal with them according to policies put in place to deal
with such cases.

The Minister appreciates your effort in raising this matter.

Kind regards

Florence Maleka
Personal Assistant

AIDS is a deadly reality. We are individually responsible to prevent the spread of AIDS 🎗

22

Minister MMS Mdladlana
Private Bag X9090
Cape Town
8000

Mr Ben Trovato
PO Box 1117
Sea Point
8060

10 May, 2001

Dear Mr Mdladlana,

Gosh, that's a hard name to type! It would be so much easier to call you Shepherd. Where did you get that name, by the way? Brenda (my wife) suggested that you grew up herding sheep or goats. I tried to teach her a little respect, but she moved out of range. I told her that most black people are deeply religious, and that your name has spiritual connotations. I'm not sure what your new name means. To be honest, I won't even attempt to spell it. But I'm sure it's something that the working classes can relate to.

Mr Minister, unemployment is the reason I am writing to you. I am fortunate to have a job. In fact, I own the company. I won't bore you with details, but let me say that we make a lot of money. And I want to give some away. That's why I am enclosing ten rand. But let's be clear on this. The money is for you personally. The big stuff will come later, and this should go to the jobless. But, at the same time, I think it is important to ensure that you are comfortable. If you are going short, it is unlikely that you will have much sympathy for those who are also struggling to survive.

By the way, what do you plan to do with these troublesome union fellows. I don't think I will be able to share my fortune with the impoverished if the dustbin workers keep going on strike. My suggestion is that you shut them down. Ban them, if you have to. Margaret Thatcher, a fine woman, you will agree, used police officers mounted on large horses to quell the unions. Perhaps we could do the same. But I suspect that dogs would be cheaper. Not to ride, of course. You might also want to consider doing something about that troublemaker, Vavi. I suspect he has his sights set on something a little grander than chief of the workers. Get your man, Buthelezi, to check him out. It wouldn't surprise me if he turned out to be Cuban.

Let me know if you are running short, and I will slip you another ten. As the Minister, it makes sense that you are at the front of the queue when free money is being handed out.

Yours truly,

....
Ben Trovato (Mr)

BRIBE GIVEN R10

23

MINISTRY: LABOUR
REPUBLIC OF SOUTH AFRICA

Private Bag X499, Pretoria, 0001, Tel: (012) 322 6523, Fax: (012) 320 1942
Private Bag X9090, Cape Town, 8000, Tel: (021) 461 6030, Fax: (021) 462 2832

Mr B Trovato
PO Box 1117
SEA POINT
8060

16 May 2001

Dear Mr Trovato

I hereby acknowledge your correspondence dated 10 May 2001.

Enclosed please find your R10.00 as it is not in the Minister's interest to accept bribes.

With best wishes.

Yours sincerely

PATRICIA A FAHRENFORT
Deputy Director: Ministry

f:\trovato160501

Mr Mike Nicholson
Hilton College
Private Bag 6001
Hilton
3245

Mr Ben Trovato
PO Box 1117
Sea Point
8060

12 May, 2001

Dear Mr Nicholson,

I heard the other day that less privileged pupils are planning to storm the country's private schools. Apparently they are upset that the government tosses a few coins your way every now and again. They seem to think the money would be better spent on state schools. Perhaps they should invade the Ministry of Education instead.

Right now, I need to know if you have been overthrown by the proletariat. My boy, Clive, is looking for a new school and Hilton College would be out of the question if he has to fight his way through teenage crack-dealers and apprentice pimps and prostitutes to get to a class of 72 glue-sniffing children.

There is no doubt that the boy will be an asset to the school. He is bright and quick on his feet. But like most adolescents, he has his defects. Clive is recovering from an unhealthy obsession with a pop singer called Marilyn Manson. He still insists on wearing cosmetics, but his nurse has it down to weekends only. I won't bore you with the details, but I can assure you that his previous principal dropped all charges when it became abundantly clear that my boy was nowhere near the device when it went off.

I am sending you ten rand on the understanding that Clive will be guaranteed entrance to your school. And there is plenty more where that came from. Enough for a new library, for example. It would have to bear my name, of course. But these are details which can be discussed later. The important thing is to get Clive out of the Institute and back into a healthy environment.

If I do not hear from you, I assume it will be in order to bring Clive around to the school on Thursday, the 24th of this month. Will 10am be convenient? Let me know.

Yours truly,

....
Ben Trovato (Mr)

CASH GIVEN R10

PS. My wife, Brenda, says she has heard that Hilton College is full of poofters. This would not suit Clive, as he is recovering from an incident. If your students are not kosher, it would be best if you returned my money.

HILTON COLLEGE

PRIVATE BAG 6001 HILTON 3245 KWAZULU-NATAL SOUTH AFRICA, TELEPHONE: (033) 343 0100 FAX: (033) 343 0080
e-mail: hc@hilton.kzn.school.za web: www.hilton.kzn.school.za
HEADMASTER: M.J. NICHOLSON B.Sc., B.Ed. (NATAL)

May 18, 2001

Mr B Trovato
P O Box 1117
SEA POINT
8060

Dear Mr Trovato

Thank you for your letter of 12 May 2001 enclosing ten rand.

I would be very happy to see you on Thursday 24th May but I will only be free from 2.00
p.m., as we have a parents function at the school in the morning.

I look forward to meeting you at 2.00 p.m. on that day.

Yours sincerely

pp M J NICHOLSON
Headmaster

MEMBER OF THE INDEPENDENT SCHOOLS' ASSOCIATION OF SOUTHERN AFRICA
MEMBER OF THE SOUTHERN AFRICAN HEADS OF INDEPENDENT SCHOOLS ASSOCIATION

Chief Executive Officer
Woolworths
93 Longmarket Street
Cape Town
8000

Mr Ben Trovato
PO Box 1117
Sea Point
8060

19 May, 2001

Dear Sir,

I am utterly alarmed.

I sent my wife, Brenda, to the shops this morning to purchase something to go with my tea. I told her to pick out something tasty. Not too filling, because I dislike feeling as if I have consumed a small elephant. Besides, I suffer from wind and excessive eating always brings out the worst in me.

Later in the day, when Brenda brought me my tea, I noticed that the snack was a small doughy affair covered in what appeared to be cheese. When I inquired further, she told me it was a "mini cheese roll". So far so good.

It was only when I went into the kitchen to instruct Brenda to refresh my tea that I discovered she was trying to kill me.

I happened to see the wrapping in which these "mini cheese rolls" had arrived. To my horror, I discovered what I had been eating. Inside my snack, which measured seven square centimetres, was an array of toxins the likes of which have never been seen outside The Young Poisoner's Handbook.

This is what my "mini cheese roll" contained:

Wheat flour, cheddar cheese, flour improver, gluten, invert sugar, yeast, emulsifier, vegetable fat, salt, acetic and propionic acid preservative.

Good God, man! Why not just package wolfsbane and sell it as imported spinach?

I assume some of these ingredients are not obtained legally. However, you at least have the good grace to print a Consumer Help Line number on the wrapping. I presume this works on the same principle as an emergency call to the city paramedics, and that a specially designed Woolworths ambulance is sent out when a man having a teatime snack falls to the ground with his internal organs imploding one by one.

Yours truly,

....
Ben Trovato (Mr)

SN Susman
Woolworths CEO/Chairman
PO Box 680
Cape Town
8000

Mr Ben Trovato
PO Box 1117
Sea Point
8060

15 June, 2001

Dear SN Susman,

When did Woolworths become a Masonic organisation?

The secrecy surrounding the identities of those who control your company is comparable to that surrounding the list of former members of the Broederbond, none of whom were ever racist.

On the 19th of May, I sent a letter of complaint addressed to the Chief Executive Officer. At that stage, I had no name to attach to the title. And now, I have no reply to attach to my complaint.

My letter concerned your mini cheese rolls. You may have heard of them.

It was only when I accidentally hacked into the Woolworths website that I discovered the truth. You are Chief Executive officer of Woolworths Holdings Limited. However, you are also Chairman of Woolworths (PTY) Limited. Very cunning indeed. Very. Small wonder that my complaint never reached you. You clearly assume the role of Chairman whenever a nasty letter is addressed to the CEO, and vice versa. Corporate schizophrenia is a cheap way of obviating the need to ever reply to an aggrieved customer.

May I remind you that you are not Sir Richard Branson.

Perusing your website almost made me lose sight of my original complaint about the potentially lethal "mini cheese roll".

"In 1993, Woolworths decided to introduce its own private label charge card. The introduction of this card substantially expanded the Company's pool of potential customers."

Thanks for the card. There's nothing quite like a shiny new card with your name on it to make you feel you have a purpose in life. However, the one thing you forgot to introduce to your expanded pool was lifeguards. These are essential if you hope to prevent your new customers from drowning in debt. I am sure you will get right on to it.

Yours truly,

....
Ben Trovato (Mr)

Woolworths (Proprietary) Limited
Reg No. 1956/000518/07
Woolworths House, 93 Longmarket Street, Cape Town, 8001. PO Box 680, Cape Town, 8000.
Telephone +27 21 407 9111

27 June 2001

Co. Ref : 74142

MR B TROVATO
P O BOX 1117
SEA POINT
8060

Dear Mr Trovato

Thank you very much for bringing your complaint to our attention. Please accept our apologies for the disappointment and inconvenience caused, as well as for the delay in replying to you.

Our chief priority is to satisfy our customers. We regret that on this occasion our service failed to comply with the high standards that you so rightfully expect.

MINI CHEESE ROLLS: Our technologist (bread department) as informed me of the following ingredient listing;

- Wheat flour (with no additives)
- Cheddar cheese
- Flour improver (wheat flour, soya flour, milk powder, glucose, enzymes, vitamin c)
- Gluten (wheat protein)
- Yeast
- Invert sugar (glucose and fructose)
- Emulsifier (made during manufacture of vegetable fat)
- Vegetable fat (made with sunflower oil)
- Salt
- Preservatives - *acetic acid (vinegar) *propionic acid (found naturally in cheese)

There are no harmful or toxic ingredients in this product as all ingredients are from natural origin.

Please accept the enclosed gift voucher to the value of R100,00 as a token of our goodwill.

Assuring you of our best attention at all times.

Yours sincerely

Z C NEUMANN (MRS)
CUSTOMER LIAISON OFFICER

WOOLWORTHS

Woolworths (Proprietary) Limited
Reg No. 1956/000518/07

Woolworths House, 93 Longmarket Street, Cape Town, 8001. PO Box 680, Cape Town, 8000,
Telephone +27 21 407 9111

9 July 2001

Mr Ben Trovato
P O Box 1117
SEA POINT
8060

Dear Mr Trovato

I have now read both your letters and our reply of 27 June. I happily admit to being somewhat of a recluse but am clearly not trying to evade contact with our customers who pay all of our salaries.

I enjoyed your letters and do take seriously the sense expressed therein. The primary part of our Food Strategy – what we call the Good Food Strategy – is to drive out all inappropriate ingredients and processes in our foods.

The food industry is notorious for using chemical processes, preservatives, flavourants etc to make goods taste stronger or last longer. We will shortly be announcing that not one of our products contains MSG. You have seen that the ingredients in this bun are all of natural source – even though some of their names sound pretty horrific. We have just managed to guarantee that all our fresh chickens do not have as part of their diets, dead chickens, which most poultry in this country does contain. We have a number of similar projects. In these sort of things one can never do enough, so we have got the team constantly driving in this direction.

I hope all this answers your queries.

Warm regards
Yours sincerely

SIMON SUSMAN
CHIEF EXECUTIVE

/ch

Mr Mzwakhe Mbuli
Leeuwkop Maximum Security Prison
Private Bag X2
Bryanston
2021

Mr Ben Trovato
PO Box 1117
Sea Point
8060

19 May, 2001

Dear Mr Mbuli,

I was taken aback to discover that The People's Poet remains behind bars. I had assumed that the nasty incident at the bank was a distant memory by now. Helen Suzman is not alone. I never believed it either. Poets do not walk around with handgrenades demanding free money. But if they did, they would want a lot more than fifteen thousand rand.
And if waging campaigns of terror were in the poet's nature, he would surely begin with publishers and literary critics.

By all accounts, you were set up because you have damaging information about people in the government. I think what really makes them angry is the knowledge that you have the capacity to turn their transgressions into rhyming couplets.

I have been dabbling in a little poetry and composed this for you.

You say you were framed
Some say you're not to be blamed
But do you eat fish
On Thursdays?

Mr Mbuli, you have probably found prison to be something of a Zen experience, and I am sure you will relate to the element of Zen tucked away inside my poem.

My son, Clive, wants to know how you get along with the other prisoners. He says the main gangs are involved in buggery and drugs, and would like to know if the poets have a gang of their own. What would the initiation ritual entail? I suppose newcomers are given thirty seconds to come up with a verse line consisting of two dactyls, one stressed syllable, another two dactyls and a final stressed syllable. But be careful! I cannot imagine that the warders would be too impressed to discover that inmates were covertly engaging in iambic pentameter when their backs were turned.

My wife, Brenda, is begging me to ask you to send her a poem. I told her to stop being such a sentimental old cow, and she poured her tea into my lap. Now I have scalded genitals. Perhaps you could send her a line or two to prevent further domestic violence.

Yours truly,

....
Ben Trovato (Mr)

07 July 2001

TO: **MR BEN TROVATO**
        PO BOX 1117
        SEAPOINT
        8060

Dear Ben

Mzwakhe thanks you for your beautiful letter and poem, that you have dedicated to him. He was very happy to hear from you, and enjoyed your correspondence enormously. He apologises for the delayed writing back to you, but there has recently been a bereavement in his family, and he needed to focus his attention on the matters at hand.

At present, all his papers are in at the Supreme Court of Appeals in Bloemfontein, and we are just waiting for a date for trial.

We are very hopeful that Mzwakhe will be home soon. He is in very good spirits and in good health.

Again, he is very grateful for your letter. Tell Clive, that it has happened, and not infrequently, that the gang leaders come to Mzwakhe's cell, to salute him. So yes, thankfully he is protected by the people, even in that terrible place.

Yours Sincerely, and with much respect and appreciation
For MZWAKHE MBULI FAN CLUB

Mark Loeb

MZWAKHE MBULI FAN CLUB
P.O.BOX 3084
PARKLANDS
2121

E-MAIL: msl@mweb.co.za
WEB SITE: www.mzwakhe.org

Chief of Staff
Survival War Games
PO Box 26174
Hout Bay
Cape Town

Mr Ben Trovato
PO Box 1117
Sea Point
8060

20 May, 2001

Dear General,

I would like to volunteer my wife, Brenda, as a participant in one of your war games. I plan this to be a surprise for her birthday, so it is important that we keep it quiet.

To be honest, I have an ulterior motive. Brenda's survival skills need polishing. She no longer seems to see my stick coming, and frequently takes it on the head. She also tends to forget that I no longer eat mini cheese rolls. And I fear that she will not survive for much longer if she keeps forgetting to raise the toilet seat when she has finished.

There is one special request, for which I am prepared to pay extra.

I would appreciate it if your men could arrange it so that Brenda is fired upon with live ammunition. I realise this sounds extreme, but let me assure you, paintballs will never drive the message home. Not with Brenda. She will simply start colour-coding her battledress.

Obviously I am not suggesting that you kill her. A bullet to the lower leg is all I need. She is one of these walk-and-talk women, and I am exhausted from being dragged around by the conversation. A flesh wound in the calf will keep her still long enough for me to explain how she can be a better wife.

Please consider the enclosed ten rand as a deposit. I will pay the remainder when the hospital calls. I will send Brenda your way the first Saturday in June.

Yours truly,

Ben Trovato (Mr)

Chief of Staff
Survival War Games
PO Box 26174
Hout Bay
7872

Mr. Ben Trovato
PO Box 1117
Sea Point
8060

Dear Sir

The general staff has reviewed your request. Whilst we are familiar with the ordeal you must be experiencing and sympathies with you we cannot for the following reasons resort to the form of training you suggest.

The solution you recommend is generated purely from a male perspective and as such will most surely be rejected by Brenda.

The results will be short lived. A temporary halt to normal female practices will generally be followed by an increased rate of activity in the very behaviors that you wish to curb.

The damage to your financial status will be immense as she exercises her freedom in various Mall excursions to make up for lost shopping time.

It is our opinion that a Joint Integrated Recovery Operation (JIRO) be planned with the full input and cooperation of your partner. Together plan a series of raids involving covert data collection on the state of the local culinary, social, travel and adventure activities available in the Western Cape region. Your physical status must be maintained therefore you will be required to undertake PT activities which require you to route march the various Cape forest trails on a regular basis.

It is our experience that given joint goal orientated missions to work towards, coupled operatives soon begin to forget the smaller less important side issues.

We look forward to your return to full coupled operative status in the not too distant future.

Best regards

Rod Panagos (JoAT)

The Manager
Cerebos Salt
PO Box 3706
Rivonia
2128

Mr Ben Trovato
PO Box 1117
Sea Point
8060

21 May, 2001

Dear Sir,

I have just returned from my doctor. He tells me that my blood pressure is higher than Herschelle Gibbs on the night before an important test match. He told me that if I hope to live much longer, I need to cut out the salt.

That's right, sir. Salt is hastening my trip to the grave. Do you use salt? I doubt it. You work with this evil substance all day. You nurture it, you trade in it, but you will never use it yourself.

I cannot eat a mielie without salt. I find it hard to even look at a boiled egg unless there is a salt cellar nearby. Forget about a pork sausage. Sir, it is pushers like you who have turned us into unwilling addicts.

You may as well turn your salt pans into fields of poppies and sell raw heroin to adolescent schoolgirls during break time. The damage you are doing is the same. Their arteries will become clogged, their blood pressure will soar, they will turn against their parents and then embrace casual sex as a means of escape. And if that does not kill them, your salt will.

Please be assured that I will be forwarding all future medical bills to your office.

May God have mercy on your soul.

Yours truly,

....
Ben Trovato (Mr)

The Manager
Cerebos Salt
PO Box 3706
Rivonia
2128

Mr Ben Trovato
PO Box 1117
Sea Point
8060

14 July, 2001

Dear Sir,

It has been almost two months since I approached you with serious concerns regarding the potential link between your salt and my death.

I can only assume that you have decided to ignore me in the hope that I collapse to the floor clutching my heart before I can send a brace of attorneys to your offices.

Well, let me assure you, Sir, that I have never felt better in all my life.

As an addict, I still cannot go without my salt fix for the day. But my mental state has improved since I last attempted to strike up a conversation with your firm.

However, my blood pressure soars when I am reminded of your arrogance. How dare you not reply to my letter? I am absolutely appalled. What gives you the right to behave like a politician? I am a customer. I buy Cerebos salt. Sometimes twice a day.

If you are prepared to send me photographic evidence that you are a salt user, I am prepared to reconsider sending you my medical bills. An ECG printout will suffice.

Yours truly,

....
Ben Trovato (Mr)

Dear Mr Trovato,

19 July 2001

I hereby wish to respond to your letter dated 14 July 2001.

Since time began, salt has been invaluable for it's preservative and flavouring qualities. Salt is physiologically necessary for the functioning of human life.

One of salt's major functions is to regulate blood volume and pressure, including the flexibility of the blood vessels.   The human heart is a big pump. When it contracts, it forces blood through the arteries of the circulatory system; that pressure is "systolic," the "top" number.

Between heartbeats, the heart relaxes. Pressure measured between heartbeats is "diastolic," the "bottom" number. When blood volume increases or the blood vessel walls don't expand enough, blood pressure increases. Normal blood pressure is less than 130/85 according to the National Heart, Lung and Blood Institute. In a population, blood pressures are a good indicator of the incidence of cardiovascular events like heart attacks and strokes.

As long ago as 2,000 B.C. when the famous Chinese "Yellow Emperor" Huang Ti recorded salt's association with a "hardened pulse," we have known of a relationship between salt and blood pressure. That's not news. Nor is the fact that manipulating sodium intake can change blood pressure in sensitive individuals, those termed "salt sensitive" (a condition with roots in both genetics and lifestyle.

For a century, medical researchers have been able to measure sodium and have documented that by increasing or decreasing sodium in the body, many people's blood pressure moves up or down in small but often-detectable amounts.

What is more newsworthy is that over the past quarter-century, we've learned that the body often makes physiologic adjustments to "correct" for such changes and preserve blood pressure at the "proper" level (e.g. changes in rennin system response or increased blood vessel stiffness or increased insulin resistance). And all this leads to the final point about salt and blood pressure: the only rationale offered for reducing salt to reduce blood pressure (in some people) is that it will lessen their risk of a heart attack or stroke.

The news today is that not a single study has shown improved health outcomes for populations on reduced sodium diets.

There continues a controversy among medical researchers about the appropriate public health response to these facts. Some argue that public policy should demand reduced sodium intakes to lower population blood pressure and, with it, the risk of heart attacks and strokes. Others point out that even significantly reduced sodium intakes produce very small population blood pressure reductions and that dietary advice should be targeted towards "salt sensitive" individuals. Yet others review the medical literature and show no documented health outcomes improvement for reduced-sodium diet.

Some consider those advocating sodium reduction to be basing their case on "junk science". Trying to put the debate in perspective, the founder of the American Society of Hypertension, Dr. John Laragh, in April 2001, summarized the situation as follows:

"Is there any proven reason for us to grossly modify our salt intake or systematically avoid table salt? Is this a proven healthy thing to do, that is, will it save us from the major goals of anti-hypertensive therapy, such as a later heart attack or stroke or kidney failure? Generally speaking the answer is either a resounding no, or that, at best, there is not any positive direct evidence to support such recommendations. And equally relevant, what are the new risks you might be taking on by avoiding salt?"

Among the points of argument from those who squabble about hypertension – as opposed to those who dismiss the arguments as irrelevant in the absence of documented health outcomes benefits – are the following:

1. Blood pressure responses to decreasing sodium are modest and disappear over time. The Trials of Hypertension Prevention, found significant improvements at six months, but they disappeared after low-sodium dieters stayed on the diet after 18 months.
2. Only a "salt sensitive" minority of the population benefits by reducing dietary salt and correcting other dietary deficiencies (e.g. potassium, calcium and magnesium) can reverse the individuals 'salt sensitivity'.
3. Reducing dietary sodium has been tried for more than two decades and the public has proven unwilling and unable to reduce sodium intakes although some medically supervised patients are able to sustain compliance over long periods of time. Other interventions such as the DASH diet high in fruits; vegetables and low-fat dairy products may be a more

realistic and effective public health intervention. Manipulating sodium on the DASH diet makes sense to some scientists, but not to others. The salt industry and food industry support the DASH Diet without salt reduction.

In any case, the researchers and dieticians continue to debate about hypertension, but a new emphasis on evidence-based medical decision-making arising in Canada and the UK – both for pharmacological and non-pharmacological interventions – suggests that the future debate may shift away from impacts on blood pressure itself to examine the more relevant policy end-point: whether a public health intervention – be it drugs or diet – actually has proven health outcomes benefits.

While the public is only now hearing about "EBM" -- evidence-based medicine – the popular press has been covering the scientific debate now for several years and the public is listening. Hopefully, we will be able to reduce the length of time converting research findings into practice and into public health policy.

I hope the above has answered your questions regarding your concerns and trust that you will not be sending us your medical bills and/or ECG printout! ☺

Yours faithfully,

Janine Bonollo
Marketing Assistant
Cerebos

Mr Barney Pityana
SA Human Rights Commission
Private Bag 2700
Houghton
2041

Mr Ben Trovato
PO Box 1117
Sea Point
8060

23 May, 2001

Dear Mr Pityana,

I hope yours is the correct agency to deal with my situation.

Brenda and I have been married for some time now. And lately she has taken
to violating my rights. The other day she deliberately poured hot tea into my
lap. She has also tried to poison me by feeding me mini cheese rolls filled with
dangerous chemicals. I have also been forced to wash my own clothes and make
my own dinner from time to time.

If we can get this to the World Court, I have a fair idea of her defence. We
should keep it quiet for now and surprise them when they take the stand. Brenda
will suggest that I have repeatedly coerced her into performing her conjugal
duties. She will say that I have slammed her fingers in the kitchen door. And she
is likely to imply that I have physically attempted to imbue her with a sense of
patriotism. This is all a pack of lies. I admit to once striking her several times to
quell a bout of hysteria, which subsequently turned out to be hay fever. However,
the symptoms are similar and one is easily mistaken.

Brenda has also hidden my favourite stick. She will try to make out that I have
used this stick on her in the past. It is a walking stick, and I frequently use it to
point out objects of interest. If it has, on occasion, connected with a part of her
body, then it is only because I have had to swiftly point to the clock to remind
her that it is teatime. This never used to happen, and I fear that her peripheral
vision is failing.

You will agree that my rights are clearly being abused, and I urgently seek your
advice in this matter. Is there perhaps one or other United Nations list on which
Brenda's name (maiden, of course) could appear? Failing that, would you be able
to inform her that her actions are being being monitored by secret agents?

It would also not hurt to mention to her that various international conventions
dealing with human rights focus specifically on the duties of a wife, particularly
insofar as they relate to mealtimes and connubial responsibilities.

Let us get this matter sorted out before disaster strikes!

Yours truly,

....
Ben Trovato (Mr)

SOUTH AFRICAN HUMAN RIGHTS COMMISSION
Entrance 1
Wilds View
Isle of Houghton,
Boundary Road
Parktown, Johannesburg

Private Bag, 2700
Houghton
2041

Telephone: 27 11 484 8300
Fax: 27 11 484 7149
Fax Commissioners:
27 11 484 8403
Fax Advocacy and
research: 27 11 484 7146
Fax Legal: 27 11 484 1360

31 May, 2001

Mr Ben Trovato
P O Box 1117
SEA POINT
Cape   8060

Dear Mr Trovato,

RE: YOUR COMPLAINT

Your letter of the 23rd inst herein refers.

We have taken careful note of the matters you raise. You will not be surprised to hear that we regret to inform you that these are not matters within the jurisdiction of the Commission. Some of the matters you raise, however, appear to be of such a serious nature that we have felt bound to refer the matter to the SAPS for appropriate action.

I trust that you and your wife will find a suitable solution to your problems.

Sincerely,

N Barney Pityana
CHAIRPERSON
cc: Western Cape Office: SAHRC
           SAPS: Sea Point

The United Nations Decade for Human Rights Education 1995 - 2005
Chairperson The Revd Dr NB Pityana; **Deputy Chairperson** SE Mabusela; **Commissioners** CRM Dlamini, K Govender, J Kollapen, Z Majodina, T Manthata, C McClain, J Nkeli, FP Tlakula, L Wessels; **Chief Executive Officer** L Mokate

SUID-AFRIKAANSE POLISIEDIENS  SOUTH AFRICAN POLICE SERVICE

AMAPOLISA OMZANTSI AFRICA

Privaatsak/Private Bag
Posbus/Post Office Box   P.O. Box 373

Verw/Ref	
Navrae/Enq Captain Verster	
Tel.nr (021) 434-7495	
Faks/Fax (021) 434-1609	
E-mail adres SEAPOINT-SAPS@saps.org.za	

OFFICE OF THE COMMANDER
SOUTH AFRICAN POLICE SERVICE
DETECTIVE SERVICES
CNR BAY RD & BILL PETERS DRIVE
SEA POINT
8001

2001-06-20

Mr Ben Trovato
P.O. Box 1117
SEA POINT
8060

RE: YOUR COMPLAINT : YOUR LETTER DATED 23RD MAY REFERS

1.   This office hereby acknowledges receipt of your letter dated 23rd May 2001.

2.   The best advice we can give to you is to go and see the Senior State Prosecutor in Cape Town.

CAPTAIN
COMMANDER : DETECTIVE SERVICES
(J D VERSTER)

SOUTH AFRICAN HUMAN RIGHTS COMMISSION
7th Floor, Volkskas Building, 132 Adderley Street
Cape Town, 8000
P.O. Box 3563, Cape Town 8001
Telephone 021 426 2277, Fax 021 426 2875

Our ref: WC\21\286

7 August 2001

Mr Ben Trovato
P.O Box 1117
Sea Point
8060

Dear Mr Trovato

DECISION REGARDING YOUR COMPLAINT

We refer to your letter as received by us on the 5th June 2001.

The Human Rights Commission is restricted by its governing Act to investigate only complaints in which allegations of a violation of a **fundamental right** are reported. Your complaint arose after 3 February 1997 and therefore the **Final Constitution (1996)** applies. The fundamental rights of that constitution are contained in the Bill of Rights in chapter two.

We have considered your case based on the information supplied to us and have not been able to find an alleged violation of any fundamental right. Your case, therefore, falls outside our jurisdiction and we cannot take it on. It is with regret that we say that we are not able to help you.

Despite your complaint not alleging a violation of a fundamental right, we are of the view that other legal rights may have been violated. We therefore recommend that you pursue other legal remedies such as applying for a protection order from any Magistrate Court in terms of section 4 of the Domestic Violence Act 116 of 1998. This Act acknowledges the fact that domestic violence is a serious social evil, which may be performed in different ways, especially in relations of domestic nature.

We wish you success in getting the remedy that you seek. We have now closed our file on this matter. However, you have the right to appeal against this decision not to take your case on. Should you wish to appeal, then you must do so within 45 days of receiving this letter by writing to:
The Chairperson, Dr Barney Pityana, The South African Human Rights Commission, Private Bag 2700, Houghton, JOHANNESBURG, 2041.

Yours faithfully

....
Victor Southwell
LEGAL AND EDUCATION OFFICER

Mr Nicky Oppenheimer
Chairman: De Beers
Private Bag X01
Southdale
2135

Mr Ben Trovato
PO Box 1117
Sea Point
8060

24 May, 2001

Dear Mr Oppenheimer,

I hear that Mad Dog Mugabe is trying to steal your land. I have also heard that
you plan on issuing a call to arms, and I would like to be among the first to
volunteer. Those thugs need a damn good thrashing, and I have had enough
practice on my Brenda to be able to hold my own when it comes to fighting for
basic human rights.

It is hard to believe that the ungrateful swine have refused your offer of 34 000
hectares. Comrade Bob says that's not enough. He says your farm is as big as
Belgium. So bloody what? Where would he be today if the family had decided to
buy the entire country?

On one farm alone, you bring in R16-million a year. I assume this is a fair boost
to Zimbabwe's foreign reserves. In fact, I think that is the foreign reserve.

Old Bobbles is clearly in the early stages of senile dementia. Have you ever
watched him speaking at a political rally? It is a terrifying sight, and you would
be well advised to send the children out of the room.

Did you ever think of hiring Ian Smith to manage your property interests? What
you need is a man who will unilaterally declare independence. It almost worked
once before. And if your farm really is as big as Belgium, you should have no
trouble getting the United Nations to recognise you. My brother, Roger, has
a printing business and he says he will quite happily do your passports and
letterheads. Brenda has suggested a coat of arms involving a deck of playing
cards. She was still babbling about clubs and spades and diamonds when I
locked her in the cellar.

The point is that we need to fight back. I am enclosing a ten rand deposit to
ensure that I get officer status. Forget about the border. We must attack by air. I
am sure a man of your means has access to parachutes and balaclavas. We will
also require weapons. But I need not tell you that where there are diamonds,
there are guns. Lots of them. Especially in Africa.

Send me the plan.

Yours truly,

....
Ben Trovato (Mr)

BRIBE GIVEN
R10

44

POST OFFICE BOX 61631
MARSHALLTOWN 2107
PHONE 27-11 (011) 833·7912
TELEGRAPHIC ADDRESS:
"SPECTRUM"

44 MAIN STREET
JOHANNESBURG
2001

1st June 2001

Mr B Trovato
P O Box 1117
Sea Point
CAPE TOWN
8060

Dear Mr Trovato,

Thank you very much for your letter. I am not sure I would go as far as you, but certainly doing business in Zimbabwe be it on the farming front or mining front, is not easy at the moment.

It was kind of you to send your R10,00 deposit to ensure that you get officer status, but I am not sure that will ever happen, so I return your money to you and will keep your letter and should anything happen, I do have your contact details!

Best wishes,

N F Oppenheimer

45

Mr Nicky Oppenheimer
Chairman: De Beers
PO Box 61631
Marshalltown
2107

Mr Ben Trovato
PO Box 1117
Sea Point
8060

29 June, 2001

Dear Mr Oppenheimer,

It was not easy, but I have succeeded in "persuading" Robert Mugabe to lay off your farms.

You may already have received the good news, and were probably wondering what caused the sudden about-face in State House.

I would appreciate it if you kept this to yourself, since the last thing I need is the media hounding me for details of my methods. With the exception of Old Bobbles, you are the only person who knows the truth.

Naturally, the ZANU-PF propaganda rags came up with this version of what happened: "The delisting comes in the wake of representations by diplomatic missions lodged with the Ministry of Foreign Affairs to have them spared."

Sure. The Zimbabwean government is known around the world for its willingness to bend over backwards to accommodate the wishes of foreigners.

A government minion by the name of Samuel Mhango said the Oppenheimer farms would no longer be seized because "they fall into the agro-industry and ranching category".

In other words, the land will not be appropriated because it is being used to farm cattle and grow crops. Unlike the 3 000 other white-owned farms up for seizure. You would think the other farmers would catch on and quickly stick some mielies into the ground. Perhaps even borrow a few goats to scatter about the place for when the inspector visits.

I do not expect any thanks for saving your farms. However, if I am ever passing by Debshan, I will pop in for a drink. Ian Smith has asked me to get him a position in the Cabinet, so I may be having another word with the President very soon.

Yours truly,

Ben Trovato (Mr)

PS. Thank you for returning my deposit. I will spend it on a tap-dancing transvestite to surprise President Sam Nujoma on his next birthday.

Sir Richard Branson
Virgin Management Ltd
120 Camden Hill Road
London
W8 7AR
U.K.

Mr Ben Trovato
PO Box 1117
Sea Point
8060

26 May, 2001

Dear Sir Richard,

Thank God for your timely intervention in our crumbling health club sector.

At the request of none other than Nelson Mandela, you stepped in and single-handedly saved an entire chain of Health and Racquet Clubs around the country. Bravo, Sir!

Every developing nation needs a Richard Branson to take care of their corpulent elite. For without them, who will become the capitalists of the future? Not the malnourished proletariat, that's for sure. They are far too preoccupied with finding food and shelter. Damn their selfish eyes.

I need not tell you that fat people rarely make good leaders. Idi Amin would not have been the genocidal maniac he was had been given unlimited access to a Virgin Active club. Because he was a pig of a man, he suffered from low self-esteem and consequently felt very little when it came to lopping off the head of anyone whose name had more than two vowels in it.

Only a true visionary like yourself knows that Africa's future lies in the gym. The critics will not understand. They will say that you are merely trying to make more money. What they fail to realise is that it is a very poor gamble to invest in a chain of health clubs in a country where people are branded unpatriotic unless they feed off giant slabs of flame-charred meat and barrels of beer every weekend. And that's just the women.

Some may even accuse you of helping to build up a new right wing, far more dangerous than your National Front could ever be. But they would be wrong.

I assume you are going to lose an enormous amount of money with this investment. Here is ten rand to make up for it. I know your heart is in the right place.

Yours truly,

....
Ben Trovato (Mr)

PS. My wife, Brenda, asks if you would be interested in investing in her brother's chain of laundromats. I reminded her that you are a knight of the realm and beat her soundly.

21 June 2001

Mr B Trovato
P O Box 1117
SEA POINT
8060

Dear Ben

Thank you for your correspondence of the 26 May 2001 addressed to Sir Richard Branson that has been forwarded to me.

We thank you for taking the time to correspond with us and hereby return your kind gesture as we are not looking to make a loss on our investment in South Africa.

Yours sincerely

IAN BURROUGHS
MANAGING DIRECTOR

VIRGIN ACTIVE SOUTH AFRICA (PROPRIETARY) LIMITED
Registration number 1993/005794/07
305 Main Road, Kenilworth, 7700 Tel. 27 21 710-8500 Fax 27 21 710 8600
Directors : I S Burroughs* A Robbins* (British) A de Wet

Mr Douglas Daft
CEO Coke
One Coca Cola Plaza
Atlanta, GA

Mr Ben Trovato
PO Box 1117
Sea Point
8060

29 May, 2001

Dear Mr Daft,

The British must have a good giggle about your name. But in my book, anyone who makes it to the top of the Coca Cola empire cannot be all that daft. My advice is to stop selling Coke in Britain. That will teach the swine. Then we shall see who comes grovelling.

I am sure you are a busy man, so I will come straight to the point. I had my neighbours (Ted and Mary Goodfellow) around the other evening for a braai. This is similar to a barbecue, except South Africans generally use the occasion to drink enormous amounts of alcohol before attacking one another over some irrelevent political or religious issue.

The evening was progressing well until I noticed that Brenda (my wife) had begun to smile a lot. Mary also began giggling, and by the end of the evening the two of them were staggering about the garden holding onto one another and shouting and laughing like two adolescents on drugs. The next day they both swore they had not touched anything apart from a dozen or so glasses of Coke each.

Ted's theory is that your company is still lacing the product with cocaine. I understand this is how you people got the rest of the world addicted in the first place. But I told him that it was very unlikely you would still be pursuing the practice today. Not with cocaine costing $50 a gram. Or so I hear. Ted said you could be using a generic.

Please let me know if twelve glasses of Coca-Cola could make a smallish woman lose all control and misbehave to such an extent that she needs to be strapped to a lemon tree.

Yours truly,

....
Ben Trovato (Mr)

49

ADDRESS REPLY TO
P. O. BOX 1734
ATLANTA, GA 30301
1-800-438-2653

July 17, 2001

Mr. Ben Trovato
P.O. Box 1117
Sea Point
Cape Town,   8060

Dear Mr. Trovato:

On behalf of Doug Daft, thank you for contacting our Consumer Information Center. We appreciate the opportunity to respond to a loyal consumer of our products.

Please be assured, our products do not contain cocaine or any other harmful substance, and cocaine has never been an added ingredient for Coca-Cola.

Thank you for your interest in our Company.

Sincerely,

Steven Ivey
Consumer Affairs Specialist

Encl: Soft Drink Nutrition
         Top Ten

NASA HQ
300 E St. SW,
Washington, DC 20500
USA

Mr Ben Trovato
PO Box 1117
Sea Point 8060
Cape Town
South Africa

29 May, 2001

Dear Sir,

I would like to volunteer to be the next civilian to go into space. I understand there may be a waiting list, but there are several reasons that I should go to the front of the line.

For a start, I am not a communist. Unlike that Tito chap who made a beeline for Moscow the moment Houston said they had a problem. Goddamn pinko liberals have no place in the space programme. It is for real men like me. And perhaps Clint Eastwood. But if he does another film with Meryl Streep, then I think he should be put on the same list as Red Dennis.

It is understandable that you will want to know why I think I am the best person to go into orbit. For a start, I am not an astronaut. This means I will not begin thinking I am God at seven million feet above sea level. I am also not afraid of heights. I am sure the last thing the control room needs is a passenger, hysterical with vertigo, refusing to let go of the International Space Station.

My main motivation for applying is that I need some peace and quiet. My wife, Brenda, has become quite intolerable lately. She seems to have developed an unhealthy liking for Coca-Cola and is becoming progressively violent. I have already been to Jamaica and visited a brothel once. I don't particularly care for football, either. The local pub has banned smoking and the park is full of prostitutes.

This leaves Outer Space.

My only concern is the meteorite factor. Should I be selected, and there is no reason to doubt it, what contingency plans are in place should the Shuttle encounter a meterorite shower? I have been afraid of flying objects ever since I was struck in the face by a blind seagull while riding my bicycle along the Sea Point promenade. I imagine a meteor could do a lot more damage than a gull. However, I assume these things are taken into account.

The only other drawback is my ability to calculate sums quickly. Mathematics was never my strong suit, and I would suggest that you not place me in a position where I would have to chart our course. I was in the Signal Corps many years ago, and would feel quite comfortable behind the radio. I presume you use the same codes as the truckers do on CB radio.

I will be in Washington early next month, and will pop in to have my suit fitted.

Yours truly,

Ben Trovato (Mr)

Aerospace Education Services Program

National
Aeronautics and
Space
Administration

NASA Education Publications
Mail Code FEO-2
300 E Street SW
Washington D.C. 20546

Thank you for your interest in NASA Educational Publications. Please find enclosed the information you requested.

This office is pleased to assist you. If in the future you need additional information about the aerospace program, please write or call again.

Publications Distribution

Oklahoma State University, Education and Research Foundation, Inc. (Contractor)

Minister Mohamed Valli Moosa
Environmental Affairs & Tourism
Private Bag X9154
Cape Town
8000

Mr Ben Trovato
PO Box 1117
Sea Point
8060

30 May, 2001

Dear Mr Moosa,

I feel it is my duty to warn you about the Spanish. Don't deal with these swine.
I hear they are after our fish. And what are they offering in return? Very little, I
expect. I have experience of the Spanish. When I was a little younger, I travelled
to Pamplona to run the bulls. It had always been a dream of mine, ever since
reading Hemmingway. I saved up just enough to get to Barcelona, and then hiked
the rest of the way.

A man wearing a black beard picked me up and threatened to take me to his
ETA commanders unless I complied with his instructions. I'm not going to go
into details because it's not an episode in my life of which I am particularly
proud. Suffice it to say that I got to Pamplona penniless and more than a little
hysterical. Fortunately, my military training came through and I was able to
take my place in the Plaza del Toro. I ran like a champion that first day. In the
afternoon I met some new friends, and we went off into the old part of the town.
Even though I had lost all of my money, I remember having a lot of sangria
to drink. I never saw the bulls again. In fact, it took someone from the South
African embassy to get me out of that disgusting cell.

And that's why I wanted to warn you about the Spanish. They will pretend to be
your friends, but then, for no reason at all, they will strip you naked and turn you
into a sexual deviant. I'm not saying that it will happen to you. But be careful
when you negotiate with these people. They will drink and laugh and have a
merry old time with you, but the moment you step out to the loo, they will pillage
your entire marine resource and take your wife too.

I'm prepared to come on board to fight the trawlers when they enter our waters.
Because enter they surely will. The blood of the conquistadors runs deep. Let us
learn from the Incas. I have basic karate training, and I beg you to let me join
the boats. Here is a ten rand deposit.

Keep our fish for us!

Yours truly,

....
Ben Trovato (Mr)

BRIBE GIVEN R10

53

MINISTRY: ENVIRONMENTAL AFFAIRS AND TOURISM
REPUBLIC OF SOUTH AFRICA
Private Bag X447, Pretoria, 0001, Tel: (27-12) 310 3611, Fax: (27-12) 322 0082
Private Bag X9154, Cape Town, 8000, Tel: (27-21) 465 7240/1/2, Fax: (27-21) 465 3216

Ref: O3/3/1   25 June 2001

Mr B Trovato
P O Box 1117
SEA POINT
8060

Dear Mr Trovato

SPANISH TRAWLERS NIGHTMARE

I wish to acknowledge receipt of your letter dated 30 May 2001.

By direction of Mr M V Moosa, Minister of Environmental Affairs and Tourism, please be advised that the Minister took note of the contents of your letter and has referred it to Mr Horst Kleinschmidt, the Deputy Director-General at Marine and Coastal Management section, for his attention and direct disposal. Mr Kleinschmidt's office telephone number is (021) 402-3911 or 3401.

Kindly expect further communication from his office in due course.

Yours sincerely

P.P. *Makolane*
FRANÇOIS ROGERS
DIRECTOR: OFFICE OF THE MINISTER

Department of Environmental Affairs and Tourism • Departement van Omgewingsake en Toerisme
Lefapha la Tikoloho le Bohahlaudi • Umnyango Wezemvelo Nezokuvakasha • Isebe leMicimbi yokuSingqongileyo noKhenketho
Lefapha la tsa Tikologo le Boeti • Umnyango Wetemvelo Netekuvakasha • Muhasho wa zwa Vhupo na Vhuendi
Ndzawulo ya ta Mbangu na Vuendzi • Lefapha la Tikologo le Bojanala • Umnŷango Wezebhoduluko Nezokuvakatjha

Marine and Coastal Management, Private Bag X2, Robbebaai 8012

Ref: V6/7
Enquiries: Dr Mayekiso
Tel: 402 3911

Mr B Trovato
PO Box 1117
SEA POINT
8060

Dear Mr Trovato

SPANISH TRALERS NIGHTMARE

Your letter dated 30 May 2001 to Minister Moosa of the Department of Environmental Affairs and Tourism refers.

We have noted the contents of your letter and will take every precaution to ensure that they do not exploit our marine resources.

Yours sincerely

Deputy Director General: Marine and Coastal Management
Date: 5/7/01

S.W.E.A.T　　　　　　　　　　　　　　　Mr Ben Trovato
Community House　　　　　　　　　　　　PO Box 1117
Salt River Road　　　　　　　　　　　　 Sea Point
Salt Road　　　　　　　　　　　　　　　8060

6 June, 2001

Dear Madame,

Brenda would kill me if she knew I was writing this letter.

However, it is not as if you are Lulu's Escort Agency. You are the Sex Workers
Education and Advocacy Taskforce, which sounds a whole lot more respectable.

My boy, Clive, is coming of age and I was hoping that your organization might be
able to help him across the yawning divide that separates the boys from the men.

Since you have an "education" component, I thought that you would be perfectly
placed to arrange for Clive to be "educated".

It need not be anything dramatic. The lad can be a tad unstable in certain
situations, and we do not want to alarm him. I would suggest avoiding leather
and latex rubber, and please ensure that no whips, chains or weapons of any sort
are easily accessible.

If at all possible, I would prefer Clive not to be left permanently scarred by the
experience. We don't want him to turn into a raving misanthropist. My memories
of entering manhood are sullied by recurring images of a naked juggler, studded
crayfishing gloves and the strong smell of antiseptic. I want his memories to be
less confusing.

At the same time, we should perhaps avoid your more seasoned lasses. We don't
want him crossing the Rubicon at the shake of a hand, if you know what I mean.
Pick out someone wholesome, but not too chaste. Fresh, yet wanton. Clive is not
likely to make the first move, unless, as I said, there is a weapon nearby.

By the way, I find it very interesting that in the local phone book there are only
two entries under "sex". One is your organization, and right above it, the Sex
Education and Dysfunction Unit. Odd, isn't it? Perhaps I should try them too.

Enclosed please find ten rand as a deposit for the girl that you will be selecting
as Clive's mentor, as it were. Perhaps it might be a good idea for me to pop
around and check her out personally. As I said, we don't want the boy to have a
relapse.

Yours truly,

....
Ben Trovato (Mr)

BRIBE GIVEN
R10

56

S W E A T

SEX WORKER EDUCATION AND ADVOCACY TASKFORCE

PO Box 373, Woodstock, 7915, Cape Town, South Africa
Physical address: Community House, 41 Salt River Rd. Salt River, Cape Town
Tel: (021) 448 7875 Fax: (021) 448 7857 email: sweat@iafrica.com

Mr Ben Trovato
P O Box 1117
Sea Point
8060

4 July 2001

Dear Sir

Herewith please find enclosed R10 which accompanied your letter dated 6th June. In response to your letter please be advised that we are a not for profit organisation working with sex workers regarding health and human rights issues.

Yours sincerely

[signature]

Jayne Arnott
Director.

57

Sex Education and Dysfunction Unit of SA
9 Montrose Avenue
Claremont
7735

Mr Ben Trovato
PO Box 1117
Sea Point
8060

6 June, 2001

Dear Madame,

I pray that you are able to help me. I have been through the telephone directory and there are only two listings under "sex". This is outrageous, considering that everyone needs it. With the possible exception of the Pope XIII in Springdale, USA. There is either too much or not enough. It is either very good or appalling. It makes you delirious with joy or leads to suicide. It relieves tension yet brings on headaches. It is everywhere and yet nowhere. I need not remind you how popular coitus is these days, and yet you and the Sex Workers Education and Advocacy Taskforce are the only entries in the book.

But no matter. I think you will be in a position to assist me. Or rather, assist my boy. You see, Clive is at a stage of his life where he needs to smell the flower of life. He needs to drink deeply from the chalice of love. The callow youth needs to feel the gentle embrace of Eros and Aphrodite. But to keep costs down, let us limit him to Eros for now.

Since you are in the field of education, I will need your best instructor. She need not be a Tantric master or a student of the Kama Sutra, but she should have the necessary skills to make sure that my lad gets across the swaying bridge between boydom and manhood.

I am pleased to see that your unit also deals with "dysfunction". Clive has been known to exhibit fairly aberrant behaviour, but I suspect this is simply his reaction to puberty. We are all pleased that the allegations of pyromania came to nothing, but it is probably best to provide a mentor who does not smoke. However, should everything about him prove dysfunctional, we may need to discuss the possibility of a refund.

Enclosed is a ten rand deposit for a suitable girl. Perhaps you can pick one out? Failing that, I can visit your offices and see if there is something that might take Clive's fancy.

Let me know soon because Clive is due for a weekend out on good behaviour.

Yours truly,

....
Ben Trovato (Mr)

BRIBE GIVEN
R10

14/6/2001

Mr. B. Trovato
P.O. Box 1117
Sea Point
8060

Dear Mr Trovato,

The Sex Education and Dysfunction Unit is not at all the kind of organisation you seem to think it is.
We are therefore not in a position to assist you in your quest.

Enclosed please find your R10.00

For Sex Education and Dysfunction Unit of S.A.

The President
The Labour Court of South Africa
Private Bag X52
Braamfontein 2017
Johannesburg

Mr Ben Trovato
PO Box 1117
Sea Point
8060

11 June, 2001

Dear Sir,

Now that democracy has crushed the workers struggle, I am sure you are a busy man. So I will get straight to the point.

It's my wife, Brenda. Ever since she saw a documentary on COSATU she has demanded to be paid for doing housework. You will agree that this is outrageous. Women were doing housework long before the communists hijacked the coming of spring. Somebody has to do the laundry and wash the dishes, even on May Day.

I have been forced to wear soiled underwear and mismatched socks for the past seven weeks. My shirts look like I have slept in them, because that's exactly what I have been forced to do since dribbling hot cocoa down my pyjamas.

Brenda is also on a sex strike. Perhaps she would relent if I offered to pay her. This matter will be coming before the Constitutional Court very soon. I do not see sex as hard labour, unless you happen to be married to that pop star fellow, Sting.

Brenda has refused to employ a domestic worker ever since she came home early and found Gladys and my boy, Clive, playing ludo in the buff.

Now Brenda has stopped doing the housework altogether. She wants a thousand rand a day to cook and clean. I told her that for a thousand rand a day I can find someone to not only wash my scants, iron my shirts and cook dinner, but who will also be willing to have gratuitous sex with me, and with a smile on her face to boot. Brenda said in that case, I should start learning Mandarin pretty damn quickly.

I have already reported Brenda's poor attitude to the Human Rights Commission. However, they involved the police, which I thought was rather unnecessary. I find justice is best served by avoiding the law and proceeding straight to the courts. Given that this is a labour matter, I am approaching you for advice. Knowing that nothing is for free, I enclose ten rand. This is not a bribe, but merely an expression of my desire to see this matter resolved as quickly and painlessly as possible.

Yours truly,

Ben Trovato (Mr)

BRIBE GIVEN R10

JUDGES' CHAMBERS
LABOUR COURTS
PRIVATE BAG X52
BRAAMFONTEIN 2017
ARBOUR SQUARE
86 JUTA STREET
BRAAMFONTEIN 2001
TEL: +27 (011) 359 5700
FAX: +27 11 403 9325

LABOUR COURTS

20 June 2001

Mr Ben Trovato

P.O. Box 1117

Sea Point

8060

Cape Town

Sir

Your letter of the 11th June 2001 addressed to the Judge President in which you enclosed a R10,00 note is hereby returned together with the R10,00 note.

Yours sincerely.

Martin

Heidi Martin

Office of the Judge President

Ms Heidi Martin
Office of the Judge President
Private Bag X52
Braamfontein
2017

Mr Ben Trovato
PO Box 1117
Sea Point
8060

14 July, 2001

Dear Ms Martin,

Thank you ever so much for your reply of 20 June on behalf of the president of the Labour Court. I had no idea that he also moonlighted as Judge President.

Reading between the lines (all two of them), I got the distinct impression that the Judge was not terribly impressed with my request for advice. Did I happen to catch him on a bad day? Was it too windy for golf? Or perhaps he had to wake up with an unrequited member, wash his own underwear, make his own breakfast and push-start his car. Somehow I doubt it. Generally, these things happen to ordinary people. Me, in particular. You do not get to be Judge President by getting down on your hands and knees and scrubbing at a mysterious fungus that has begun growing around the base of the toilet.

You get to be Judge President after years of either putting people in jail, or keeping them out of jail. During that time, you get to make enormous amounts of money. And eventually, you develop the Necessary Attitude. This entails ignoring requests for advice from ordinary folk who might have been in jail once or twice, but whose trials never lasted long enough to generate the kind of money that advocates expect to make.

The Judge President appears to have a particularly well developed Necessary Attitude. Not only did he send my ten rand back, but he also instructed you to return my letter. Did he do this because he could not even lower himself to scrunch it up and toss it into the bin? If so, why did he not instruct you to do that? I do not need my letter back. I have a copy. I always keep copies of everything I write to anyone in the legal profession. I am all too familiar with the tippex-photocopier-lawsuit trap. As, I am sure, is the Judge.

But as a married white man, I am accustomed to rejection.

What really worries me is the manner in which my letter was returned. It was concealed in a giant brown envelope marked "Recycle". I presume this is part of the government's futile strategy to win the green vote. In this country, it is easier to buy the bunny-huggers than woo them. Very few people are impressed with the word "Recycle" any more. But that is beside the point. What I am more concerned about (apart from finding a way to dispose of this enormous envelope) is the fact that you spent six rand (R6) on postage. Six rand for one sentence. My original letter cost one rand forty (R1,40). I understand that in the government's frenzy to create jobs, there is not always time for secretaries to fold a letter to fit a smaller envelope. But, Ms Martin, the extra effort could save the taxpayer millions. In our economy, size does count. Let's get folding!

Yours truly,

....
Ben Trovato (Mr)

PS. There is no need to show this to the Judge President.

Judge Fikile Bam
President: The Land Claims Court
Private Bag X10060
Randburg
2125

Mr Ben Trovato
PO Box 1117
Sea Point
8060

11 June, 2001

Dear Judge,

I am renting a modest house on a small piece of land. However, my neighbour lives on a plot the size of Luxembourg and his house resembles the Challenger space shuttle.

I would like to claim this property for myself.

I suspect he is an absentee landlord, since the lights are hardly ever on. This should make it easier for judgement to be delivered in my favour.

I need to know if we can get this through the court before October, as I am planning to host an end-of-winter party. My current patio is only large enough to accommodate the neighbours (Ted and Mary Goodfellow), and if my claim succeeds I will be able to squeeze in at least 400 people. You will appreciate that I need to get the invitations out early.

Would you advise that I take occupancy while the alleged owner is out of the country? I assume the Land Claims Court operates on the "nine-tenths of the law" principle. I have studied the house and with the help of a sturdy ladder and a pair of industrial bolt-cutters I can be in before papers are even filed.

Although I have no ancestral claims to this particular piece of land, I do have two dogs who need a fair amount of space for their morning run. And if you are anything of an animal lover, I am sure you will put in a word with the judge presiding over this matter.

I plan on being in Johannesburg soon. Perhaps I could buy you lunch? Let me know how you are placed for early July.

Yours truly,

Ben Trovato (Mr)

The Land Claims Court

Judges' Chambers

Randburg Mall • (Opposite Post Office) • Cnr Hill St & Kent Ave • Randburg • 2194
Private Bag X10060 • Randburg • 2125 • Tel: (011) 781-2291 • Fax: (011) 781-2217
http://www.law.wits.ac.za/lcc

11 July 2001

Mr Ben Trovato
PO Box 1117
Sea Point
8060

Dear Mr Trovato

I acknowledge receipt of your letter dated 11 June 2001 and thank you for it. I apologise for the delay in responding but I was working in Bloemfontein at the time and have only returned recently to attend to correspondence that came during my absence.

The jurisdiction of the Land Claims Court is limited and is confined to considering claims for restitution of rights in land to persons dispossessed of such rights after 19 June 1913. The dispossession must have been as a result of the application of past racially discriminatory legislation or practices. The procedure, in your case, would have had to be started in the Land Claims Commissioners' office in Cape Town and not directly with the Court.

I am consequently able to accept your lunch invitation certain that the absentee landlord will not thereby have occasion to apply for my recusal should his estate one day be up for restribution.

Yours faithfully

FC Bam
President (Land Claims Court)

Justice Arthur Chaskalson
President of the Constitutional Court
Private Bag X32
Braamfontein
2017

Mr Ben Trovato
PO Box 1117
Sea Point
8060

11 June, 2001

Dear Judge Chaskalson,

From what I hear, you are a man who understands the law. Presumably you are married, and are therefore also a man who understands the needs of men. Not in the way that some judges understand the needs of men, of course. I hasten to add that I am not prejudiced in one way or another. However, a judge who has little need of female company might not be ideally placed to advise me on my rights.

Judge, I have been married for a number of years. And my Brenda has always been an active participant on the connubial front. Well, to be honest, she has on more than one occasion needed a little encouragement to partake of the conjugal bliss. Fortunately, the neighbours stopped notifying the police once they realised that I was simply exercising my marital rights.

And it is to do with these rights that I am approaching you.

Brenda has frozen up on me. At first I thought it might be a circulation problem, and I attempted to open up her veins with a rigorous slapping. Well, that certainly got her blood up, if nothing else. She retrieved my stick from where she keeps it hidden and set about my lower body. She only stopped when she suspected that I was enjoying it, but I can assure you that I dislike a beating as much as the next man.

Like you, I am from the old school and feel it undignified to beg for sex. There can be few things less appealing than a grown man grovelling for his wife's favours. So I have refrained from mentioning it. And so has she. An indecent amount of time has lapsed, and fearing rebuffal, I remain on my side of the bed and she on hers.

Being a judge, it is unlikely that your wife would dare to attempt such an infringement. And I am sure you will agree that Brenda is violating my constitutional rights. Although I have not seen it personally, my neighbour (Ted Goodfellow) assures me that there is a clause in the Constitution dealing with frigid spouses.

Since I am getting no relief at home, would you suggest that I seek it in the Constitutional Court? I am not asking for free advice. Here is a ten rand note as a token of my gratitude.

Yours truly,

....
Ben Trovato (Mr)

BRIBE GIVEN
R10

THE CONSTITUTIONAL COURT

4 July 2001   1/4/18

Mr B Trovato
P O Box 1117
SEA POINT
8060

Dear Sir

REPRESENTATIONS

Your letter dated 11 June 2001 addressed to the President of the Constitutional Court was delivered his absence of the president from the Court.

The president has now returned. He has asked me to return to you the R 10,00 enclosed with your letter.

Yours faithfully

D C C DU PLESSIS
DIRECTOR: CONSTITUTIONAL COURT

BRAAMPARK FORUM II 33 HOOFD STREET, BRAAMFONTEIN, JOHANNESBURG 2017
PRIVATE BAG X 32, BRAAMFONTEIN, 2017
TELEPHONE: (011) 359-7458 or via Switchboard (011) 403 - 8032 FACSIMILE: 403 - 6524
WEBSITE: http://www.concourt.gov.za/

The Chief Librarian
Gay & Lesbian Archives of SA
PO Box 31719
Braamfontein
2017

Mr Ben Trovato
PO Box 1117
Sea Point
8060

12 June, 2001

Dear Chief Librarian,

Living in Cape Town, I get the impression that there is an enormous ongoing swing towards homosexuality so you must be very busy archiving the newcomers and I won't keep you long.

My Brenda has gone cold on me, and I was wondering if you kept family trees in your archive. I suspect her complete lack of interest in sex has something to do with men in general, and I need to trace her genealogy. At first I thought she had simply found me physically repulsive. But then my neighbour, Ted Goodfellow, said it was more likely that a genetic timebomb had exploded deep inside her. I was taken aback, to say the least. Is this what women mean when they say their clock is ticking?

I need to find out if Brenda has a homosexual lurking in the upper branches of her tree. Her maiden name is French. Once, while we were courting, she confessed to having had a crush on a girl at school. I laughed it off, and said the French have always been a bit suspect. Talk about self-fulfilling prophecies.

I urgently need to know if this celibacy business is a passing phase or something a lot more serious. Please run a check on her and let me know as soon as possible.

Yours truly,

....
Ben Trovato (Mr)

PS. While you are at it, could you punch in the names "Sam Nujoma" and "Robert Mugabe"? I remember seeing a photograph of the two of them holding hands, and I have always wondered how deep their friendship really was. My interest is purely academic, as I think they are both fine leaders and solid democrats.

The Gay and Lesbian Archives (GALA)
PO Box 31719
Braamfontein
2017
Gauteng
South Africa
Fax\phone: + 27 (11) 717-4283\4
email: galasa@pixie.co.za
Web: http://www.wits.ac.za/gala

20 June 2001

Ben Trovato
PO Box 1117
Sea Point
8060
Cape Town

Dear Mr Trovato,

Thank you for your recent enquiry addressed to the Gay and Lesbian Archives and your thoughtful concern about our time consuming preoccupation with documenting the lives of the known and suspected.

I regret to say that we do not have family trees and genealogies in our archive – and a great pity, as we are simply unable to engage in the "nature" / "nurture" debate on the basis of our extensive collections of organizational records, and the papers of individuals who have kindly housed their personal memorabilia with us.

We do of course have material on Sam Nujoma and Robert Mugabe, but this tends to be drawn from the public domain and does not offer any further insight into the heady eroticism of their domestic affairs.

Thank you for your interest in our work, I enclose some additional material.

Sincerely

Graeme Reid
Coordinator

The Chief
National Coalition of Free Men
PO Box 129
Manhasset, NY 11030
USA

Mr Ben Trovato
PO Box 1117
Sea Point 8060
Cape Town
South Africa

15 June, 2001

Dear Sir,

I have been looking far and wide for a little advice, and I think your organisation may be able to provide that sympathetic ear.

The problem is my Brenda. We have been married for some time. But that's not the problem. I suspect that she is trying to destroy me. Nothing like coming at me with a steak knife, you understand. It is far more subtle than that. A pot of scalding hot tea "accidentally" dropped in my lap. A mini cheese roll filled with "tasty" ingredients. Another night of trying to prepare my own dinner. Another week of wearing dirty underwear. But that is the least of it.

Brenda has taken to using sex as a weapon. She was always a tiger in bed. Well, a lynx, at the most. Now she is roadkill. And tabby cat, at that.

I can cope with the dangerous psychological games and petty assaults, but I am struggling to come to terms with the withdrawal of conjugal rights. I tried to get her in the mood the other night, but she turned my own stick on me.

Would you suggest that I begin begging for her favours? This kind of thing always seems somewhat undignified. It might be acceptable if you have only one night left to live, but in my view it is a little extreme if you are married and hope to reach old age still doing it.

Where does your organisation stand on frigid spouses? I have approached the president of our Constitutional Court with the same question, but I fear that his answer will be dictated by thousands of militant jack-booted members of the Right to Hairy Armpits Society.

I also wrote to the chief of our Human Rights Commission, a certain Mr Barney Pityana, suggesting that we take the matter to the International Court of Justice as a groundbreaking test case. Do you know what he did? He reported me to the local police.

So not only do I spend every night celibate and hungry, but I cannot sleep for fear that the front door will be kicked down by burly thugs in camouflage who will drag me into the street dressed in unclean pyjamas and clearly sporting an unrequited member for all the neighbours to see.

At this point, any advice would be welcome.

Yours truly,

....
Ben Trovato (Mr)

cc. UK Men's Movement
    We, The People

69

July 2, 2001

Dear Mr. Trovato:

First let me say our position is that any man who has entered into a willing relationship with a woman based on traditional ideals, ie., she will stay home, cook and sew, has a perfect right to expect that she will keep her obligations.

However, in recent years there have been some changes. Women have been given the moral approval to break their contracts. Moreover, the idea of conjugal rights is, in most western nations, no longer valid. In most places it has been replaced by spousal rape laws and/or wife abuse legislation. And where no fault divorce laws exist the man no longer has any moral right to have any sexual expectations (nor does the wife, for that matter).

The man takes the brunt of all of this, because he is most likely to be at the losing end of a property settlement (some women's groups would disagree with this) and/or most likely to be the one to have to pay alimony and child support.

Having said this, you do not have a legal problem at this moment. Bringing yourself to the attention of the legal authorities has only served to put them on notice. This will probably not work well for you if your wife makes some kind of complaint. Keep courts, human rights commissions, police, etc., out of your affairs for now.

Your first order of business is to do whatever you have to in order to secure your position legally, financially and socially. You will need to build a social network of supportive and knowledgeable friends. To accomplish this you should join and support any father's rights group you can find near you (even though you may not have children). You should attend meetings and get to know people. You need a social support group of friends.

You also should shop around for a competent divorce attorney who can tell you how to arrange your affairs, can guide you through the law and who will be ready to respond if your wife sues for divorce. It may be more advantageous for you to sue first for divorce. But don't do anything right away. Divorce attorneys have very bad reputations and you want to be able to consider any advice you get with your friends.

Your second order of business is to explore truthfully what is happening to your marriage, assuming that you are not anxious to get divorced, but actually want to repair things. This is going to require some deep communication. I am going to assume that both of you lack the skills on your own to bring this about.

In our experience, most of the men we hear about don't get any warning from their wives that they are going to get sued for divorce. In our experience the man is lead to believe that nothing is wrong until his wife has all of her affairs (first order of business, above) in order. The man is then taken completely by surprise and is slow to defend himself because he is experiencing disbelief, becomes depressed and has no idea where to turn for help. In your case you are getting plenty of signals. Non verbal as they are, your wife is clearly trying to communicate something. Our advice is to seek professional counseling. This first step is something that you need to do first without your wife. Approach your wife later with the help of a therapist.

Finding a father's rights group in South Africa might be difficult. The first place to start is with the librarian in the reference room of a local library. Write to the Children's Rights Council, 300 I Street, North East, Suite 401, Washington, DC, USA 20002. They maintain an international directory. You can call them during business hours at (202) 547-6227 or FAX (202) 546-4272. You can also use the internet to try and find a group, but this will be laborious. If you do not own a computer you will have to find a librarian who can show you what to do. If there are no father's rights groups, join anything where you can make friends with other males.

Good luck, and don't assume your wife hates you. At the same time be prepared to go to war and to protect your assets.

Yours truly,

Joe Hill
National Coalition of Free Men
PO Box 129
Manhasset, NY 11030
EMAIL: ncfm@ncfm.org

The Manager
Commission Services
PO Box 7943
Pretoria
0001

Mr Ben Trovato
PO Box 1117
Sea Point
8060

27 June, 2001

Dear Sir,

I see that the Independent Electoral Commission is looking for someone to run the show. Well, you need look no further. I am your man. Should you be reluctant to take my word for it, allow me to explain why I am the best person to handle the vital post of Chief Electoral Officer.

I have more experience than most when it comes to elections. I have stood in more queues outside more polling booths than I care to mention. During the 1980s, much of the population chose to stay at home drinking beer and watching football on the telly whenever Election Day came around. That's fine for some, but I was out there in rain or shine casting my vote for a better South Africa.

With all the changes in 1994, I thought my voting days were over. We had always been led to believe that communists hold elections once every 200 years. To my surprise, we have been asked to line up and make our mark several times since then. And I have gladly done so. Several times in each election, in fact.

Perhaps I should not be telling you this, but it is the only way I can demonstrate my qualifications for the job. Seven years ago, I discovered a way to vote repeatedly at a number of polling stations in the same election. Being a confirmed democrat, I felt this was the least I could do to help prop up the system.

You will be pleased to know that I am not at all partisan when it comes to politics. I always spread my X around as much as possible. Every party on the roll gets at least one of my votes. But some (who shall remain nameless!) may get up to seven or eight, depending on how many polling stations I can reach before Brenda notices that I am missing and starts filing for divorce on the grounds that I am presumed dead.

I realise that you are an "affirmative action employer", but I believe that being white is a minor infraction compared with the wealth of experience that I would bring to the IEC.

Here is ten rand to help you slip my application to the top of the pile. Vote for me!

Yours truly,

....
Ben Trovato (Mr)

BRIBE GIVEN R10

INDEPENDENT ELECTORAL COMMISSION

Ref : CEO068

6 August 2001

Mr Ben Trovato
PO Box 1117
Sea Point
8060

Dear Mr Trovato

APPLICATION FOR POSITION OF CEO : ELECTORAL COMMISSION

Thank you for your interest in applying for the position of the Chief Electoral Officer of the Electoral Commission. Given the high interest that has been expressed for this position, we regret that your application was not successful this time.

The IEC wishes you success in your future endeavours.

Again, thank you for your interest in our organisation.

Sincerely yours

E Düring

MS E DÜRING
MANAGER : COMMISSION SERVICES

Ps. Please find attached your R10·00.

missioners:
ia Bam (Chairperson) ● Herbert Vilakazi (Deputy Chairperson) ● Thoko Mpumlwana ● Fanie van der Merwe ● Justice Ismail Hussain
on House, 260 Walker Street, Sunnyside, Pretoria ● PO Box 7943, Pretoria, 0001 ● Tel (012) 428-5700 ● Fax (012) 341-5292

Mr Des Lindberg
Chairman: Theatre Managements of SA
PO Box 2348
Houghton
2041

Mr Ben Trovato
PO Box 1117
Sea Point
8060

8 July, 2001

Dear Mr Lindberg,

Congratulations on being elected to lead such a powerful organisation. The last I heard of you, you were singing about a seagull called Nelson. You have certainly come a long way since then! Not that the song wasn't without merit. It had a catchy tune, but you clearly never lived in Sea Point when you wrote it. If you had, you might have been inclined to pour even more oil on the screeching, scavenging bastard.

Since you are now a man of the arts, I was hoping you would be interested in producing my latest one-act play.

The curtain goes up to reveal a young man sitting on a chair. He is naked apart from a long, black coat and military boots.

He looks straight ahead.

After twenty minutes, he reaches inside his coat, takes out a butcher's knife and plunges it into his chest. He falls to the floor, dead.

The curtain drops.

A literate audience will immediately recognise the work as a dramatic allegory on the futility of life. I am prepared to direct it if you wish.

I plan to be in Johannesburg soon, and I will pop into your office to discuss the details.

Enclosed is ten rand to buy the props. Something with a serrated edge would be perfect.

Yours truly,

....
Ben Trovato (Mr)

PS. Brenda, my wife, sends regards to Dawn. She says she wants to know what is her secret. I asked her what she meant by that, but she only raised her eyebrows and accidentally dropped a cup of hot tea in my lap.

CA$H GIVEN
R10

74

Full Member of

Ben Trovato,
P.O.Box 1117
Sea Point
8060

Dear Ben,

Thank you for your letter, and your congratulations. This reply will probably take
weeks, since the snail mail is just that. E-mail is quicker.

Your proposal for a one act play is presumably satirical, as I am reluctant to believe that
your are sufficiently depressed about the human condition to want to charge the public
good money for the drama you describe! Anyway there are not many literate audiences
around any more! Not up here anyway.

Do you get to see much theatre there in the colonies? We are given to believe that the
Cape is the breeding ground for lots of innovative theatre. Have you seen either of Fiona
Coyne's plays (Baxter)? We loved her work, which we saw in Grahamstown recently.

Meanwhile we have invested the ten rand note in a new breadknife for our kitchen. The
last one was stolen!

Hope your lap is recovering from the nasty hot tea accident. Love to your wife Brenda.

Thanks for writing,

Yours truly

DES LINDBERG

CAT

DES & DAWN LINDBERG • CABARET AND THEATRE

49 St Patrick Rd Houghton 2198 ☐ P O Box 2348 Houghton 2041
Tel (011) 487-1800 Fax (011) 487-1993
Cellular - Des 082-900-5315 Dawn 082-900-7527

E-mails: des@desdawn.co.za : dawn@desdawn.co.za : catoffice@desdawn.co.za; Web: www.desdawn.co.za

The Director
AFF
PO Box 2265
Bonita Springs, FL 34133
USA

Mr Ben Trovato
PO Box 1117
Sea Point 8060
Cape Town
South Africa

12 July, 2001

Dear Sir,

The other day my neighbour and I were having a couple of beers and talking about all the things we haven't done in our lives. One of them is to join a cult. I understand that you are a former cult member, and are obviously in a much better position to point out the best cults on the market.

Ted agrees with me that we should steer clear of anything that involves small animals like ferrets or gerbils. We would also not be interested in initiation rituals that involve pain (to us). And let's avoid Marilyn Manson. The rest is open for discussion.

We realise that many cults attract dangerous types like L Ron Hubbard, George W Bush and the strange Reverend Moon. Would you recommend that we start our own? This way, we can create the rules and control the membership. It sounds a lot safer. We were thinking of something quite esoteric, like a doomsday cult. However, we would want to avoid having to preside over mass suicides every solstice.

South Africa would be perfect for a new cult, because people seem to believe anything you tell them. It may seem hard to swallow, but there was once a cult called the National Party run by a handful of men in suits who managed to convince forty million people that they were not civilised enough to have the vote. But they never managed to hypnotise everyone. Some escaped and began blowing things up to get the others to snap out of it. Unfortunately, people like Hendrik Verwoerd and PW Botha gave cults a bad name.

Ted and I want to be members of a non-evil cult. However, we would also prefer to avoid the goody-goody cults, of course. That would take away the undercurrents of danger and mystery. We may as well join the Rotary Club, in that case. Perhaps something between the Jehovah's Witnesses and the Taliban.

We want to move quickly before we are too old to bend down for the rituals, so it would be appreciated if you could give us your advice without delay.

Yours truly,

....
Ben Trovato (Mr)

July 31, 2001

Mr. Ben Trovato
PO Box 1117
Sea Point 8060
Cape Town
South Africa

Dear Mr. Trovato,

We received your letter of July 12, 2001. I think there must be some mistake, as to what we do, because we are not able to assist you with your request.

If you are connected to the internet you can consult our web site (www.infocult.org) which will give you an idea of our services.

Sincerely,

Mike Kropveld
Executive Director

Mr Geoff Stovold
Secretary of Jorrocks Hunt Club
Summersales Barn, Blackham
Tunbridge Wells, Kent TN3 9TS
U.K.

Mr Ben Trovato
PO Box 1117
Sea Point 8060
Cape Town
South Africa

13 July, 2001

Dear Mr Stovold,

My sources tell me that a vicious campaign is being waged against you after
you issued death threats against people opposed to fox hunting. If this is true,
then allow me to extend my sympathy and support. How dare these people? Do
they not realise who they are dealing with? For heaven's sake, we have access
to powerful guns and fast dogs! You and I both know that in the event of a
confrontation, even the fox will be on our side.

Are you aware that these thugs have named you on the Internet? This means that
over a billion people have access to your personal details. I cannot even begin
to imagine what manner of telephone calls you and your poor family have been
receiving. And they call us terrorists?

The bunny-humpers have effectively imposed a fatwah on you. Perhaps
you should write a book badmouthing Islam and get round-the-clock police
protection. If that does not work, please be assured that you have friends out
here in Africa. This is, after all, the original home of the Great White Hunter.

There are still plenty of animals to kill over here. Just the other day, an entire
family of warthogs crossed through my garden. It would be quite easy to sit on
the porch with a brandy in one hand and an Uzi in the other. One wouldn't even
build up a sweat!

If the Noah's Arkists begin making your life intolerable, I would recommend that
you head out this way until the pressure is off. I'll get Brenda to make up the
spare room.

The alternative would be to wait until you can see the yellow of their bellies, and
then pick them off one by one. It is quite easy to get away with this sort of thing
out here. But I suppose it is unlikely that the Tunbridge Wells police will turn a
blind eye.

Bag a fox for me!

Yours truly,

....
Ben Trovato (Mr)

Mr. Ben Trovato,
PO Box 1117,
Sea Point 8060
Cape Town
South Africa

30 July 2001

Dear Mr. Trovato,

Thank you for your kind letter dated 13th July last. I would like to take this opportunity of correcting some of your statements. I have not made and would not make any death threats against anyone. I may not agree with many of the views held by those opposed to fox hunting in the UK but I would defend their right to hold and express those views. I do not agree with the use of violence in a democratic country such as the UK to further political agendas and I would not take this course of action myself.

There are unfortunately a small minority of people willing to carry out violent acts, allegedly in "support of their cause". There are others disinclined to violence themselves but prepared to encourage those that are, hence the web site. In my view these people are much like football hooligans, more interested in causing a ruck and mayhem than any 'cause' or game. There is not much one can do except work with the police and grin and bear it.

The sad thing that I often reflect upon is that I am probably closer to the views held by many of the anti-hunt people than the ordinary British Joe Public. Clearly we disagree on foxhunting. However, I am very much against causing unnecessary suffering to animals and in my view much of this is to be found in inhumane farming practices and thoughtless petkeeping. I myself take as much care as possible to only consume meat products that come from an humane farming environment and I won't have a caged animal in the house.

Yours sincerely,

Geoff Stovold

Major-General RJ Beukes Mr Ben Trovato
Chief of the SA Air Force PO Box 1117
Private Bag X199 Sea Point
Pretoria 8060
0001

17 July, 2001

Dear General Beukes,

I understand the Air Force has taken charge of President Mbeki's spanking new Boeing Business Jet. Congratulations! I am sure the president has had enough of travelling on SAA. I know I have. Getting his own plane is bound to put him in a better mood. And this will be good for all of us.

I also hear that the aircraft was delivered in a "green" state. As a flying man yourself, I need not point out that this means the interior must still be fitted. I see the plane itself costs R300-million. Quite a bargain, if you ask me! I was alarmed to discover, however, that R108-million has been set aside for interior decorating.

I have good news for you. My wife, Brenda, is offering to do it for just one million rand! A remarkable saving of R107-million, which could perhaps be spent on a presidential boat of some kind.

When I was younger, I bought a Kombi which Brenda fitted out beautifully with covered seats and fine curtains. And I am sure you will agree, General, that there is really not that much difference between a Boeing Business Jet and 20 VW Kombis placed end to end.

Brenda has some wonderful ideas which she would like to share with you. She wanted to write this letter herself, but there is no telling what could happen if you allow your wife unfettered access to a computer that is connected to the Internet!

She says that for the curtains separating Business Class from the poor brutes at the back, she would like to use lemon yellow diaphanous sheers held back by snakeskin straps tied in pussycat bows. As a counterpoint, she suggests rich saffron animal prints to cover the seats. She also says it is vital that feng shui protocol be observed, since the last thing you want to do is unbalance President Mbeki's chakras while he is travelling.

We will be in Pretoria sometime in August. Brenda wants to bring a few fabric samples around to your office. Let us know a convenient time.

Right now, I have to go out and do something masculine.

Yours truly,

....
Ben Trovato (Mr)

KANTOOR VAN DIE HOOF VAN DIE SA LUGMAG
OFFICE OF THE CHIEF OF THE SA AIR FORCE

Privaatsak X199 Pretoria 0001
Private bag

7 August 2001

Mr Ben Trovato
PO Box 1117
Sea Point
Cape Town
8060

Dear Sir

Thank you for your interesting letter dated 17 July 2001.

As you would know, purchasing aircraft involve many processes. Therefore your letter was forwarded to the acquisition team for consideration.

Kind regards.

(R.J. BEUKES)
CHIEF OF THE AIR FORCE: LIEUTENANT GENERAL

The Director
SA National Parks
PO Box 787
Pretoria
0001

Mr Ben Trovato
PO Box 1117
Sea Point 8060
Cape Town
South Africa

17 July, 2001

Dear Sir,

I understand that on 1st October, SA National Parks will be declaring open season on the Himalayan tahrs that are destroying Table Mountain.

About time, too! I could never understand why there was such an outcry over the operation. You and I both know the tahrs are not from this fine country. Our police force has shown us how to treat illegal aliens, and we should follow their example. Even though there are only 50 left on the mountain, they are frightening the tourists. Nobody wants to go for an afternoon stroll and come across a herd of giant goat-like creatures with slitty red eyes, deadly horns and bristling manes. Besides, if the tahrs were given free reign, Table Mountain would eventually be reduced to a pile of rubble that even a child could step over. Either way, we lose the tourists.

I would like to play my part in making Table Mountain safe for our children. Although I am not a hunting man by nature, I would like to be given the chance to bag a tahr. My neighbour has an Uzi submachine gun that he brought back from a visit to Israel some time ago, and he is prepared to lend it to me. This would be ideal, as my aim has not been the same since my wife "accidentally" poked me in the eye with a crochet hook.

By spraying small knots of tahrs, I could quite easily bring down three or four at a time. Naturally, I would not want to spoil the fun for everyone else. Perhaps you might want to consider quotas. Five per man would be fair.

Speaking of vermin, is there any chance that we can have Table Mountain's dassie population declared undesirable? I was up there the other day and had to fend off a brute the size of a lynx. He came at me while I was eating my lunch. Fortunately, I had my military training to fall back on. But not everyone knows how to deal with an overweight, one-eyed, snaggle-toothed rodent whose brain is rotten with altitude sickness. Dassies could be second prize for those who don't make the tahr hunt. It might even appeal to the tourists. I suspect the Germans would be up for it.

Anyway, enclosed is ten rand to get me on the list. Let me know if I have to wait until October. I am quite keen on getting in a little practice right now.

Yours truly,

Ben Trovato (Mr)

BRIBE GIVEN
R10

Tel: +27 21 701 8692 • Fax: +27 21 701 8773
Shop A1, Ground Floor, Westlake Square
cnr Steenberg Road & Westlake Drive, Westlake, 7945
✉ P.O. Box 37, Constantia, 7848
email: capepeninsula@parks-sa.co.za
web site: www.cpnp.co.za

Cape Peninsula
National Park

CP 90/3/7

22 August 2001

Mr Ben Trovato
P O Box 1117
Sea Point
8060

Dear Sir

RE: HIMALAYAN TAHRS

Your letter received from the Ministry of Environmental Affairs and Tourism refers:

Many thanks for your interest in the Tahr Issue. As there will be no opportunities for members of the public to participate in the process of removing the Tahrs from Table Mountain, we herewith return your R10.

With kind regards

PARK MANAGER

cc Francois Rogers – Ministry Environmental Affairs and Tourism

The Managing Director
7-Eleven Convenience Stores
PO Box 711
Epping 1
7460

Mr Ben Trovato
PO Box 1117
Sea Point
8060

18 July, 2001

Dear Sir,

You may have noticed the vicious winter storms that are lashing Cape Town. You may even have felt the icy chill of the night air. On the other hand, you might not have. As a very wealthy man, you probably emigrate during this terrible time of year. On the other hand, with over a hundred shops under your command you probably don't get out much.

When you leave the office to return to a cold house, do you pick up a bag of rooikrans firewood that is "specially grown and packed for 7-11"? I bet you R10 (enclosed) that you do not. I bet that you go home and switch on the heaters. But if you do decide to make a fire, I bet you get your wood from the corner café (same bet). I will tell you why you do not use 7-11 wood. Because it is wet. The rooikrans wood sold in your shops does not burn. It is soggy. It gurgles and spits when you try to burn it. I have invested huge sums in firelighters in an effort to keep a feeble flame flickering in the grate.

What the hell do you do with the wood? Do you have staff hosing it down before putting it on the shelves? Do not even think of blaming it on the rain. I have bought wood from your shops when the weather has been dry for weeks. And the rooikrans still bubbles and hisses and carries on like it is my cat that I am using for fuel. I would probably have more luck burning my cat. At least the hair would burn.

You call yourselves convenience stores? I have never been so inconvenienced in my life. Around the city, men have stacked the fire, tossed a match into the kindling and cuddled up for a romantic night on the honeymoon rug. It always ends badly. The poor girl has to put on layer after layer of clothing until she is of such gargantuan proportions that any passion is extinguished faster than the rooikrans. The man, of course, is still on his knees at 3am blowing and cursing long after his paramour has given up and gone to bed.

Men do not react well to fires going out on them. Especially not when a woman is in the room. On a scale of shame, it is second only to erectile dysfunction. We have been impressing the opposite sex with our fire-making skills ever since we discovered the stuff. And we are not about to stop now. Give us dry wood. Or else.

Yours truly,

....
Ben Trovato (Mr)

PS. If I am correct in assuming that you do not use your own rooikrans, you owe me R20. If not, send me a photograph of you lighting a rooikrans fire and keep my money.

84

SEVEN~ELEVEN CORPORATION
SA (Pty) Ltd
Reg. No. 1989/04849/07

Head Office/Warehouse P.O. Box 711   Tel: (021) 5351-711
711 Cochrane Ave.   Goodwood 7460   Fax: (021) 5350-711
Epping 1   Cape Town   E-mail: info@7-11
7460   Website: www.7-11.co.za

Winner Franchisor of the Year 1996

28/8/2001

P.O.Box 1117
Sea Point
8060

Att   :   Mr. Ben Travato

Re   :   Complaint –7/11 Rooikrans Wood

Dear Mr. Travato,

Please be so kind as to furbish us with your street address, we would like to deliver a gift to you in person, as mentioned in our reply letter to your complaint.

Unfortunately you did not mention any street address as well as a telephone number for us to contact you.

I thank you

Your sincerely

Natasha Filipe
Customer Complaints Dept.

SEVEN~ELEVEN CORPORATION
SA (Pty) Ltd
Reg. No. 1989/04849/07

Head Office/Warehouse
711 Cochrane Ave.
Epping 1
7460

P.O. Box 711
Goodwood 7460
Cape Town

Tel: (021) 5351-711
Fax: (021) 5350-711
E-mail: info@7-11
Website: www.7-11.co.za

ATTENTION: MR BEN TRAVATO
P.O. BOX 1117
SEA POINT
8060

28 July 2001

Dear Sir

RE: WET WOOD

I was born behind a cash register in my father's café 32 years ago. Since then, I have been an active member of the Company and General Manager thereof for the past 10 years now. In all my time in retail, I have received thousands of customer complaints, but none, I assure you, none, have been as witty and as well written as yours.

I have tabled your letter for both our executive meeting and our weekly Franchisees meeting and you can only imagine the response received.

On a more serious note, however, I must apologize, most sincerely, for any inconvenience caused. I personally have been a buyer of our Rooikrantz wood for many years now. We pride ourselves on our quality and size of each individual piece especially, so much so that we are wiling to put our brand name on it. As a family, we braai with Rooikrantz wood religiously on a weekly basis. We too have realized that the wood is green and have addressed it with our supplier. Within 2 weeks the "new" grade of wood will infiltrate the market place and we have been assured that the problem will be corrected.

We have your address via your letter sent and if you will allow us the opportunity, we would like to have a senior area manager deliver you some of our new wood with a bottle of red wine and 2 wine glasses so that you may make another attempt at rekindling your flame.

Thank you for the time and effort to write us – it is customers like yourself who help us to improve our business.

Yours sincerely

Elia Hadjidakis
GENERAL MANAGER

Managing Director: George Hadjidakis

Commissioner Wilson Toba
Eastern Cape Police
Private Bag 6020
Port Elizabeth
6000

Mr Ben Trovato
PO Box 1117
Sea Point
8060

23 July, 2001

Dear Commissioner,

I read in the local paper that the Eastern Cape police have arrested an Australian couple in possession of dagga. Congratulations on the good work!

They were travelling on a luxury coach from the Wild Coast to Cape Town when eagle-eyed officers from Idutywa realised that something was afoot. And when they stopped the bus and searched everyone aboard, their worst suspicions were confirmed.

The two Australians (aged 26 and 27) had 95 grams of marijuana secreted in their luggage. Thank God your men acted swiftly. There is no telling what horrors would have been unleashed upon the Mother City had the drug dealers managed to get through with their deadly cargo intact.

Even though the Eastern Cape is the poorest province in the country, I am sure you will agree that we do not need dope fiends coming in and spreading their Australian dollars around our impoverished communities.

The police roadblock and search by armed men must have provided a valuable lesson to every tourist on board that bus. The flora of the Eastern Cape is to be admired, not smoked. Where would the Transkei be if it was opened up to narco-tourism? Before long, even the lowly cattle-herder would have a double-storey home, two cars and a holiday bungalow in Clifton. And what kind of message would that send out, I ask you?

I understand the hopheads were due to fly home to Australia the day after they were apprehended. Talk about the nick of time! Had they escaped, word would have spread like wildfire around Sydney. You would have woken up one day to find the entire Wild Coast swamped by yawling mobs of antipodean jugglers, fire-eaters and other assorted freaks of nature.

Keep the Eastern Cape pure!

Yours truly,

Ben Trovato (Mr)

SOUTH AFRICAN POLICE SERVICE ✦ **SUID-AFRIKAANSE POLISIEDIENS**

My reference / My verwysing	12/2/4
Enquiries / Navrae	ASST COMM. HAYES / CAPT CHENGAN
Tel	041-3946121
Fax / Faks	041-3946932

OFFICE OF THE PROVINCIAL COMMISSIONER
SOUTH AFRICAN POLICE SERVICE
P/BAG 6020
EASTERN CAPE
PORT ELIZABETH
6000

7 August 2001

Mr Ben Trovato
PO Box 1117
SEA POINT
8060

Dear Sir

 APPRECIATION : MEMBERS OF THE SA POLICE SERVICE : IDUTYWA

1.   This office takes cognisance of your letter dated 23 July 2001.

2.   A copy thereof is being forwarded to the Area Commissioner Queenstown for his attention and the commendation of the Station.

Kind regards.

_____ **DEPUTY PROVINCIAL COMMISSIONER**
f\\PROVINCIAL COMMISSIONER : EASTERN CAPE
n\\PROVINSIALE KOMMISSARIS : OOS-KAAP
T H HAYES

avr\\Chengan\\2001\\8

88

Mr Frank Khan
Director of Public Prosecutions
Private Bag 9003
Cape Town 8000

Mr Ben Trovato
PO Box 1117
Sea Point
8060

23 July, 2001

Dear Mr Kahn,

I may have been misinformed, but word has it that you are a decent man.

I decided to write to you after hearing the appalling news that a judge has made prostitution legal. As a family man, I feel sure that you do not support this decision. On the other hand, our beaches are awash in half-naked women and the bars are full of men in skirts. If this kind of degeneracy is allowed, perhaps it does not overly concern you that I will now be forced to fend off hordes of drug-crazed tarts every time I stop at a traffic light in Sea Point.

We need to crack down hard before the moral fabric of our society gets a run in it. My neighbour and I had been considering forming a vigilante outfit, but Commissioner Lennit Max warned me against exposing myself. So I have another suggestion. I will pick up prostitutes and take them directly to your office. I suspect that I will have to operate mainly at night, so I need to know if there would be a problem should I drop them off at your home. I am sure you will advise me against taking them to the police, since that would be like delivering pizza to a starving man.

You will probably find out sooner or later, so I may as well be the one to tell you. I suspect that my wife, Brenda, is peddling her flesh somewhere along the Atlantic seaboard. Betraying my wife to the authorities does not come easily, but it must be done. Brenda's depleted libido has led me to suspect that she is taking her favours elsewhere, and is so thoroughly exhausted by the evening that she cannot even cook a meal, let along fulfill her other nuptial duties.

If my suspicions are accurate, it will only be a matter of time before Brenda is among those safely locked in the back of my bakkie. If I had to let her go, the others would accuse me of nepotism. This places me in the rather difficult position of having to leave my wife in your charge. I urge you to treat her as gently as possible. I anticipate making three or four runs a night. By Christmas, even the pope will be able to walk down Somerset Road with his Catholic sensibilities intact. I may need to switch cars now and then, so I would appreciate any help your office could give me in this regard.

Please forward me your home address so I can begin the operation as soon possible.

Yours truly,

....
Ben Trovato (Mr)

THE DIRECTOR OF PUBLIC PROSECUTIONS
UMLAWULI WEZOTSHUTSHISO WOLUNTU
DIE DIREKTEUR VAN OPENBARE VERVOLGINGS

Tel:	(021) 480 2411	**e-mail :** chiefclerk@justice.gov.za	**Reference no:** CPK/00/0363
Fax:	(021) 424 7825	**Internet:** www.ag-wcape.gov.za	**Enquiries:** Mrs A Lotz

Mr Ben Trovato
P O Box 1117
SEA POINT
8060

The Director of Public Prosecutions:
Cape of Good Hope
Private Bag 9003
CAPE TOWN
8000

2001 -08- 2 9

Dear Sir

Receipt of you letter dated 8.8.2001 is acknowledged.

Yours faithfully

F W KAHN SC
DIRECTOR OF PUBLIC PROSECUTIONS: CAPE OF GOOD HOPE

Mr Gerald Majola
United Cricket Board
PO Box 55009
Northlands
2116

Mr Ben Trovato
PO Box 1117
Sea Point
8060

13 August, 2001

Dear Mr Majola,

Congratulations on your new initiative to give young players an opportunity to make the national side. Those marijuana-smoking hooligans have had it their own way for far too long. If it were up to me, they would all be packed off to Jerusalem to learn a little humility.

I understand the plan is to create an A team which will be used as a breeding ground for new talent. You will be pleased to know that I have a promising young player in mind. His name is Clive, and he is my son. The lad has shown a remarkable eye for a ball ever since he could walk. By the age of seven, he could reach the neighbour's bedroom window with a rock bigger than his fist. And I once saw him send the cat a good 20 metres across the lawn with one well-placed stroke from my walking stick. If the animal had been smaller, the size of a cricket ball, it would have been over the boundary for sure.

Clive is busy undergoing specialised training at the moment, but we hope to have him back before the end of the month. I can have him in Johannesburg by early October, and he will be more than ready to tackle India when the side arrives in April.

It is possible that Clive may wish to liven up the dress code a little, but should you prefer everyone in the team to wear the same outfit, I am sure we will be able to reach a compromise. However, I suspect that a fast bowler wearing camouflage might be just the thing we need to catch the Aussies on the wrong foot.

I see Percy Sonn has been re-elected as president of the UCB. Please send him my congratulations. I am glad to hear that he will be keeping his day job as head of the elite Scorpions Unit. He is just the man we need to clean up a sport that has been awash in narcotics and blood money for way too long.

Enclosed is ten rand to secure Clive a position in the A team. And there is more where that came from. Much, much more. I expect to see you in Johannesburg soon.

Yours truly,

....
Ben Trovato (Mr)

BRIBE GIVEN R10

Wanderers Club, North Street, Illovo, 2196
P.O. Box 55009, Northlands, 2116
Facsimile : (011) 880-6578, Telephone (011) 880-2810
www.cricket.co.za
E-Mail : ucbsa@ucb.co.za

23rd August 2001

Mr. Ben Trovato
P.O Box 1117
Sea Point
8060

Dear Mr. Trovato

Further to your letter to Mr. Gerald Majola dated 13th August 2001:

The South African "A" side is chosen from the pool of deserving players who have worked their way through the ranks via participation in the provincial cricket system. Please phone me if you require further information.

Enclosed please find your R10 – perhaps you should donate it to the SPCA?

Yours sincerely,

ROSALYNNE GOLDIN
Marketing Director
United Cricket Board

The Manager
SPCA
PO Box 3
Plumstead

Mr Ben Trovato
PO Box 1117
Sea Point
8060

4 September, 2001

Dear Sir or Madam:

This probably makes little sense to you, but the SPCA is in line to benefit by the United Cricket Board's rejection of my son, Clive, for the South African "A" side.

Rather than make use of my lad's considerable ball skills, Rosalynne Goldin, the UCB's Marketing Director, feels that I should instead donate money to the SPCA. I cannot fathom it out, either.

I can only assume that the UCB, possibly Mr Gerald Majola himself, is in need of a pet of some kind. Perhaps you should send him something that is not trained to retrieve things. I should imagine the last thing Gibbs and the boys need is a highly trained gun dog intercepting the ball before it gets to the boundary. Unless they are fielding, of course, in which case I suggest something small and fast. Preferably not a bull terrier, since you would need to slit its throat to get it to open its mouth and drop the ball.

Whatever you do, please do not send the UCB a sniffer dog. The team is in enough trouble as it is without the mascot tearing their luggage apart every time they go on tour.

We should also not lose sight of the fact that Mr Majola may very well be a cat person.

I am enclosing R20.

Keep up the good work.

Yours truly,

....
Ben Trovato (Mr)

CA$H GIVEN
R20

THANK YOU

CAPE OF GOOD HOPE
DBV
SPCA
KAAP DIE GOEIE HOOP

FR/FI No. 003-244 NPO
Registration No. 1939/013624/0

website
http://www.spca-ct.co.za
e-mail
fundraising@spca-ct.co.za
enquiries@spca-ct.co.za

1st Avenue
Grassy Park

P.O. Box 3
Plumstead
7801

021-705 3757

021-705 2127

13 SEP 2001

Mr B Trovato
P O Box 1117
SEA POINT, CAPE TOWN
8060

Dear Mr Trovato

On behalf of all the animals in our care, a very sincere thank you for
your wonderful donation of R20.00. Your concern makes it possible for
us to restore some poor, unwanted animal's faith in human kindness

Unfortunately animals cannot speak up for themselves and they just
have to bear whatever treatment is handed out to them and that is why
it is so important to have a friend like you, someone who really cares
and who is prepared to do something practical to help.

So thank you once again for your gift. I hope you'll consider making
the SPCA your favourite charity as we need all the support that people
like you can give. Our best to you for the rest of 2001, happy in the
knowledge that your donation has helped an animal in need.

Your Receipt Reference Number is 40296.

Yours faithfully
CAPE OF GOOD HOPE SPCA

FRANCES DORER
FUNDRAISING

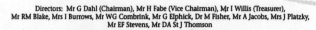
ESTABLISHED 1872 • FOUNDER SOCIETY OF THE SPCA MOVEMENT IN SOUTH AFRICA
EXECUTIVE MEMBER OF NATIONAL COUNCIL OF SPCA'S • WORLD SOCIETY FOR THE PROTECTION OF ANIMALS • ASSOCIATED WITH RSPCA

We Speak for, Protect & Care for Animals

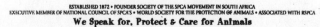

Minister Helen Zille
MEC Education
Private Bag X9161
Cape Town
8000

Mr Ben Trovato
PO Box 1117
Sea Point
8060

14 August, 2001

Dear Ms Zille,

I was driving in the city yesterday when I happened to catch a glimpse of the day's headlines. I rarely buy the paper, and prefer to skim the front page of newspapers while waiting for the lights to change. I find I sleep easier if I have no idea of what is going on in the world. Ignorance certainly can be bliss! Which brings me to the matter at hand.

Quite frankly, Minister, I was horrified to see that you are mounting a campaign to introduce "call girl schools"!

I assume you are basing your idea on the recent decision by that depraved judge in Pretoria who has just legalised prostitution. I implore you, Ms Zille, to rethink your decision. For the sake of the children. And some of the men.

I know you are a dedicated and competent Education Minister, but I suspect this time you have been led astray by degenerate advisors with a vested interest in flooding the city with well-educated women of easy virtue.

There is enough whoremongering going on in parliament, and the city can ill afford to create another tightly knit community of strumpets with degrees.

I suspect that my very own wife has become a fille de joie, and encouraging the competition to improve their education will mean longer hours and even less chance that she will have the energy to fulfill her connubial responsibilities.

I doubt very much that call girl schools will be welcomed by gentlemen who seek out the company of ladies of the evening. At one stage or another, most men need a break from educated women. And the last thing they need is for the trollop to begin pondering what Descartes really meant when he said cogito, ergo sum when all they want to do is get her knickers off.

My neighbour feels particularly strongly about the issue and wishes to stage a protest outside your offices. Please let me know which day would be convenient.

Yours truly,

Ben Trovato (Mr)

Telefoon
Telephone   (021) 467-2523
IFoni

Faks
Fax   (021) 461-3140
IFeksi

Verwysing
Reference   3/1/9
ISalathiso

Ministerie van Onderwys

Ministry of Education

I-Ofisi yoMphathiswa wezeMfundo

Mr B Trovato
PO Box 1117
SEA POINT
8060

Dear Mr Trovato

Thank you for your delightful letter to Minister H Zille dated 14 August 2001, the content was noted with appreciation. You raise very interesting and pertinent questions and it makes for rather thought provoking reading.

The Provincial competencies on education are mainly focussed on primary and secondary school education. The training you refer to, should first be analysed and specific needs should be established. Would it for example be regarded as "in service training"; what level of qualification would it be, a diploma course or a degree; where would it fit in, - Hospitality or Business Studies?

I am however slightly puzzled by your reaction and I cannot decide whether it is the ignorance you refer to in your letter, (which I doubt), or is it as they say in Latin a *lapsus oculus* or is it a legitimate Freudian slip?

What ever contributed to your reaction, never believe everything your eyes see - the matter under discussion was actually "all girl schools".

You are most welcome to contact me should you wish to discuss the matter further.

My kindest regards to Mrs Trovato.

EDDIE KIRSTEN
HEAD: MINISTRY
DATE: 21 - 8 - 2001

MELD ASSEBLIEF VERWYSINGSNOMMERS IN ALLE KORRESPONDENSIE / PLEASE QUOTE REFERENCE NUMBERS IN ALL CORRESPONDENCE / NCEDA UBHALE IINOMBOLO ZESALATHISO KUYO YONKE IMBALELWANO

GRAND CENTRAL TOWERS, LAER-PARLEMENTSTRAAT, PRIVAATSAK X9114, KAAPSTAD 8000
GRAND CENTRAL TOWERS, LOWER PARLIAMENT STREET, PRIVATE BAG X9114, CAPE TOWN 8000

96

Minister Mosiuoa Lekota
Ministry of Defence
Private Bag X427
Pretoria
0001

Mr Ben Trovato
PO Box 1117
Sea Point
8060

30 June, 2001

Dear Mr Lekota,

I would like to applaud your decision to introduce voluntary conscription. While I may not understand the concept, I still think it is a damn fine thing.

My boy, Clive, will soon become an adult. Oddly enough, with the help of the Russians.

But as you well know, Manhood entails more than losing your foreskin, virginity or way home after a night out with the lads. It includes a sense of duty. Some may say that patriotism is the virtue of the vicious, but you won't hear that kind of talk around my house.

You and I are both military men and yet we were never awarded rank of any kind. I served in 2 Signals Regiment and after two years I emerged much the worse for wear and still a common signalman. You were technically the enemy in those days, so your military experience might have been somewhat different. But since you have no rank attached to your name, it is safe to assume that you were also passed over in favour of those who happily ran off into the bush with grenades dangling like ripe avocados from their belts.

As a signalman, I was expected to be able to tell red from green, learn Morse Code and type 35 words a minute. I never understood the need for this, since the army itself moved at well under one word an hour. I am also colour-blind, which might account for the disaster at Cuito Cuanavale in 1989. And the only Morse I could ever remember was dotdotdot...dashdashdash...dotdotdot. This probably explains why the only border I ever crossed in those two years was the one between the Transvaal and Natal, as I hitchhiked home for another illegal weekend in Durban.

But back to Clive. I want him to spend some time in the army. However, we need to keep him away from your General Andrew Masondo. I saw him being interrogated on the programme Third Degree the other night, and I could not sleep for two days afterwards.

I may as well tell you that I have approached a foreign army with a view to placing him there. And I am awaiting a response from a paramilitary outfit inside this country. But I would prefer it if our very own national army could introduce him to the real world. The SADF is, in a sense, my alma mater. The only difference is that most graduates do not harbour lifelong grudges that can only be appeased by slaughtering their professors.

Yours truly,

....
Ben Trovato (Mr)

PS. My wife, Brenda, has just suggested that the army might not even accept white boys any more. I called her a racist pig and chased her out into the garden. But she always manages to find her way back in. It's the damnedest thing.

Minister Mosiuoa Lekota
Ministry of Defence
Private Bag X427
Pretoria
0001

Mr Ben Trovato
PO Box 1117
Sea Point
8060

15 August, 2001

Dear Mr Lekota,

Belated congratulations on your 53rd birthday! I hear you celebrated it on a game farm near Bloemfontein. Nothing wrong with that. People are free to spend their birthdays wherever they wish. Especially in a democracy. It might be different in Cuba, though.

I read in the paper that you spent the day hunting. Well, of course you did. You are, after all, the Minister of Defence. If you were the Minister of Tourism you would probably spend your birthday snorkelling naked at Lake St Lucia. But you are not. So we don't expect that kind of behaviour from you. There is something infinitely reassuring in knowing that the man in charge of our army, navy and air force is out there killing things on his birthday. God forbid that you had to be photographed playing Putt-Putt.

Your spokesman also mentioned that you shot two buck with a single bullet! This certainly proves that you are more than man enough for the job. How on earth did you do it? The last time I heard of something like this happening was when John F Kennedy was shot. Do you remember the magic bullet? Lee Harvey Oswald fired just once, and JFK was hit by the same bullet at least half a dozen times. It was the damnedest thing. I'm not disputing your story, but are you absolutely certain that you were the only person on the grassy knoll?

My neighbour has another version of events. He says you were probably hunting with an AK-47, and that you panicked and opened up on automatic when a herd of blesbok broke cover on your left flank. He says your spokesman is spin doctoring, because hunting with weapons designed for conventional warfare is frowned upon by the purists. Just like trout fishermen have a problem with people who arrive at the river with splinter grenades and a tungsten steel gaffing hook. But who cares what these loony liberals think, anyway?

Your spokesman also pointed out that it wasn't a clean kill. You are probably wondering why he had to mention this. I hate to say it, but your remarkable feat is tarnished by the news that it took several bullets in the back of the head to finish off the job. Having to execute two wounded antelope is not something that you want everyone to know about. I say get rid of the man. He is clearly a mole planted by the Green Party. Never mind what people say. Killing is your business, and business is good. Here is R10 for your birthday.

Yours truly,

....
Ben Trovato (Mr)

CA$H GIVEN
R10

99

Tel: (012) 355-6101

Fax: (012) 355-6139

Enquiries: Mr. B. P. Molefe

Private Bag x427

Pretoria

0001

23rd August 2001

Dear Mr. Trovato,

It is with a thrill that I received what you called "belated congradulations" for my 53rd birthday. You were very generous not only with your commendations but also with the present.

Your letter was full of repartee and pleasantries which left me in a light mood. For all these, I send my profound thanks and wish you all the best in future.

Sincerely,

Mr. M. G. P. LEKOTA
(MINISTER OF DEFENCE)

Embassy of Japan
Sanlam Building, 2nd floor
353 Festival Street
Hatfield
0083

Mr Ben Trovato
PO Box 1117
Sea Point
8060

29 July, 2001

Dear Ambassador,

I see that one of your government officials has described Minke whales as the "cockroaches" of the sea. I could not agree more. Dirty, great things cluttering up the ocean. Fortunately, they don't fly at your head when you least expect it. Getting struck by an airborne Minke could certainly ruin a good day's fishing.

The Minke are vermin. Scum of the seas. They are forever lying there, half-submerged, waiting for a yacht to come along. Many a sailor has cursed the smirking Minke while watching his boat sink from sight. They are also far too big. Any fish that weighs 15 tons is a freak of nature. Nothing short of grotesque. They upset the feng shui of the ocean and deserve to die.

I cannot understand why the members of the International Whaling Commission refuse to lift the 16-year ban on commercial hunting. We don't even need them around. They scoff all the shrimp and float around in the shipping channels idly belching from their blowholes. And the whales are no better.

I think it was a stroke of genius on the part of your government to tell the world that you are still catching Minke whales, but only for "scientific research". I have no doubt that you have plenty of people in white coats who study the meat as it is chopped into 1kg blocks and sold to fish and chip shops around Japan. Given the fact that 2 500 tons of blubber are consumed in your country every year, I find it remarkable that there are so few fat Japanese. Although the sumo wrestlers probably take more than their fair share.

As you know, whale season here in the Western Cape is almost upon us. In fact, a few Southern Rights have already been spotted in False Bay. I have an old hand-held harpoon that has been in my family for generations, and I have been thinking of giving it a whirl. If I manage to bag a medium sized cockroach, I am prepared to have it transported to the embassy at my own cost. What would you say to R1 000 a ton? Translate that into yen, and you've got a damn fine deal.

In the meantime, here's R10 in "development aid". Use it wisely.

Let's stamp out the whales!

Yours truly,

....
Ben Trovato (Mr)

Embassy of Japan

P.O. Box 11434 Hatfield 0028
Pretoria Republic of South Africa

Tel: (012) 342-2100
Fax: (012) 430-3922

Mr. Ben Trovato.
PO Box 1117
Sea Point
8060

We refer to your letter dated 29 July, 2001 concerning the Japanese research activity on whales. We appreciate the interest shown in whales and I would like to inform you that we are quite open and willing to discuss this subject. However, it would be somewhat difficult to do so if one's opinion is based on inaccurate information.

Allow me the courtesy to explain and provide you with background information on whale research.

Whaling is no longer an issue of species conservation as was the situation in the 1970's, when several whale species had been over-harvested and the effective measures to protect the endangered species were awaited. The International Whaling Commission (IWC) did an outstanding job on this subject in the mid - 1970's, to protect blue whales and other endangered species, and Japan highly appreciates its effort.

However, since the 1980's the situation has changed as non-endangered whale species also became protected by the IWC, despite the fact that the IWC Scientific Committee has calculated that some whale species were quite abundant. In the 1990's, scientists calculated that the global whale population (35 species) consumes 280 - 500 million metric tons of fish and crustacea every year. This amount is 3 - 6 times as much as is fished by human beings worldwide, as the annual world fishery production is around 90 million metric tons. The ecological relevance of the total protection of whale should be reviewed under these circumstances.

Also, it should be noted that any form of resource use contains a certain level of cost and risk to the environment. For example, an increased production of crops could result in further reduction for dwindling natural forests. Cattle raising consumes more fossil energy than whale hunting while producing the same amount of protein. Under these circumstances, it is not productive to attack one form of resource use by citing particular risk or cost to the environment. Rather, we should assess the wide variety of risks and costs associated with various activities, compare their cost/benefit to each other and choose the optimum way to balance the human activities.

Japanese research on whales is designed to unveil the population dynamics and ecological roles of this species by means of lethal and non-lethal method. Also, regarding this research, we should like to point out the following information as being the correct understanding of the situation.

The IWC has never concluded that this research does not address any critically important research needs. The report of scientific review (which was completed at the special meeting of the IWC Scientific Committee in May 5000) on this research program, along with the previously obtained research results, is open to the public through the IWC, Cambridge, UK.

The by-product of the research (i.e. whale meat) is sold in the market, but it does not create any profit. A non-profit research institute, which carries out the research program, sells the by-product in order to cover a portion of its research cost. The rest of the cost is covered by government subsidy. Please note that the International Convention for the Regulation of Whaling requests that by-products from the research be full utilized so far as practicable.

For more information, please visit http://www.whalesci.org/ (Institute of Cetacean Research, Tokyo, Japan) and http://ourworld. compuserve.com/homepages/ iwcoffice/ (the International Whaling Commission, Cambridge, UK).

The environment is a high priority in Japan and, in fact, our government spends more than $750 million annually for environmental conservation programs. This amount well exceeds those of major European countries and we are proud of our commitment. In the same token, we believe a limited harvest of non-endangered whales can be consistent with the concept of the sustainable use and the resource conservation of the earth.

The Embassy of Japan will openly respond to this matter in an orderly approach based on objective facts.

Lastly, kindly find herewith attached your kind donation towards Japanese development aid. We are, unfortunately, not in a position to accept the attached donation as the Government of Japan does not allow any of its bodies to accept any form of donation as worthy as it may be.

Sincerely Yours

S Sakata
First Secretary
Embassy of Japan

Ambassador Thomas Borer
Swiss Embassy
Schweizerische Botschaft
Otto von Bismarck Allee 4A
DE 10557 Berlin
Germany

Mr Ben Trovato
PO Box 1117
Sea Point 8060
Cape Town
South Africa

7 July, 2001

Dear Mr Ambassador,

I understand that the Germans are growing increasingly anxious about what they term your "behaviour". From what I can make out, their anxiety is related to your beautiful wife, Shawne, a horse, a red miniskirt, the American flag and a tattoo. And, of course, a pile of glossy photographs that appeared in one of Germany's few magazines that do not dwell on intimate parts of the human anatomy.

How dare they question your suitability to represent your country in their country? Is it written anywhere that diplomats and their spouses have to behave in a particular fashion? Well, I suppose it is. But that is not the point.

You and Shawne have been tagged as Switzerland's "most glamorous diplomats". Nothing wrong with that. The stuffy old corps could certainly do with a little livening up. Apparently, you have also earned something of a reputation as "partygoers" in Berlin. In my book, there is something considerably more civilised about going off to a party than going off to invade Poland.

I believe your wife was Miss Dallas in 1992 and Miss Texas in 1994. I hear that she also came second in the Miss America contest. And the Germans expect her to play the shy, retiring diplomat's wife who is capable of dishing out little more than the canapés?

Ever since Boris Becker became an illegitimate father in a broom closet, the German authorities have been scrambling for the moral high ground. What they seem to forget is that had you been Thomas Borer the hashish dealer who fled from Zurich to the slums of Berlin with an exotic woman who was approached to pose naked for a top German porn magazine, they would have been the first to buy a copy on their way home to wives who do unmentionable things with the family bratwurst just to get noticed.

It must be quite a challenge to represent a country known for its cheese, watches and cowardice in times of war. Here in South Africa, we think you and your wife are pioneers blazing a new trail for the diplomats of the future. Do you have any advice I can pass on to our own diplomatic corps? Most of them are former terrorists, so we need not worry about any moral high ground here.

Down with double standards!

Yours truly,

....
Ben Trovato (Mr)

Shawne Fielding

Dear Ben Trovato,   September 4, 2001

Thomas gave me you letter and you are hysterical, I really wonder who you truly are
or if you parents had a great affinity for the Italian language knowing you would be
such a talented writer.

In any event thanks for the kind words and the belly laughs. I wish you all the very
best, health, happiness and continued success.

Sincerly,

Shawne Fielding
Shawne Fielding

Shawne Fielding

Mr Gerald Morkel
Western Cape Premier
Private Bag X9043
Cape Town
8000

Mr Ben Trovato
PO Box 1117
Sea Point
8060

23 July, 2001

Dear Mr Morkel,

My wife, Brenda, says that you are simply a figurehead and that is why we never hear anything from you. Or about you, for that matter. I tried to teach her a little respect for her elders, but I ended up with a scalded groin.

We are simple people, and I for one would like to be able to give my smart-aleck liberal neighbour a convincing reply when he asks what you do with your day. Help me out!

The other reason I am writing to you is to find out if a recent survey of your cabinet's reading habits is accurate.

Your favourite book is the bible. Fair enough. The premier needs all the help he can get. But Hennie Bester, the minister of community safety, also says the bible is his favourite book. Piet Meyer, minister of transport, sport and recreation, names the bible as his favourite book. So does Pierre Uys, minister of local government and development planning. And the bible is agriculture minister Gerrit van Rensburg's favourite book.

Nearly half your cabinet cites the bible as their favourite book? That is quite remarkable. I would be surprised if any political grouping outside the Vatican could match that.

Keep on crusading!

Yours truly,

Ben Trovato (Mr)

Mr Gerald Morkel
Western Cape Premier
Private Bag X9043
Cape Town
8000

Mr Ben Trovato
PO Box 1117
Sea Point
8060

29 August, 2001

Dear Mr Morkel,

I have yet to receive a reply to my letter of 24th July in which I questioned the accuracy of a survey stating that almost half of your Cabinet cites the Bible as their favourite book.

May I point out that ignoring the common folk is a very unchristian practice. But ignoring people like me is downright dangerous. I am not without influence.

May I remind you of the words of Steven in Acts 7: 51-52: "You stiff-necked people, uncircumcised in heart and spirit, you always resist the Holy Spirit."

Should any of your Cabinet ministers need a break from the Good Book, please ask them to get in touch with me. I have an extensive personal library and I would be happy to lend them a good read.

If you like, I can bring a selection of fine fiction to your offices. How does next Thursday suit you?

Yours truly,

....
Ben Trovato (Mr)

Kantoor van die Premier
Office of the Premier
I-ofisi yeNkulumbuso

Reference
Verwysing
Isingqinisiso   PM9/2

Date
Datum   2001 -09- 1 2
Umhla

Mr Ben Trovato
P O Box 1117
SEA POINT
8060

Dear Mr Trovato

By direction of Mr G N Morkel, Premier of the Western Cape, I acknowledge receipt of both your letters, the content of which has been noted.

Please accept the apology of the Office of the Premier for not replying to your first letter more promptly. I want to assure you that the Premier's favourite book is the Bible. My Premier goes to the Good Book during breaks and does not need a break from it. My Premier would also never judge a fellow man, but would leave judgements to God.

Kind regards

CHRIS KOOLE
DIRECTOR : PUBLIC RELATIONS

Privaatsak X9043, Kaapstad 8000   Private Bag X9043 Cape Town 8000
       Tel: +27 21 483 4705/6   Fax: +27 21 483 3421

Afrikaner Weerstandsbeweging
PO Box 274
Ventersdorp
2710

Mr Ben Trovato
PO Box 1117
Sea Point
8060

28 June, 2001

Dear Deputy Leader,

I was wondering if you chaps are still going, now that Mr Terreblanche is on long leave.

The reason I ask is that my boy, Clive, is approaching Manhood and is in dire need of a little toughening up. He was showing distressing signs of confusion concerning his gender, but I am happy to say we have managed to break him as far as the lipstick goes.

Within a month of two, he will need military training. I served in 2 Signals Regiment myself, and I can honestly say that a couple of years in the SADF left me a changed man.

I heard on the news the other day that the SANDF was planning to introduce voluntary conscription. This is about as confusing as sticking an N into the middle of the name to prove that the army no longer goes wandering off into neighbouring countries.

Then I saw an interview with General Andrew Masondo on telly the other night, and I realised that if I sent Clive off to the army, one of them would not make it out alive.

That is when I thought of the AWB. I recall that you have an army of your own. Tequila, I think they are called. Do they still exist?

Clive needs to learn the meaning of patriotism. He needs to grasp the significance of a uniform (although Brenda was wrong to burn his favourite camouflage skirt – it set him back considerably). He also needs to learn the value of spending time with boys his own age. I am not sure who he hangs around with at the Institute, since parents are denied access to information of virtually any kind. However, I am confident that his so-called friends are little more than pale shadows of the strapping, courageous patriots of Tequila.

I know in my very soul that the Tequila Youth can teach Clive a thing or two. However, I must mention that he is still a virgin. I am in the process of helping him across that particular hurdle. And once his voice has dropped an octave or two, he is all yours.

Please let me know if he can make the January intake.

Yours truly,

....
Ben Trovato (Mr)

110

AWB   Verwysing MOS/I/7/01

22 November 2001

Dear Mr. Trovato

We acknowledge receipt of you letter dated 28 June 2001. We are being flooded with mail and although we want to reply to all the letters and e-mails right away, it is humanly impossible. Please accept our sincere apology.

Concerning your situation with your son, it is a tragedy that out sons and daughters isn't receiving the training and discipline they so desperately need. Non-the less, we can't allow them to go and die, fighting a war for countries we regard as enemies. Hopefully the situation will change in future.

The government banned military training to non-government organizations and we won't be able to assist you with military training. If you and your family can assimilate with the history and strife for freedom of the Boer people, you are more than welcome to join our movement. Membership is subject to approval.

If however you want to support our cause without being a member you can do so by helping us financially. We are busy reorganizing the movement and need financial assistance urgently. Our banking details are as follow:
Afrikaner Weerstandsbeweging (AWB); ABSA Bank; Ventersdorp Branch; Branch code: 334-539: Account number: 2250142016

Cheques or postal orders, to the above address are also welcome. Please send them with registered post.

Thank you for your support. We hope to hear from you soon.

Boer greetings

A. Mostert (Editor: Storm)
Communication Administrator

The struggle that our fathers begun will rage till we've conquered.

STORM

NR. 9   AWB NUUSBRIEF / AWB NEWSLETTER   DES - JAN 2002

Posbus 4712, Kempton Park, 1620   Tel. / Faks. (011)975-3129 / 083 206 1291   E-pos: storm@awb.co.za

"Ek vermaan u om getrou te wees tot die dood toe aan u tradisies, aan u godsdiens, aan u taal en aan u volk, mag God met u almal wees totdat ons mekaar weer sien."

Kommandant Joseph (Jopie) Johannes Fourie

GELOFTEDAG
Is dit nog nodig?

www.awb.co.za

INFORMATION PACK

Lord Jeffrey Archer
Belmarsh Prison, Western Way
Thamesmead
London
SE28 0EB

Mr Ben Trovato
PO Box 1117
Sea Point
8060
Cape Town
South Africa

21 July, 2001

Dear Lord Archer,

How odd to think that you are languishing in a prison cell! You have many supporters in South Africa who are appaled at the manner in which you have been treated. As a teenager I liked nothing better than curling up with A Twist of Sand or A Grue of Ice. In view of what has happened, I suggest your next book be titled A Miscarriage of Justice.

Four years for perjury? Out here in the colonies, we find that sort of sentencing to be completely outrageous. To go to jail for that long, one would have to murder one's mother-in-law and then attack the police when they came to investigate. Even then, one could get away with it by pleading Diminished Responsibility on the grounds that one had been drinking cheap brandy since dawn. Perjury is treated like a littering offence. Most of the time we don't even bother turning up for the sentencing.

So what if you lied about the harlot? That's what men are supposed to do. You can be sure that if Hugh Grant had not been caught with his pants down, he would not have gone around town bragging about his charming encounter with Ms Divine Brown. As far as I can make out, the only difference is that you made a lot of money out of taking the Daily Mirror to court for daring to suggest that you had lain with a woman of ill repute. That took balls, if I may say so. In my experience, fake diaries and false alibis are generally foolproof. Did someone rat you out? Give me his name. I know people who deal with scum like that.

As a one-time deputy chairman of the Conservative Party, I would have expected that Maggie and John Major would have pulled a few strings to get you off. Then again, the Tories are earning something of a reputation as fair weather friends. Do you plan on switching to Labour?

And now they want to strip you of your title? I see a certain Sir Teddy Taylor (Tory) suggests that people like you should be "quietly excluded" from the House of Lords. Should that happen, I suggest you take a leaf out of Sir Guy Fawkes's book.

What is this latest fabrication that you stole millions of pounds destined for Kurdish refugees in Iraq? I see it's another Tory who has the knives out on this one. You managed to raise over 57 million pounds for the Kurds. Now that they've spent it all, they claim to have only received 250-thousand pounds. But it would not surprise me if the authorities took the word of a goat-herding nomad over yours. These are strange times, indeed.

I am enclosing a ten rand note. Tell the thug running the tuck shop that it's worth fifty pounds. When things settle down, let me know if you need anything else.

Yours truly,

Ben Trovato (Mr)

113

JEFFREY ARCHER

5th October 2001

Strictly Personal & Confidential

Dear Mr Trovato

I must first apologise for the delay in replying to your kind letter to Lord Archer.

Jeffrey has read your letter and wanted to respond personally, but I hope you will understand that he has been overwhelmed with the number of letters he has received, and so has asked me, on this occasion, to reply on his behalf.

The past few months have been, and continue to be, a grueling and unpleasant experience for him and his family, and your willingness to write gives him strength at this difficult time.

Yours sincerely

Alison Prince
Personal Assistant to Jeffrey Archer

The Centre for Conflict Resolution
Bertram Place
31 Orange Street
Gardens
8001

Mr Ben Trovato
PO Box 1117
Sea Point
8060

22 May, 2002

Dear Sir,

I was pleased to hear that the thirteen "highly-dangerous" Palestinian militants
were finally given safe passage out of Bethlehem without any more blood being
spilled. That's what I call conflict resolution! Five weeks in any church is enough
to break anyone's spirit. More than most, they deserved to begin their exile in
sea-facing rooms at the Flamingo Beach Hotel in the resort town of Larnaca on
the idyllic island of Cyprus.

I am not one for joining causes, but I am in considerable need of a break. My
wife, Brenda, would also appreciate a little time apart. I was hoping you could
advise me on the best course of action.

I intend occupying a church (something small, possibly in Bellville) on the
second Wednesday in June. Would you suggest that I notify the city council in
advance? I would also appreciate any suggestions you may have with regard to
selecting a church. Should I go for something high profile, like Roman Catholic,
or keep it simple and hole up with the Latter Day Saints? Would a Synagogue be
a bad idea?

For this to work, I would need a few armed men to watch the front door. It
wouldn't be a proper siege, otherwise. I don't mind if amateur gunmen want
to come alone. But they would have to bring their own weapons. Do you have
anyone on your membership list who might be interested? I won't be able to pay
them, but I will buy lunch.

I am also looking for a negotiator who could get me out before the weekend and
into a suite at the Table Bay Hotel by cocktail hour. I am sure you could put me
in touch with people who are qualified in this field of work.

I eagerly await your advice and assistance.

Yours truly,

Ben Trovato (Mr)

**CENTRE FOR
CONFLICT
RESOLUTION**

Association incorporated
under Section 21

Centre for Conflict Resolution
University of Cape Town
c/o Rhodes Gift Post Office
7707
South Africa
Tel: +27 21 422-2512
Fax: +27 21 422-2622
e-mail: mailbox@ccr.uct.ac.za
http://ccrweb.ccr.uct.ac.za

2002/15/lm

Dear Mr Trovato

Thank you for your letter of 22 May.

I was sorry to hear that you and Mrs Trovato are in need of a little time apart.

Given the nature of the Centre for Conflict Resolution, and notwithstanding your kind offer of lunch, I'm afraid that I do not have many amateur gunmen at my disposal.

My recommendation regarding a suitable church is that you consider the chapel at Pollsmoor Prison. In the long run this would save you much inconvenience in travel arrangements and would give you access to a large number of amateur gunmen. You are unlikely to get a sea-facing room but the mountain views are excellent and the cocktail hour can be quite merry.

Best wishes

LAURIE NATHAN
Executive Director

Dr Ben Ngubane
Minister of Arts, Science and
Technology
Private Bag X9156
Cape Town 8000

Mr Ben Trovato
PO Box 1117
Sea Point
8060

23 May, 2002

Dear Dr Ngubane,

Congratulations on the fine work you are doing. My wife, Brenda, says you are her favourite politician.

I was hoping you might be able to help me with a query. My neighbour, Ted, is planning to hold a fish braai for a group of important overseas visitors in the near future. We were discussing the menu over a couple of beers when he struck upon a brilliant idea. Why not include a coelacanth to go with the snoek and steenbras! It has novelty value and the bigger ones look capable of feeding at least four people.

I seem to remember your ministry announcing that there was a coelacanth run at Sodwana Bay on the North Coast. I hope they haven't been fished out already. I was at St Lucia once and had to fight my way through hordes of blood-crazed rednecks guzzling brandy and gutting fish right there in the shorebreak.

If the fish are still biting, could you advise me on the best bait for coelacanth? Given their history, they are probably smarter than your average kabeljou. You can't really go wrong with fresh squid, but for all I know the coelacanth can't stand the taste of squid. And the last thing I want is to be stuck out at Sodwana with something on the end of my hook that actually repulses the fish.

Any suggestions would be much appreciated. In return, I'll let you know what coelacanth tastes like!

All the best.

Yours truly,

....
Ben Trovato (Mr)

Dr Ben Ngubane
Minister of Arts, Science and
Technology
Private Bag X727
Pretoria 0001

Mr Ben Trovato
PO Box 1117
Sea Point
8060

29 June, 2002

Dear Dr Ngubane,

I am still waiting for a reply to my letter of 23rd May. I am sure the response has gone astray in the mail, since you have never struck me as a person who deliberately ignores people simply because they happen to be taxpayers.

You may recall that I was inquiring about the possibility of catching one or two coelacanth for a very important braai that my neighbour is planning.

I urgently need to know if they are still biting in the St Lucia area. I would hate to make the trip all the way there only to find that the Boers have taken everything.

I anxiously await your response.

Thank you and keep up the good work.

Yours truly,

Ben Trovato (Mr)

MINISTRY: ARTS, CULTURE, SCIENCE AND TECHNOLOGY
REPUBLIC OF SOUTH AFRICA
Private Bag X727, Pretoria, 0001, Tel: (012) 337 8376 Fax: (012) 324 2687
Private Bag X9156, Cape Town, 8000, Tel: (021) 465 4850/70, Fax: (021) 461 1425

05 July 2002

Ref: AS(0734-2002)

Dear Mr Trovato

POSSIBILITY OF CATCHING ONE OR TWO COELACANTH

On behalf of Dr B S Ngubane, Minister of Arts, Culture, Science and Technology, I acknowledge receipt of your letter dated 29 June 2002.

Minister Ngubane has taken the liberty of referring the matter to his Department for further attention.

Kind regards

MR MABETHA L RALEBIPI
ACT ADMINISTRATIVE SECRETARY

Minister Charles Nqakula
Ministry of Safety and Security
Private Bag X9080
Cape Town
8000

Mr Ben Trovato
PO Box 1117
Sea Point
8060

23 May, 2002

Dear Minister,

Allow me to congratulate you on your appointment to Minister. I hear that crime is already down. Congratulations! You must have some reputation on the streets.

I cannot imagine that you are terribly thrilled with the Constitutional Court's ruling that police may no longer open fire on fleeing suspects. I thought all judges were heavily armed gun freaks. Perhaps that was just in the good old days. Democracy seems to have brought with it a new crop of limp-wristed liberals who believe that it's enough for a policeman to shout "Stop, or I'll...I'll chase you!"

I can't remember when last I saw a policeman running anywhere. There was one moving quickly on foot near my home the other day, but it turned out that he was rushing to get to the bottle store before it closed. Crime fighting now becomes a matter of survival of the fittest. I expect many criminals will be spending their free time in the gym. Perhaps you should consider striking a deal with Virgin Active. Undercover cops could watch the bikes and work out on the treadmill at the same time.

I understand that the ruling also extends to civilians. My neighbour, Ted, has asked me to ask you to clarify something. If someone is running away, and you want to shoot them, would it be alright to run faster than them, overtake them and then turn around and shoot them from the front? In this situation, the target is no longer fleeing. He is running directly towards you, unless he swerves. Did the Constitutional Court say anything about suspects running in a crab-like fashion? What if the suspect is fleeing, but while he is running away he turns quickly and starts to run backwards? What happens then? What about this. A suspect takes off and you give chase, but you are equally fit. Or unfit. You manage to pull up alongside him but can't quite get in front. Is it acceptable then to shoot him in a leg just to slow him down a bit? Or should one simply keep shouting at him in a non-threatening manner until he sees the error of his ways? Ted also wants to know if all else fails, is he legally entitled to throw his weapon at the fleeing suspect's head?

Please could you provide a little clarity before there is a nasty accident.

Best of luck in your new job.

Yours truly,

....
Ben Trovato (Mr)

Minister Charles Nqakula
Minister of Safety and Security
Private Bag X463
Pretoria
0001

Mr Ben Trovato
PO Box 1117
Sea Point
8060

29 June, 2002

Dear Mr Nqakula,

I am still waiting for a reply to my letter of 23rd May. I am sure the response has gone astray in the mail, since you do not strike me as a person who deliberately ignores people simply because they happen to be taxpayers.

If you recall, I was requesting clarity on the Constitutional Court's ruling that decent people may no longer open fire on fleeing suspects.

It is absolutely imperative that the position is explained more clearly. There are a few suspects who loiter outside my house every day, and I need to know what my rights are when it comes to opening fire on them.

I hope your reply makes it through the mail this time.

Keep up the good work.

Yours truly,

....
Ben Trovato (Mr)

DEPARTMENT: SAFETY AND SECURITY
REPUBLIC OF SOUTH AFRICA
Private Bag X463, Pretoria, 0001. Tel: (012) 339 2800. Fax: (012) 339 2820
Thibault Arcade, 231 Pretorius Street, Pretoria
tshwete@saps.org.za

4 July 2002

Dear Mr Trovato

RE – FIRING AT FLEEING SUSPECTS

Your letter dated 29 June 2002, regarding the aforesaid refers.

Kindly note that your letter will be brought to the attention of the Minister in due course. You will receive further correspondence in this regard shortly thereafter.

Your patience in this matter is appreciated.

Kind regards.

KRISHNEE KISSOONDUTH
ADMINISTRATIVE SECRETARY (DIRECTOR)

Reference: 3/2/1(55/2001)

DEPARTMENT: SAFETY AND SECURITY
REPUBLIC OF SOUTH AFRICA
Private Bag X463, Pretoria, 0001. Tel: (012) 339 2800, Fax: (012) 339 2820
Thibault Arcade, 231 Pretorius Street, Pretoria
tshwete@saps.org.za

29 July 2002

Dear Mr Trovato

RE – FIRING AT FLEEING SUSPECTS

Your letter dated 29 June 2002, regarding the aforesaid refers.

Kindly note that this office has no record of your letter dated 23 May and you would therefore not have received a reply. Further, the Ministry has been informed by the National Commissioner of the South African Police Service as follows:

"It would appear that you are seeking clarity on the Constitutional Court's ruling on Section 49 of the Criminal procedure Act, 1977 (Act No 51 of 1977). The Constitutional Court's ruling is clear and precise and needs no amplification. The Constitutional Court stated (on pages 45 – 46 of the ruling) the following:

(a) The purpose of arrest is to bring before court for trial persons suspected of having committed offences.

(b) Arrest is not the only means of achieving this purpose, nor always the best

(c) Arrest may never be used to punish a suspect.

(d) Where arrest is called for, force may be used only where it is necessary in order to carry out the arrest.

(e) Where force is necessary, only the least degree of force reasonably necessary to carry out the arrest may be used.

(f) In deciding what degree of force is both reasonable and necessary, all the circumstances must be taken into account, including the threat of violence the suspect poses to the arrester or others, and the nature and circumstances of the offence the suspect is suspected of having committed; the force being proportional in all these circumstances.

(g) Shooting a suspect solely in order to carry out an arrest is permitted in very limited circumstances only.

(h) Ordinarily such shooting is not permitted unless the suspect poses a threat of violence to the arrester or others or is suspected on reasonable grounds of having committed a crime involving the infliction or threatened infliction of serious bodily harm and there are not other reasonable means of carrying out the arrest, whether at that time or later.

(i) These limitations in no way detract from the rights of an arrester attempting to carry out an arrest to kill a suspect in self-defence or in defence of any other person."

I trust that this information will address your concerns.

Kind regards.

CHRISTINE MGWENYA
CHIEF OF STAFF

Mr Ian Leach
The Royal Johannesburg &
Kensington Golf Club
PO Box 46017
Orange Grove 2119

Mr Ben Trovato
PO Box 1117
Sea Point
8060

25 May, 2002

Dear Mr Leach,

I am writing to you with a view to getting my boy, Clive, onto your membership list. I understand that as far as golf clubs go, yours is among the best. Perusing the names of your staff as well as those serving on the committee, I was pleased to see that there no natives among them. I am not a racist, but golf clubs are, by definition, elitist. You do not want to throw membership open to the general hoi polloi. Not unless you want thugs like OJ Simpson strolling the links.

Clive is in his teenage years and has shown a remarkable eye for a ball. He was in line for a position with South Africa's A cricket team, but the institute was unable to sign his release papers in time. I am pleased to report that the lad is now nearing the end of his treatment, and will be looking for something to take his mind off a few nasty incidents that occurred when he was younger. Golf would be perfect.

It might be advisable to let Clive play a few solo rounds before putting him in a foursome. He needs to get back into the swing of things, so to speak. I would not want strangers putting him off his stroke before he is completely ready. I presume you do not allow women to become members? A golf course is no place for the fairer sex. However, I have no objection to them preparing the drinks and snacks at the clubhouse. But it is better for all concerned if they stay off the greens. I am sure you will agree.

Enclosed please find R10 to help Clive to the front of the line. There is more where this comes from. The clubhouse's new Trovato wing is not beyond the realms of possibility!

I look forward to hearing from you soon.

Keep your putter straight!

Yours truly,

....
Ben Trovato (Mr)

BRIBE GIVEN
R10

ROYAL JOHANNESBURG &
KENSINGTON GOLF CLUB

3 June, 2002

Dear Mr. Trovato

We do not know who you are and are not sure whether the tone of your letter is serious or meant to be a joke.

The values of our Club do not coincide with the values expressed in your letter and we therefore regret that we have no interest in pursuing membership at our Club for your son.

Thank you for your enquiry and we return your R10 note.

Sincerely

IAN LEACH
Chief Executive Officer

The Director
Two Oceans Aquarium
PO Box 50603
Waterfront
8002

Mr Ben Trovato
PO Box 1117
Sea Point
8060

5 June, 2002

Dear Sir,

I understand from contacts on the Cape Flats that the Two Oceans Aquarium is looking for certain marine specimens. Well, I am your man. I am in touch with a wide network of informal fishermen who have the entire Atlantic seaboard covered.

I am able to provide you with the finest perlemoen you can ever hope to come across.
Quantity is not a problem. I can easily get you enough for an exhibition tank and more to spare. For ethical reasons I can't say much, but as a marine man yourself, you must already know that the taste of a fresh abalone is almost better than sex. They are not much to look at, I admit. If you want to order a few for one of your tanks, I suggest that you daub the outer shell with streaks of luminous waterproof paint. It makes them look far more exotic. There's not a lot you can do if they choose to suck up against the glass, of course. Should that happen, try to warn tour guides to keep the children away. I have seen married men turn celibate at the sight.

I can get you all the old favourites – lobster, rock cod, red snapper, tuna etc. But I am sure you have more than enough of those on your hands. What about a coelacanth? I am in negotiations with the Ministry of Science and Technology to bag a few. I suggest you get your order in now.

If you need something cheaper, there is always the dusky dolphin. As you know, we have more than we can handle in the Western Cape. Dolphins I can do for five hundred apiece. I prefer to deal in job lots of six. A dozen gets you a complimentary penguin.

Get your order in now before the Spanish pillage the lot!

Yours truly,

Ben Trovato (Mr)

Two Oceans

AQUARIUM

Dock Rd Victoria & Alfred Waterfront

P.O. Box 50603 Waterfront 8002

Cape Town South Africa

Tel (021) 418-3823/4   Fax (021) 418-3952

E-mail aquarium@aquarium.co.za

http://www.aquarium.co.za

12th August 2002

Dear Sir

Thank you for your letter of 5 June 2002. We have our collecting and sourcing of the specimens which we need very satisfactorily in place and are not in a position to take up your offer.

Yours faithfully

p.p.

E.A. FEARNHEAD
Managing Director

The Director
Koeberg Nuclear Power Station
Private Bag X10
Kernkrag
7440

Mr Ben Trovato
PO Box 1117
Sea Point
8060

11 June, 2002

Dear Sir,

I read in the paper that you have put a 26-year-old woman in charge of safety. Dear God, what were you thinking! This is a nuclear reactor we are talking about, not an arts and crafts shop. I am all for equal rights, but the women I know are quite happy to be put in charge of little more than the kitchen.

Women do not even know how to change a plug. Not because they are incompetent, but because their brains are wired differently to ours. Your 26-year-old is no different. Sooner or later, she is going to get confused. Too many flashing lights, gauges and bleeping noises will automatically shut down vital parts of her brain. She only has to press the wrong button and it's goodbye Cape Town.

My neighbour, Ted, says we probably won't even feel a thing. He says it will be like a blast of very hot air and then a millisecond later our flesh and bones will be vapourised. Painless, he assures me. Well, sir, let me tell you that I am far from assured.

What if this woman finds her husband with another man? Do you have any idea what these people are capable of in their quest for revenge? Most of them would not hesitate to destroy an entire city to teach that two-timing bastard the lesson of his life.

Are you prepared to provide me with some sort of guarantee that I will not wake up one morning to find a giant wave of deadly gamma rays heading up my street?

I may have to consider moving my family to somewhere safer, like Durban. At least the Zulus would never put a woman in charge of a nuclear reactor.

Please reconsider the appointment. Tell the woman that it was a clerical error, then fire one of the clerks. If she demands some sort of position, put her in charge of catering.

I anxiously await your words of reassurance.

Yours truly,

....
Ben Trovato (Mr)

Koeberg Nuclear Power Station

Melkbosstrand, Cape

Private Bag X10
7440 Kernkrag
South Africa
Telephone (021) 550-4911 (Int'l +27 21 550-4911)
Telefax (021) 550-5100 (Int'l +27 21 550-5100)

ESKOM

24 July 2002

Dear Mr. Trovato,

Thank you for your letter and the light relief that you have introduced into my day!

The fact that you have taken the trouble to put pen to paper is commendable in as much as you do appear to have more than a simple passing interest in Koeberg and its relationship with the community it serves. I would personally welcome a visit from you to convince you why you will never have to expect the "blast of hot air"; (and please bring your neighbour, Ted along!) I promise that I won't let any of the women at Koeberg know that you are here, just in case they exercise their "quest for revenge".

Yours sincerely,

PETER HROZESKY
POWER STATION MANAGER

130

Mr Peter Prozesky
Manager:
Koeberg Nuclear Power Station
Private Bag X10
7440 Kernkrag

Mr Ben Trovato
PO Box 1117
Sea Point
8060

5 September, 2002

Dear Mr Prozesky,

Thank you for your reply of 24th July to my letter expressing concerns about
appointing a slip of a girl to ensure the security of the power station.

I was about to take up your offer of a visit to the facility to set my mind at rest
when a band of thugs from Greenpeace beat me to it. But instead of going
through the front door like normal people, they chose to go over a five-storey wall
surrounding the facility. They even had time to unfurl banners reading "Nukes
Out Of Africa" and "Koeberg Sucks".

Where on earth was the girl while all this was going on? Painting her toenails?
On the phone to her mother complaining that all men are bastards? She should
have been lying belly down in a trench on the beach lobbing mortars at the
foreign invaders. Why was she not leading a fixed bayonet charge the moment
the marauders set foot on land?

I am horrified that you were unable to prevent your security from being breached
by a bunch of limp-wristed, lentil-munching bunny-huggers in little colour-
coded rubber boats and lilac jumpsuits. What happens if real men storm the
installation? Would you all drop your tea and run shrieking into the suburbs of
Melkbosstrand? A fine lot of good that would do.

My wife, Brenda, wants to move to Richards Bay because of this fiasco. I have
told her that in the event of an explosion, Knysna would be far enough away. Do
you agree?

If you are able to convince Brenda that it is still safe to stay on in Cape Town,
my neighbour and I would be prepared to lend Koeberg a hand to keep the
vegetarians out. I am a trained Signalman and two semaphore flags are all I need
to give the city ample warning of an impending attack. Ted is a sniper. Put him
on the roof with his favourite weapon and he could pick off a tourist on Robben
Island. Not that he would, of course. All I am saying is that your sea-facing
perimeter would
be secure.

Brenda has already started to pack. Please let me know urgently if it is safe to
stay in the city. And if it is, when do you want Ted and I to report for duty?

Best of luck.

Yours truly,

....
Ben Trovato (Mr)

Dear Mr Trovato

Once again I must thank you for the interest shown in Koeberg's ongoing
business. Particularly , I must thank you for the magnanimous offer of the
services of Ted and yourself in the protection of this national asset against the
dark forces of evil that would conspire to bring anarchy to the world ! I am truly
heartened to know that there are people out there who are unselfishly prepared to
step into the breach and to conduct themselves with honour and dignity.

Turning to the recent visit to this establishment by the lilac jump-suit brigade,
it is perhaps unfortunate that the media and our eco-terrorists seemed to
have missed a fundamental point entirely. This is that Koeberg is actually the
most "Green" and "peaceful" form of bulk energy production available in this
country! Koeberg is the only energy processing plant in RSA that is completely
accountable for ensuring that its waste products will be collected and safely
looked after for future generations. In Europe, where 20% of electricity comes
from Koeberg's sister plants, there is an avoidance of 20 billion tons of
greenhouse gasses per year ! So, our misguided bunny huggers have, as the
Afrikaans put it so aptly, "die pot mis gesit!" (and we all know that this leaves a
bit of a mess for the rest of us to clean up).

I wish to assure you that your and Ted's services won't be needed just yet.
On the day of the "Green invasion", Koeberg's own armed Rambo-brigade was
timeously in attendance. When faced with a smiling, young (and not unattractive)
New Zealand lassie climbing over the wall, saying "I come in peace", they
disappointedly had to find some other use for their itchy trigger fingers! (I'm sure
Ted would sympathise). So, there was no real need for our lady operator to begin
to break a sweat, let alone to strap on her bandoleers.

You can assure Brenda that her personal health would be far better served by
living in Melkbosstrand than in Richardsbay. Remind her of the rather large
industrialization in and around that part of the world. I personally would find the
choice of domicile a very logical and easy one to make for my family.

Once again, I invite you to come for a cup of tea and a personal tour. Oh, and
unless you have a rubber duck and matching jump-suit, and are accompanied
by a bevy of suitably attired female attendants, I would recommend you use the
front door.

Regards

PETER R. PROZESKY
POWER STATION MANAGER

The Director
SANCA
PO Box 70389
Durban
4067

Mr Ben Trovato
PO Box 1117
Sea Point
8060

23 June, 2002

Dear Sir,

I read in the paper the other day that a young chap by the name of Castro Chiluba (the son of former Zambian president, Frederick) has been sent to jail for six months for possessing cannabis.

I have a son who is approaching the age where he might well begin experimenting with illegal substances. He has already experimented with pretty much everything else i.e. cross-dressing, arson etc. I would appreciate your expert advice.

The Chiluba boy was arrested at a nightclub with twenty (20) kilograms of cannabis. He appealed for leniency on the grounds that he was merely a consumer, not a trafficker. I am no prude. In fact, I tried the stuff myself when I was younger. Please keep this to yourself. If my wife, Brenda, knew about my past she would have me arrested.

I am trying to find out if 20 kilograms is an average amount for a youngster to take with him when he goes out to the disco on a Friday night. I am asking because I think responsible parents should be able to tell when their offspring are drifting into the twilight world of drug abuse.

If Clive says he's going out and I spot him leaving the house with one of those large, black bin-bags slung over his shoulder, should I worry? What if he says he's going to meet a friend at the pub and comes out of his room wearing his backpack? He may try something more devious, of course. Is it physically possible for a young lad to conceal 20 kilograms of marijuana inside his clothing without it being noticed? I tried it with piles of my neighbour's freshly mown lawn, and I managed to get at least seven kilograms into my brooks and down my shirt before he spotted me and threatened to call the police.

I realise there is a possibility that you may tell me that there is nothing to worry about. That kids are growing up much faster these days. And that 20 kilograms today is like four grams in our time. Maybe this is what it takes for Clive's generation to loosen up and have fun. Please let me know if I should begin strip-searching the boy when he goes out.

Yours truly,

....
Ben Trovato (Mr)

cc. Cape Town Drug Counselling Centre

SANCA
Lulama Treatment Centre
Warman House Adolescent Unit
185 Vause Road, Berea, DURBAN, 4001
Tel: 202-2241, 202-2274 Fax : 201-4643
E-mail : lulama@mweb.co.za

Sanca Durban
Alcohol and Drug Centres

SANCA
Prevention Services
Penthouse Out-Patient Clinic
236 - 9th Avenue, Morningside, DURBAN, 4001
Tel: 303-2202 Fax : 303-1938
E-mail : antidrug@mweb.co.za

ALL CORRESPONDENCE TO THE DIRECTOR, SANCA, P.O. BOX 70389, OVERPORT, DURBAN, 4067

03 July 2002

Dear Mr Trovato

Thank you for your letter & your interest in drug abuse. At least, you've maintained your sense of humour, something we really need to do in these challenging times! I will do my best to deal with the various matters you've raised & hope that your concerns will be appropriately addressed.

- I'm glad to hear you're not a prude, & with reference to past indiscretions, you may rest assured that your wife cannot have you arrested in terms of the Drugs & Drugs Trafficking Act (No 140 of 1992). Unless, of course, there's something you're not telling us!!
- If the report on the young man in possession of 20kg of cannabis is true, then the logistics of transporting the stash conjure up images of a Monty Pythonesque nature! What a relief that this is not typical behaviour. Apparently, centuries ago, the nomadic peoples of central Africa made minor tribal law-breakers smoke dagga until they passed out, as a punishment. This led to "green fever", the dagga equivalent of a "babbelas". Imagine what 20kg would do! More seriously, he must have been dealing. Enclosed please find a copy of our booklet on this drug : "Questions & Answers on Dagga" for your reference.
- Strip searching your son as a preventative measure sounds innovative and may be seem tempting when you are faced with a cross-dressing arsonist who shows signs of trying anything once. However, this would most probably have the judges of our constitutional court shaking their august heads in disapproval. Your local branch of SANCA has trained professionals who could guide you in what we term "constructive confrontation", which is a communication strategy for dealing with dysfunction.

I trust this information is helpful. Hopefully by now, your neighbour has calmed down over your creative & informative experiment with his grass cuttings! Thank you for sharing this experience with us.

Yours sincerely

Claire Savage (Mrs)
Senior Information Officer

PS A friend of mine is quite a fan of yours. Thanks for writing! I guess you know only too well, that laughter is the best medicine (drug?)!

THE CAPE TOWN DRUG COUNSELLING CENTRE

03 July 2002

Dear Mr Trovato,

Thank you for your enquiry.
I enclose a booklet which should provide you with some perspective and direction on drug issues.

Regarding your question about 20 kilos of dagga - this is a large amount of dagga, and I presume he would run the risk of being charged with dealing if he was carrying that amount.

Hope you find the information helpful.

Yours faithfully,

Cathy Karassellos
Clinical Psychologist

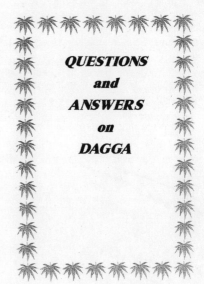

QUESTIONS
and
ANSWERS
on
DAGGA

Minister Ngconde Balfour
Minister of Sport
Private Bag X869
Pretoria
0001

Mr Ben Trovato
PO Box 1117
Sea Point
8060

28 June, 2002

Dear Minister Balfour,

Congratulations on taking that old fertiliser farmer, Louis Luyt, to task for his views on the state of rugby which appear in a book co-written by other Afrikaner dissidents. As you so rightly point out, they are nothing but "apartheid dinosaurs" who are trying to "sew mayhem and division" among rugby fans.

I have been a rugby player for most of my life, but was forced to leave the field forever when an old war injury started playing up. But my spirit remains true. And this latest fracas has certainly got the mayhem rising up inside me!

Luyt might have been president of the Rugby Union for fourteen years, but that was at a time when the only black people allowed into Ellis Park Stadium were those bearing trays of beer and biltong.

Luyt has the cheek to issue a statement calling you "uncouth" and "lacking intelligence"! He goes on to say that it's unconstitutional and libelous for you to call him a racist. Then accuses you of racism! The man is clearly confused.

He also says you single-handedly lost South Africa the Olympic Games and the Soccer World Cup. I suppose you are also to blame for the weak rand. And no doubt you had a hand in the plane crash that killed Hansie Cronje. In fact, where were you the day Kennedy was assassinated?

Luyt calls you an "overweight, bloated and big-mouthed minister". That is outrageous. I will bet any money you like that if you both hit the scales, he would turn out to be the whale.

I enclose ten rand towards any libel action you might take against that horrible man.

Yours truly,

....
Ben Trovato (Mr)

CA$H GIVEN
R10

MINISTRY: SPORT AND RECREATION
REPUBLIC OF SOUTH AFRICA
Private Bag X869, Pretoria, 0001, Tel: (012) 334 3100, Fax: (012) 321 8493
Private Bag X9149, Cape Town, 8000, Tel: (021) 465 5506/7/8/9, Fax: (021) 465 4402

12 August 2002

Dear Mr Trovato

Allow me to express my appreciation for the enthusiastic manner in which you support sport and rugby, in particular.

It is quite obvious that you follow South African sport with more than a passing interest and that you are abreast of developments within sport. I found your comments with regard to Dr Louis Luyt very interesting and wish to thank you for the support you have given to me personally.

I have received both your letters but due to the fact that the letter dated 28 June 2002 arrived at a time that my office shifted from Cape Town to Pretoria during the parliamentary recess, I was not in a position to respond immediately. My office attempted to reach you by telephone but this was not possible as you are not listed. In fact, only two companies are listed in the Cape Peninsula telephone directory under the name of "Trovato" and they could not assist me in tracing you.

Nevertheless, thank you for your kind gesture of contributing financially towards what you refer to as "libel action" that I might consider. I have no intention of considering such steps and wish to suggest that you permit me to forward the donation to a project in Cape Town providing sport opportunities for street children.

Your kind-hearted gesture will contribute towards our ideal of providing sport for all in the country. I would love the opportunity to speak to you personally at some time. Could you oblige by calling Graham Abrahams at tel. 021 465-5506 in order for such an arrangement to be made?

I look forward to your response.

Kind regards

BMN BALFOUR
Minister of Sport and Recreation

137

The Manager
Classic FM
PO Box 782
Auckland Park
2006

Mr Ben Trovato
PO Box 1117
Sea Point
8060

14 June, 2002

Dear Sir,

I came across your station the other day while attempting to intercept extraterrestrial communications and was momentarily distracted by a catchy little Gershwin tune. All well and good. But suddenly, without warning, you began playing Bach! Dear God, man, do your presenters have such little regard for those of us who fought in the war?

Johann Sebastian Bach was a German. Have you forgotten the lessons learned at Leipzig? Can you ignore the role he played in propping up the despot Prince Leopold of Kothen? And let me assure you, it was no coincidence that Bach was the favourite composer of one A. Hitler. The bloodline ran deep.

I lost many friends to the guns of the cursed Afrika Corps. And I, myself, played no small part in the downfall of Field Marshal Erwin Rommel. You may recall that the death of the man known as the Desert Fox was reported as a suicide. That is about as far from the truth as you can get. But it appears that your station is not interested in the truth. I am old now, but that does not mean you can get away with tormenting us.

I expect an explanation from you, failing which I will have no alternative but to report you to the International War Crimes Tribunal.

Never forget the men of the 21st Division! We died for you. And your family.

Thank you.

Yours truly,

....
Ben Trovato (Mr)

CLASSIC fM
102.7

12 August 2002

Dear Mr Trovato

I have not replied to your letter of the 14th of June, due to the fact that I did not receive your communication. Are you sure that you have the correct radio station? – Classic fM has a Gauteng radio license and listeners can only listen to the station on DSTV in Cape Town.

I have noted your concerns about the station playing the music of J.S.Bach. I sympathize that any memories are hurtful. It is however our station policy to continue playing the music of Bach as there is no direct link between Bach and the Nazi era.

Yours faithfully

Mike Ford
Classic fM(SA) Pty Ltd

The Chairman
Film and Publication Board
Private Bag X9069
Cape Town
8000

Mr Ben Trovato
PO Box 1117
Sea Point
8060

14 June, 2002

Dear Sir,

I wish to lodge a complaint about the film, Spider-Man. It is misleading and dangerous. I have always believed that documentaries, by their very nature, are obliged to tell the truth. That they are there to present us with the facts, not lie to us. For that reason, I went along with an open mind, keen to learn something new.

Indeed, I found it fascinating. I was particularly impressed with the cameraman's uncanny ability to be in the right place at the right time. How on earth he noticed the spider dropping down from the roof in the museum is anyone's guess! I imagine he has worked with Sir David Attenborough in the past.

Mr Peter Parker seemed very at ease with having a camera around the whole time. And a good thing too, or we might never have got to witness that incredible transformation.

As a documentary, I found it enlightening (although the music was a little loud in places). And what a coup to finally prove the existence of the Green Goblin! I notice that the sceptics are no longer quite so vocal.

For a week after seeing the film, my neighbour and I collected spiders from the garden. We got at least twenty different kinds into a shoebox. Last Thursday, I waited until Brenda went shopping and then put the box into the microwave oven. I used a low setting so as not to fry the creatures, but just high enough to give them a quick dose of radiation. When I took the box out, most of them were curled up stubbornly refusing to move. But five were hopping about like kangaroos. I quickly poured them down my shirt and waited expectantly. Nothing happened. But later that evening, I noticed a small red mark on my stomach. I went to bed so Brenda wouldn't notice. In the morning, I crept into the bathroom to see my new muscles. However, there was little change. Then I tried squirting high-tensile silk at my sleeping wife. I went through a range of hand movements, but nothing would come out of my wrists. Brenda awoke to find me wiggling my fingers in her face. She reacted badly. And so did I, when I realised that the makers of Spider-Man had perpetrated a deception of monumental proportions.

I urge the Film and Publication Board to either ban this film or have it reclassified from Documentary to Fiction Feature. Please let me know your decision as I may need to take further action.

Yours truly,

....
Ben Trovato (Mr)

140

19 June 2002

Dear Mr Trovato

Thank you for your letter of 14 June 2002. I am sorry that you feel betrayed, deceived and misled. The truth, actually, is plainer than the nose on the Green Goblin.

In the first place, the cameraman happens to be in the right place at the right time because this is a recreation of what actually happened. This is Spidey, better known as the "Webslinger" or "Your Friendly Neighbourhood Spiderman", in flashbacks. We took you back in time, Ben. (How ironic that you should not know this since you share the same name as Spidey's dear old uncle.)

Yes, we managed to expose the Green Goblin. Just in case you missed it. Osborne Enterprises survived and dear old Harry will emerge as the new Green Goblin to avenge his poor old papa's untimely demise.

I am sorry that you failed to duplicate Spidey's powers but maybe you forgot that he got his powers through a spider that was exposed to gamma radiation, not unlike Dr Bruce Banner's alter ego, the Incredible Hulk. Microwave radiation is not gamma radiation. Microwaves involve a range of radio frequencies between about 1GHz to about 300GHz. (To convert from frequency to wavelength, just divide the speed of light 300 000 000 meters per second by the frequency in cycles per second.) You will need a particle accelerator, not a microwave, to produce gamma-rays. (Of course, the Universe is the biggest particle accelerator available but it already belongs to someone else. Unfortunately, the Board, as a secret Government organization, may not loan its own particle accelerator. IN fact, nobody knows if the Board even has a particle accelerator. Its use for the purpose of viewing videos and DVD's for "censorship" was a stroke of genius to hide the fact that it is a particle accelerator.)

I feel I should also warn you about squirting high-tensile silk at wives, whether your's or of others'. In our experience, high-tensile silk has a sophoroforic-aphrodasiaic effect and we have tried to warn people not to use it without protection, especially in view of the need to maintain one-child nuclear families to avoid over-population. Remember, with great power comes great responsibility.

I am also able to confirm that we have reclassified the film as documentary fiction, which is neither documentary nor fiction but truth fictionalized to protect the innocent.

Please remember that Spidey was bitten by an arachnid and not a spider. If you have not already done so, please release all the spiders you have captured.

Your friendly neighbourhood "censor" board.

Iyavar Chetty

141

Mr Bertus Celliers
Armscor
Private Bag X337
Pretoria
0001

Mr Ben Trovato
PO Box 1117
Sea Point
8060

12 July, 2002

Dear Sir,

I understand that Armscor is selling one of its Daphne Class patrol submarines.

I am very interested in purchasing it. My neighbour and I have already come up with plans to convert it into an aircraft. The shape of the sub makes an ideal fuselage. Ted is very good at metalwork and he has designed a pair of wings to fit the Daphne. Since submarines already have a propeller, we need only replace it with a larger one. We would also need to fit a pair of sturdy wheels to the underside. The controls themselves are very similar. Up, down, left, right. What more do you need?

But anyone can turn a submarine into an aircraft. Our plan is far more sophisticated.

The craft is going to be aeronautically amphibious. It sounds like a highly technical term, but all it means is that our Daphne will be able to operate in both the air and the water. Most aircraft are ill-equipped to fly under water. Considering the number of planes that end up in the sea, this is obviously a major design flaw.

Ted has designed the wings to fold back on themselves. It's the same principle that the Japanese use to make hand-held fans. This means that once the plane is over the ocean, or any large stretch of water, we will be able to retract the wings and go into a steep dive without any fear of death. By the time Daphne penetrates the surface of the water, she will look identical to any other submarine of her class. Except her propeller will be much bigger. Because of this, we estimate that she will be able to travel at speeds of up to 300kph underwater. Using that velocity, Daphne will be able to burst from the ocean and in less than a second the wings will be fully deployed and she will continue flying through the air.

We intend patenting the design, but we are prepared to talk if Armscor is interested in the prototype.

Please let me know as soon as possible if we can pay for the submarine at Simon's Town. Or would you prefer we send a cheque to your office? I have enclosed ten rand as a deposit. There is much more where that came from.

Long live the pioneering spirit!

Yours truly,

....
Ben Trovato (Mr)

 **ARMSCOR**

2 August 2002

RE: Daphne Class Patrol Submarines

Sir,

Your letter to Mr Bertus Celliers dated 12 July 2002, refers.

Thank you for your interest. It is with serious concern that we take note of
your project plan. Although we find the theory behind the plan sound, we feel
compelled to point out the following:
The submarine was designed and built to operate in, and under the sea. This
specific design was chosen due to it's exceptional stealth caracteristics whilst
submerged. Our concern lies in the fact that the craft might not display the
same stealth profile in flight, especially whilst flapping its retractable wings
(we assume this forms an integral part of your design). Furthermore, due to its
stealth caracteristics, air traffic control might not be able to identify it on radar.

The second concern that we have is with fuel efficiency. Whilst we understand
and accept the fact that your design will be super fuel efficient when you dive at
a puddle with folded wings, our concern mainly lies with what happens between
the time that you burst from the ocean surface until the time you reach the apex
of your flight. In this regard, we would suggest pumping vast amounts of Nitrous
Oxide (laughing gas) into the "fuselage". It won't make the craft more fuel
efficient, but you could potentially have a good laugh at the fuel bill.

All jokes aside, thank you for your letter. It has had its intended effect of
entertaining us in our (all too often) serious work environment.

Faithfully

GJ van Staden
Senior Manager
Defence and Industry Support

 **ARMSCOR**

23 July 2002

REGISTERED MAIL

SALE OF DAPHNE SUBMARINE – SPEAR

Dear Sir,

Thank you for your letter of 12 July 2002, the contents of which have been noted.

Copies of the advertisement published in the Sunday Times and Rapport of 21 July 2002 regarding the sale of the submarine concerned are attached for your information.

Your Ten Rand note (Number: DR 2781179A) included with your letter as a deposit, is also returned since it does not comply with tender conditions.

Yours faithfully

L.P Celliers (Bertus)
Manager: Corporate Communication Division

This Ten Rand note no DR2781179 A issued by the
South African Reserve Bank is the sole property of
Mr Ben Trovato with the indicated postal address of
PO Box 1117, Sea Point, 8060.

Certified as a true version of the situation on this day,
the 22nd of July 2002 at 14:00

L P (Bertus) Celliers
Manager: Corporate Communications
Armscor

Free Gun South Africa
PO Box 31532
Braamfontein
2017

Mr Ben Trovato
PO Box 1117
Sea Point
8060

23 June, 2002

Dear Sir,

I have been thinking of emigrating ever since my wife, Brenda, was set upon by two burly men from the local neighbourhood watch. It emerged later that they had mistaken her for a housebreaker. While trying to wrestle free from a lethal stranglehold, she tried telling them that she had a key for the front door. But they laughed and said it's the easiest thing in the world to make copies. She is still wearing a neck brace.

My neighbour, Ted, suggested that instead of emigrating I should get myself a gun. I had my doubts until he told me about your organisation, Free Gun South Africa. He said you provide people with complimentary weapons. I asked him why you would do this, and he said it's because you are good citizens who care about people.

If Ted is telling the truth (for once in his life) would it be possible for you to provide me with more information? I have never owned a gun, so it would be easier for me to choose if you had some sort of catalogue that I could look through.

I have always liked the look of a machine-gun. Ted says I would probably get my picture in the newspaper if I went about wearing a bandolier filled with shiny cartridges. I would also be ready for the armed response people when they launch their next attack.

Even though the gun is free, please accept the enclosed R10 towards postage costs.

Let's go hunting!

Yours truly,

Ben Trovato (Mr)

BRIBE GIVEN
R10

FOR A SAFE AND SECURE NATION

02 July 2002

Dear Mr Trovato

Thank you for your letter dated 23 June 2002. Unfortunately your friend misled you by saying we are giving out guns for free. We are a non-violent organization,

Gun Free South Africa is committed to making a material contribution to building a safe and secure nation, free from fear, by reducing the number of firearms in society. Should you need more information about GFSA visit our website : http://www.gca.org.za

Enclosed is your R10 that you said was donation towards postage costs.

Yours sincerely

HB Magubane
Administrator

Mr Chris Koole
Director: Public Relations
Office of the Premier
Private Bag X9043
Cape Town 8000

Mr Ben Trovato
PO Box 1117
Sea Point
8060

June 5, 2002

Dear Mr Koole,

You may remember me from a previous correspondence in which I offered Premier Gerald Morkel a selection of alternative reading matter to take his mind off the weighty business of running the province.

Your reply was: "My Premier goes to the Good Book during breaks."

It must have been distressing for you to discover that Mr Morkel was, in fact, going to German fraudster Jurgen Harksen during breaks.

You also said: "My Premier would never judge a fellow man." I could not agree more. Mr Morkel has certainly shown himself to be a man singularly lacking in judgement.

When he was demoted to Mayor, did you go with him? Or are you now serving our new Premier, Peter Marais? Hang on. Hasn't Mr Marais resigned for getting a little too boisterous with the ladies? Gosh, it's hard to keep up.

I understand Mr Morkel has given up his ceremonial duties as mayor. This must leave him with plenty of time. Especially since Harksen is behind bars. Would you suggest I bring a selection of good fiction around to his office?

Hope to hear from you soon.

Yours truly,

Ben Trovato (Mr)

Mr Ben Trovato
PO Box 1117
Sea Point
8060

Chris Koole
Directr: Public Relations
Communication Services
PO BOX 659
8000

7 June 2002

Dear Mr Trovato

I remember our last exchange of letters. I am no longer serving the Premier of
the Western Cape and have nothing to do with the Unicity where Mr Morkel, my
former boss now serves as Mayor – be it with or without ceremonial functions.
This response is in my personal capacity.

With reference to former Premier Morkel and Harksen I find it strange that you
have already tried, found guilty and sentenced someone (Mr Morkel) who has not
even been heard by the Desai commisson of inquiry. For that matter it seems you
have come into the habit of judging and sentencing people before they have been
allowed to defend themselves (Mr Marais).

If someone whispered in my ear that you, or whoever, were a former con-artist
who had done pensioners out of their lively hood should I just believe it? And if
the accuser were a prison inmate or a know crook believing such a story would
seem even more far fetched. Accusations remain just that if they are not tried in
court. They can then be proven to be defamatory or true. If some-one telephones
you a hundred times a day on your cellular 'phone does that mean you were in
contact with the caller – even if you did not answer?

Even if Harksen is behind bars he probably still has his cellular 'phone
– remember Boesak? You are entitled to your opinion, but let me assure you, and
this is from me to you – heart to heart – Mr Morkel is a devout Christian and
has set himself high standards. He worked 18 hours a day for this province. If
he, like Hansie Cronje, is found to have stumbled along the way – and the funny
thing is that all this money talk does not involve personal gain – then he will
be judged accordingly. I know Mr Marais well as a former minister and assure
you that he too was a hard working man, a good manager and passionate about
helping the less fortunate. He too has not yet been tried. And if it comes to pass
that he has been too "boisterous", he too will be judged accordingly.

I am still a civil servant employed by the Provincial Administration and true to
our code of conduct, steer clear of getting involved in political forays.

Thank you for your letter. I enjoy your humorous (do 'n detect a degree of
sarcasm?) style of writing.

Yours truly,

Chris Koole (Mr)

The Chief Executive
SASOL
PO Box 5486
Johannesburg
2000

Mr Ben Trovato
PO Box 1117
Sea Point
8060

30 June, 2002

Dear Sir,

I was watching the telly the other night when a SASOL advertisement came on. I almost fell out of my chair, such was my dismay.

The advert featured a multi-racial group of children. But this is not what horrified me. Let me tell you that I very nearly choked on my cognac when I heard the song that was being played. You know what I am talking about. It is beyond comprehension that you could choose a song by that communist band, The Beatles.

As if that is not bad enough, you go one step further and select something sung by that drug-addled bisexual hippy John Lennon. In case you have forgotten, let me recite the chorus for you: *"I get high with a little help from my friends."*

Dear God, man, what were you people thinking? This is an advertisement for a company that produces petroleum products. What message are you sending out? Are you deliberately encouraging our children to spend their time at the corner garage sniffing petrol fumes when they could rather be in self-defence classes learning how to stay alive in today's violent and promiscuous society?

Are you in competition with the glue companies?

I used to mix with a crowd of petrol-sniffers when I was young and foolish, and I have seen what this stuff can do to an undeveloped mind. I will never forget Bennie van der Ploeg, a bright kid who used to get top marks until he started hanging around the local Shell pretending to pump up his bicycle tyres and ending up slumped semi-conscious from inhaling long and hard at the pumps. Bennie is a vegetable today.

You simply cannot tell the younger generation that they have friends at SASOL who will help them get high.

Please let me know what you intend doing to remedy the situation. I will not hesitate to lead a boycott of all SASOL products. If you have to have music in your advertisements, I suggest you use a wholesome band. Stay away from sluts like Britney Spears and that other dusky one with the devil in her eyes. A little Sinatra would not hurt anyone.

I look forward to hearing from you soon.

Yours truly,

....
Ben Trovato (Mr)

The Chief Executive
SASOL
PO Box 5486
Johannesburg
2000

Mr Ben Trovato
PO Box 1117
Sea Point
8060

4 August, 2002

Dear Sir,

I have not yet received a reply to my letter of 30th June. I am sure it has gone astray in the mail, since you must surely be aware of the potential consequences of ignoring members of the public who make regular use of Sasol products but who are quite capable of switching to another company's products without any qualms whatsoever.

You may recall that I expressed my concern about Sasol's latest television advertisement which features a Beatles song calling on people to get high with a little help from their friends. Making matters worse, the advert features young children who hardly need encouragement to take mind-altering drugs.

Should I not hear from you in this matter, you will leave me no choice but to approach the Advertising Standards Authority, the Broadcasting Complaints Commission and my neighbour, Ted Goodfellow, who is a veteran of consumer boycotts.

Thank you.

Yours truly,

....
Ben Trovato (Mr)

reaching new frontiers

19 August 2002

Dear Mr Trovato

Thank you for your letter of 4 August 2002. Brenda Kali, Sasol's Manager Group Communications and Public Affairs, responded to your 30 June 2002 letter on 11 July, 2002.

I have noted your concerns along with the numerous positive responses received by Sasol regarding Sasol's latest television and other media advertisements.

Yours sincerely

P V Cox

Ms Brenda Kali
Sasol – Public Affairs
PO Box 5486
Johannesburg
2000

Mr Ben Trovato
PO Box 1117
Sea Point
8060

24 August, 2002

Dear Ms Kali,

You may remember my letters of 30th June and 4th August in which I expressed concern about your latest advertising campaign. However, it is possible that you may not remember sending your "reply" to me.

I have since heard from your boss, Mr Cox, who tells me that you responded to my letter on the 30th of June.

Ms Kali, we both know that you never wrote that letter. The entire affair reeks of a cover-up that goes all the way to the top. Would you be prepared to take a polygraph test stating that you did, in fact, reply to my letter? And that you actually posted said reply? The mail service is extremely efficient in this country. I can testify to that. Perhaps it slipped to the bottom of your handbag. Have you checked?

All I want is your response to my complaint. I am not even complaining about the amount of benzene, vinyl chloride and methylene chloride that you put in your petrol. Nor do I particularly care that the good folk of Sasolburg are inhaling air mixed with nearly one hundred thousand tons of hydrogen sulphide, hydrogen dioxide and a whole bunch of volatile organic compounds. So long as our children are not encouraged to get high with a little help from their friends.

I am sure you have kept a duplicate of your "response" to my concerns. I suggest you make a copy, pop it into an envelope, slap a stamp on it, make sure my address is on it and slip it into a mail box. The post office insists that these steps be followed for them to do their job properly.

Let's hear from you this time.

Yours truly,

....
Ben Trovato (Mr)

Police Commissioner Lennit Max
Private Bag 9004
Cape Town
8000

Mr Ben Trovato
PO Box 1117
Sea Point
8060

3 July, 2002

Dear Commissioner,

Congratulations on the fine job you are doing. I have not seen a single crime committed before my eyes in almost two months. There was a time that we were unable to move without tripping over a rapist or murderer. In fact, the only crime I have witnessed lately was when the National Party's Marthinus van Schalkwyk stole the job of premier! My neighbour was so outraged that he wanted to lay charges of theft. I managed to convince him to stay out of it and pretend that he saw nothing.

Even though you appear to have crime well under control, I am concerned about the younger generation. They do not seem to possess the values that have been instilled in men like you and I. This morning I was going for a stroll along the Sea Point promenade when I came across two teenagers openly kissing on a bench! I am no prude and have done my fair share of canoodling. But always in the privacy of my own home. It seems that even smooching has changed since our days. At first, I thought the girl on the promenade had passed out and was being given mouth-to-mouth resuscitation, such was the frantic urgency with which he was setting about her. Had an alien from outer space landed just then, he would have thought this was a planet of people who ate one another.

You may have read in the paper the other day that the Iranian police arrested 30 girls and boys during what they called a "depraved" birthday party. It turned out that the youngsters were dancing with each other. As you know, this is not allowed under sharia law. That is what makes Islam such a wholesome religion. The youngsters were given fines, suspended jail sentences and up to 70 lashes each. It may sound a little on the harsh side, but these kids will certainly think twice before engaging in such degenerate behaviour in the future.

Dancing may appear to be an innocent pursuit to many of us. But, just as dagga leads to heroin, mixed-gender dancing leads to unprotected sex and Satanism. And the Iranians know this better than most.

Would it be possible for your men to step up their raids on parties in some of our residential areas? I know of several homes near me that are used for drinking and dancing over weekends. I will provide the addresses if you can guarantee me protection.

Down with hedonism!

Yours truly,

Ben Trovato (Mr)

South African Police Service *Suid-Afrikaanse Polisiediens*

| Private Bag Privaatsak | X9004, CAPE TOWN / KAAPSTAD, 8000 | Fax : Faks : | (021) 417-7336 |

---

15 July 2002

Dear Mr. Trovato

YOUR LETTER DATED 3 JULY 2002

1. On behalf of the Provincial Commissioner, I hereby acknowledge receipt of your letter dated as above. The Commissioner has noted the content thereof with thanks and once again expresses his sincere commitment to the effective combating of crime in the Western Cape.

2. Whilst some, like yourself, may view it as lamentable, our fine constitution does not permit the criminalisation of displays of public affection or dancing and the enjoyment of music. This of course, as long as the former does not amount to public indecency (where nudity is usually a prerequisite) or the latter interfere with the serenity and peace of others. If I may make so bold, I do feel that the punishments which you propose are a trifle harsh, even in view of the intense emotions which the actions in question appear to arouse in you.

3. Nevertheless, please feel free to contact my office should you wish to meet with me in order to discuss your concerns in depth. To this end, my contact details are as follows:

   Tel. (W):(021) 417-7388
   Fax:(021) 417-7389

4. In view of your previous generosity, I gladly enclose R10-00 to cover your travel expenses.

5. Please convey my kindest regards to Brenda and Clive. I trust all is well with the lad.

Yours sincerely,

SUPERINTENDENT
f/PROVINCIAL COMMISSIONER: WESTERN CAPE
M W ROMBURGH

155

Supt. M Romburgh
SA Police Service
Private Bag X9004
Cape Town
8000

Mr Ben Trovato
PO Box 1117
Sea Point
8060

22 July, 2002

Dear Superintendent Romburgh,

Allow me to congratulate you on your fine police work. You are indeed a sleuth
of the first order! In my original letter, I made no mention of my wife or son. And
yet you passed on your regards to both Brenda and Clive. It would not surprise
me at all to hear that your colleagues refer to you as The Human Bloodhound.
It is no wonder that you have made Superintendent. In fact, I shall be writing
to the Minister of Safety and Security recommending that he promote you
to Inspector General. But please do not get your hopes up. The minister is a
Communist and I was trained by this country's finest military theorists to regard
these people with extreme prejudice. However, since his first name is Charles
and not Vladimir, it is more likely that he only brings out his dog-eared copy of
Das Kapital at cocktail parties and not while he is at work.

Clive is now out of the institute and is doing relatively well. I gave him the
R10 that you so kindly sent me, and now you are his hero. He says that when
he grows up he wants to join the Uninformed Branch. I presume he means
Uniformed Branch. He also says that he wants to thank you personally, but this
might not be a good idea as I suspect he wants to extort more money out of you
so he can buy the latest Eminem album.

I could not help but notice that you are less than enthusiastic about my
suggestion regarding the imposition of lashes on youngsters caught flagrantly
disregarding all moral sensibilities. As you so rightly point out, the Constitution
prevents it. But this only applies while you are in uniform. My neighbour and I
are becoming informal vigilantes, much like informal parking attendants but with
Hawaiian shirts and more muscle. We would be honoured if you joined us on one
of our outings. Ted's wife, Mary, provides the snacks and Brenda does the drinks.
The risk of poisoning always livens things up a bit! We are a little short on
equipment so bring what you can. However, if you are unable to afford a cattle
prod, one will be provided for you free of charge.

Best wishes,

....
Ben Trovato (Mr)

PS. A man of your investigative talents should be able to find out Jackie Selebi's
real name. Let me know what you get.

156

The Instructor-in-Chief
Arthur Murray School of Dancing
PO Box 2505
Rivonia
2128

Mr Ben Trovato
PO Box 1117
Sea Point
8060

4 July, 2002

Dear Instructor-in-Chief,

Ever since I was a little boy I have wanted to learn how to dance. I once made the mistake of mentioning this to my father. He got his gun (a Walther PPK), took me outside and started firing into the ground around my feet. When the magazine was empty, he looked at me and said: "See. You don't need lessons."

These days he is too old to shoot straight. Besides, I would never tell him that I am considering joining your outfit. The shock would probably kill him. On second thoughts, perhaps I will tell him. But I am straying from the point. Before I am crippled with arthritis, I need to feel what it is like to swing a woman about on the dance floor. I tried it once with my wife, Brenda, but she thought I was attacking her and chased me through the house with my son's aluminium baseball bat.

The Arthur Murray School of Dancing is renowned. So it makes sense that I come to you first. But one thing is troubling me. When I mentioned my intentions to my neighbour, he was quick to warn me against it. Ted says that Arthur Murray was responsible for opening up the drug trade in America. He says Murray was the man who made contact with Pablo Escobar and began smuggling tons of cocaine straight out of Bolivia. Not only that, but Murray was also selling guns to both the Medellin and Cali cartels. I asked him if he was sure he had the right Arthur Murray, and he nodded and tapped his nose. Old Ted knows a thing or two, but I wanted to check with you before I sign up with my local dance studio.

Please let me know if your Mr Murray was ever a drug-smuggling gunrunner. Is he still alive? I would hate to find myself involved in a front company for the global narcotics trade.

I anxiously await your response.

Yours truly,

....
Ben Trovato (Mr)

The Instructor-in-Chief
Arthur Murray School of Dancing
PO Box 2505
Rivonia
2128

Mr Ben Trovato
PO Box 1117
Sea Point
8060

4 August, 2002

Dear Sir,

It has been a month since I wrote to you enquiring about the possibility of joining one of your schools, and I have not yet had a reply. I know that you expect people to dance to your tune, but that is no reason to ignore us.

If you recall, I had expressed concerns about Mr Murray's background. It has been suggested in certain quarters that your Mr Murray had more than a passing interest in the global drug trade. And that the dancing schools are merely money laundering fronts.

I have managed to convince my wife that we need to learn the foxtrot, the tango and all those other exotic styles that made Fred Astair and Ginger Rogers the most romantic couple in all of Hollywood history. But not at the expense of our freedom.

Once again, I await your assurances that we will not be arrested as accomplices if we join one of Arthur Murray's dancing schools.

Thank you.

Yours truly,

....
Ben Trovato (Mr)

IAN D. McCALLUM
LICENSEE

Arthur Murray Studio

13th August, 2002

Dear Mr. Trovato,

I refer to your two letters dated 4th July and 4th August which have been passed on to me by my franchisee in Johannesburg.

Firstly I must apologise for the delay in replying but this is due to the fact that on reading your first letter I was completely amazed and bewildered by it's content. On a second reading I was convinced that someone was playing a joke on us. However, I assume this now not to be the case as you have enquired once again.

In the 44 years that I have been part of the Arthur Murray organization I have never once heard any type of insinuation that Mr Arthur Murray was involved in any way whatsoever with the drug trade in America.

I started my Arthur Murray career in London and had the opportunity of meeting both Arthur and Kathryn Murray on a couple of occasions. I have always had tremendous admiration for the man who started the finest social dance organization in the world and can assure you that I would not have had anything to do with a company whose founder had drug smuggling or gunrunning implications.

My late husband Ian McCallum started the Arthur Murray organization here in South Africa in 1955. He was a man of great integrity and honesty and would certainly never have been associated with a company which had a 'shady' history.

You are quite right when you state "the Arthur Murray School of Dancing is renowned". We are, without doubt, the largest and most successful social dance organisation in the world. The A.M. studios in South Africa are held in very high esteem by our head office and board of directors in America.

Over the years our studios in South Africa have taught hundreds of thousands of people to dance. Apart from achieving a high dance standard our students have fun, gain confidence, make new friends and develop a whole new social life. We have always prided ourselves on being a huge Arthur Murray family and in a few cases are presently teaching fourth generation of families.

In view of the high reputation the Arthur Murray organization has here in South Africa and around the world I find it absolutely inconceivable that anyone could associate it with drug smuggling, gun running or money laundering.

However, may I suggest that if you still have reservations concerning Mr. Arthur Murray (who incidentally passed away some years ago) you could contact our Head Office in Coral Gables, Florida. U.S.A. for further assurance.

I am absolutely delighted to hear that both you and your wife would like to take dance lessons with us and, should you decide to do so, I look forward to meeting you in the near future.

We have two Arthur Murray studios in the Cape Town area, one in Bellville and the other in Table View. They are both owned by Mr. & Mrs. Burger Herbst. Mrs. Herbst (known as Miss Lynn) runs the Bellville branch whilst Mr. Herbst runs the Table View studio. They have a wonderful team of proffesional instructors and I know you will be very well taught and looked after.

I suggest you call Miss Lynn on the above telephone number to make an appointment to visit the studio of you choice, to learn more about our activities and to participate in a complimentary half hour lesson for both you and your wife. I can assure you that you are under no obligation to enroll with us if you are hesitant in any way.

May you and your wife have many happy hours of dancing ahead.

Yours sincerely,

SYLVIA McCALLUM
MASTER FRANCHISEE

c.c.Mr. & Mrs. Herbst.

The Manager
Babcock Equipment
PO Box 3498
Johannesburg
2000

Mr Ben Trovato
PO Box 1117
Sea Point
8060

4 July, 2002

Dear Sir,

I am sure you are a busy man, so I will be brief.

I was at a function the other night and overheard a group of men talking about Babcocks. At first I thought they were comparing size, as men are inclined to do after a few drinks. But listening more closely, it turned out that they were in fact discussing something called Babcocks.

To be honest, I have no idea what a Babcock is. I know what a shuttlecock is because I used to play the game with my sister. Everyone knows what a weathercock is for, although I have yet to see one pointing in the right direction. A cockalorum is a self-important little man and a cockatrice is a legendary monster, part snake and part rooster, that can kill with a single glance. It sounds like my wife, Brenda. I know that cockshy refers to a game involving coconuts and not men who avoid public urinals. And I know that a cockabully is a small freshwater fish from New Zealand and a cockup is what happened when Marthinus van Schalkwyk became premier of the Western Cape.

But I do not know what is a Babcock.

I tried to get information from several sources in Cape Town, but down here any mention of the C-word leads to pursed lips and invitations which I could not possibly accept.

Enlighten me, please.

Yours truly,

Ben Trovato (Mr)

GAUTENG
P.O. Box 13902
Witfield 1467
Tel: +27 (011) 826 6511
Fax: +27 (011) 823 2030

KWA-ZULU NATAL
P.O. Box 190
New Germany 3620
Tel: +27 (031) 705 2733/42
Fax: +27 (031) 705 2532

MPUMALANGA
P.O. Box 170
Middelburg 1050
Tel: +27 (013) 246 2867
Fax: +27 (013) 246 2863

WEBSITE: www.babcockpeq.co.za
E-MAIL: enquiries@babcockpeq.co.za

WESTERN CAPE
P16-18 Willow Road
Stikland 7530
Tel: +27 (021) 946 2655
Fax: +27 (021) 946 2656

FREE STATE
P.O. Box 2007
Bloemfontein 9300
Tel: +27 (051) 432 3302
Fax: +27 (051) 432 3351

MPUMALANGA
P.O. Box 5296
Nelspruit 1200
Tel: +27 (013) 755 2130
Fax: +27 (013) 755 1934

25 July 2002

Dear Mr Trovato

I refer to your letter dated 4 July 2002, querying what a Babcock is.

To be quite truthful, we are as confused as you are as to the origin and meaning of a Babcock. The matter gets even more baffling when you consider that our company was originally founded in the USA some 120 years ago under the appellation Babcock & Wilcox. At many board meetings over the years we have pondered whether these gentlemen were the founders of our company, and if so, were they more than just friends?

We have come to recognize that to go on speculating is futile and that by electing to work for Babcock we take on the burden of being made fun of by our competitors and idle gossip mongers. Maybe the reason why we are so successful and have seen the start of two centuries is that we have been forged through the fires of ridicule and humiliation.

Yours sincerely

FRANK REID
MANAGING DIRECTOR

PS:It is interesting to note that we have often been misnamed as Badcock, which has taken great presence of mind to deal with but in the final analysis we feel that a Willingcock is better than a Badcock or even Nocock at all!

Mr Peter Matlhare
CEO SABC
Private Bag X1
Auckland Park
Johannesburg

Mr Ben Trovato
PO Box 1117
Sea Point
8060

9 July, 2002

Dear Mr Matlhare,

I wish to complain about the lack of decent pornography on SABC television channels.

Instead, we get endless moronic soaps featuring people with names like Jade and Sasha. That is if we aren't being forced to sit through documentaries on the mating habits of the endangered Amazonian screwworm.

Sir, the spark has gone out of my marriage. My conjugal rights continue to be violated and I am at the end of my tether. Brenda (my wife) needs to be snapped out of her celibate state. I am convinced that a bit of porn on the old telly would do the trick. She has to be reminded that other people still engage in this practice. And that coitus is not something played on the deck of a cruise ship.

Every night, I try to keep Brenda in front of the television for as long as possible in the hope of catching a glimpse of some gratuitous copulating. I once heard of a programme called Fellatio, which sounded promising. But it turned out to be a talk show involving some dreadful woman with a similar name.

As the man in charge of the public broadcaster, I am sure you have the power to instruct one of the channels to begin showing more sex. Not just a flash of thigh, but the real rumpy pumpy stuff. And not too late in the evening, please. I tend to nod off around ten.

Please let me know if you are prepared to help save my marriage.

Thank you and God bless.

Yours truly,

....
Ben Trovato (Mr)

PS. Enclosed please find R10 to help speed up the process.

SABC Public Relations
Private Bag X1
Auckland Park
Johannesburg

Mr Ben Trovato
PO Box 1117
Sea Point
8060

23 August, 2002

Dear Sir or Madam:

I wrote to the SABC on the 9th of July and have not yet had a response. As a person who diligently pays his television licence, I am outraged by your capacity to ignore people.

You may recall that I was enquiring about the possibility of the SABC showing programmes of a more adult nature. I am not talking about Days of our Lives, here. Think Emmanuel with less dialogue and fewer clothes. There are many people of my generation who need their marriages spiced up by something a little raunchier than Dawson's Creek.

As licence-payers, you are obliged to listen to us. Let me know if you plan on doing something about it.

Let's hear from you this time.

Yours truly,

....
Ben Trovato (Mr)

PS. Any idea what might have happened to my ten rand that I sent along to help speed up the process? You might want to check Mr Matlare's top drawer.

BRIBE RETURNED

S B C
AUDIENCE LIAISON
Corporate Affairs

Room 2302 Radiopark
Henley Road
Auckland Park
Johannesburg
Private Bag X1
Auckland Park 2006
Tel: 27 11 714-5178/3821
Fax: 27 11 714-4508
e-mail: moan@sabc.co.za

30 August 2002

Dear Mr Trovato

Thank you for your letters of 9 July and 23 August. The second of these was delivered to the Labour Relations department, and the postal worker who showed such initiative is being considered for promotion. I apologise for taking so long to reply to your first letter. The delay was occasioned by deliberations at executive level on the possibility of granting your request, and on the best use of your contribution. Ultimately, however, the consensus was that since the SABC already screens so much pornography, expending a further ten rand on it would simply be an extravagance. I therefore regretfully return your R10 note, although we were tempted to use it to buy another season of Dawson's Creek.

I have gathered from your letter that you believe there is no hard pornography on our television channels, so I can only conclude that you have been watching at the wrong time. Unlike other broadcasters, who believe that pornography belongs in the small hours, we have been innovative and placed it mainly in the morning. Our research has shown that many married people tend to nod off around ten at night, which might be at the root of their celibate state, so we like to catch them when they are still invigorated and the kids are off to school. Just to give you a taste of what is on offer during the day:

- The Little Mermaid: a titillating young siren, if somewhat fishy. Perhaps not as stimulating for Brenda, but Neptune does some interesting things with his trident.
- Aladdin: getting it off on a wild magic carpet ride.
- Bare in the Big Blue House: you may have been misled by the spelling error ('Bear') in the title, for which we apologise. Blue, as the title indicates.
- Black Beauty: for those who like to add some colour to spice the conjugal encounter.
- Dragonballz: a must for Brenda. This is in the afternoon, placed specially for women whose partners would like a hot (as opposed to lukewarm) welcome home.

Perhaps a simple change of viewing habits would do the trick. We wish you many happy returns of your conjugal rights.

Yours sincerely

DOROTHY VAN TONDER
Manager: Compliance & Liaison
Policy & Regulatory Affairs

PS You might want to check whether Henry Root has copyrighted his original concept. If so, this R10 may well come in handy.

The Manager
Mount Nelson Hotel
76 Orange Street
Cape Town
8001

Mr Ben Trovato
PO Box 1117
Sea Point
8060

9 July, 2002

Dear Sir,

I hope you are able to assist me.

My neighbour and I popped into your fine establishment one morning about a week ago for a quick snort to give the day a little more clarity. Unfortunately, we overstayed our welcome. As far as I recall, dinner was about to be served by the time a friendly member of your staff showed us to the parking lot.

Since then I have been accosted by my wife demanding to know where the garden gnome has got to. Then it struck me. I had taken the gnome along to your hotel, but he failed to return home with me. I cannot say for sure what possessed me to bring him along for a drink, but I dare say the idea made sense at the time.

He is just under a metre high (tall for a gnome) and as last seen wearing a pointy red hat and blue lederhosen. He had a fishing rod, but my friend tells me that I was using it as a swizzle stick so it may no longer be attached to his hand.

Quite frankly, I could not care less about the gnome. But my wife insists that I find it. She seems to think that it has some kind of sentimental value because her sister's husband gave it to us as a wedding gift. I have always thought that as far as presents go, giving someone a garden gnome is the same as giving someone a voucher for a free consultation with a physician who specialises in sexual dysfunction. This probably explains why Brenda spends more time with the gnome than she does with me. Although I am sure that their relationship is nothing more than platonic, she seems to miss Little Big Man (her name, not mine).

Please could you check with your lost property people to see if they have our gnome?

Thank you.

Yours truly,

Ben Trovato (Mr)

MOUNT NELSON HOTEL

1 0 0
YEARS
1 8 9 9 - 1 9 9 9

2 August 2002

Dear Mr Trovato

RE: GARDEN GNOME:

Thank you for your letter dated 9 July 2002.

Unfortunately after having checked all possible areas and spoken to relevant staff members, we have been unable to trace your missing garden gnome.

Should we find "Little Big Man" we will be in direct contact with you. Sorry that we cannot respond with better news.

Yours sincerely

Odette Arbuthnot
PA to Hotel Manager

The Manager
Sabi Sabi Private Game Reserve
Sabie Sands 2
Skukusa

Mr Ben Trovato
PO Box 1117
Sea Point
8060

9 July, 2002

Dear Sir,

Your resort comes highly recommended. A friend of minor Italian nobility said if there is one place on earth that he would want to die, it is Sabi Sabi. Personally, I am in no rush to die. But I suppose if one were seeking an early death, one would choose a place that is full of dangerous man-eating animals. One would not, for example, recommend a health spa as the best place in which to die, no matter how luxurious the surroundings.

But getting back to business. I urgently need to take my wife, Brenda, away for a week. The pilot light of my marriage has gone out. The geyser is cold. But I still have gas in me. Plenty of it. All I need is a spark. The explosion is guaranteed. And I suspect that Sabi Sabi could well prove to be my personal Ground Zero. However, before I make a reservation, there are certain things on which I need clarity.

Since the pilot light has been extinguished, I will need fuel to stoke the fire. In my case, this means role-playing. When I was courting Brenda, she once asked me to dress up as a Rastafarian bongo player. I arrived at her house wearing a Caribbean print shirt and imitation dreadlocks, not really knowing what to expect. It wasn't long before she began playing Bob Marley tunes and plying me with a powerful rum punch. Later, she rolled a marijuana cigarette and brought out a drum from beneath her bed. To be honest, it was the best evening of my life.

But that was before the Ice Age descended. Now, Brenda needs to be coaxed back into the tropics. And what better place to do it than surrounded by the eroticism of the bush?

Before I make a reservation, I thought it only fair to check with you whether there will be any problems. Even though my Italian friend tells me that Sabi Sabi is a very liberal place, I would not want to be confronted by heavily armed khaki-clad game rangers just as the fun begins. My plan is to pick up the bongos on the second or third night. It's best to give Brenda a chance to settle in before I turn on the power. I assume that you have marijuana on the premises. Or would you suggest I bring my own? I realise there is a chance that the Rastafarian game may no longer work. As a precaution, I will bring along my Raging Bull outfit. It worked in Pamplona many years ago, and there is no reason why it should not work at Sabi Sabi. All I need is a clear run of about 20 metres.

Please let me know if my needs are acceptable to management, as I have to book soon.

Yours truly,

....
Ben Trovato (Mr)

SABI 🦏 SABI

24 July 2002

Dear Mr Trovato

Thank you for considering Sabi Sabi for your special romantic weekend. We are able to offer you our Rhino Horn suite, consisting of a very large bedroom, luxurious bathroom with sunken double jacuzzi and sumptuous lounge, all interconnected by a 30 metre passage. This, we feel, would more than adequately accommodated for your Pamplona bull run, (or "buffalo" run, as we prefer to call it).

As far as your request for Marijuana is concerned, we at Sabi Sabi are particularly concerned about conservation and ecology, and to this end, no exotic shrubs are either planted, cooked, eaten or smoked on the property. However, through extensive research, we have identified a number of indigenous plants and herbs, such as Bushman's Tea (Cathaedulis) and Sausage Tree (Kigelia Africana), which experienced guests, such as yourself, have informed us are infinitely more potent than marijuana. We will be happy to supply you with as much of these as you feel you may need.

Although you expressed a degree of negativity towards health spas, may we take the liberty of advising you of the benefits of our Earth Nature Spa for your specific needs? We believe that our specially trained therapists and masseurs will make your stay with us even more memorable, and take some of the pressure off yourself. The treatment we recommend consists of a detoxifying and energizing seaweed wrap, after which you and Brenda would soak in a double hydro jet bath before being given our ultimate sensual massage in our twin massaging room. You would both be brought to the brink of pleasure at which time we would bundle you off to your suite. This could save you a lot of energy, and would also avoid your having to pack at least one Rastafarian style outfit in your luggage.

Please let us know if there is anything else we could do to make your stay at Sabi Sabi more combustible.

Yours faithfully

Patrick Shorten

Mr P Shorten
MANAGING DIRECTOR

Mr Andries Viljoen
CEO: South African Airways
Private Bag X13
Johannesburg Int. Airport
1627

Mr Ben Trovato
PO Box 1117
Sea Point
8060

17 July, 2002

Dear Mr Viljoen,

My wife and I are frequent fliers. I have family in Palermo and friends in Northern Ireland. Brenda has business associates in Lagos and her father lives in Monaco. We also have holiday homes in Venice and Portugal.

South African Airways has always been our carrier of choice. Brenda and I have never been anything but satisfied with the service. The only exception was during a trip to London when a steward reached for my tray and "accidentally" grabbed my willy instead.

We are due for a trip soon and I was about to call my travel agent when my neighbour, Ted, said that he hoped we got there safely now that SAA had begun hiring pilots from the township. He was surprised to hear that I did not know about your new policy. He said there is one man who worked as a baggage handler at Lesotho Airways and who is now the captain of an SAA jumbo jet.

I am not a racist, but Brenda is decidedly nervous about flying overseas on an aircraft captained by a man who might have been up all night beating his wife and carousing in a shebeen.

I could not care less what he does in his personal life, but I have seen how these people drive taxis and I doubt that my heart is strong enough to survive fourteen hours of swerving violently across the Atlantic. Even if he does it in nine. Just the thought of cutting in front of other planes on the airstrip makes me nervous.

Do you think we should take a chance on your chap from the location, or would you advise that we switch airlines for safety's sake? I suppose there would not be much chance of a darkie getting into a Swiss Air cockpit. From what I hear, they are not even allowed into the country.

We would appreciate your suggestions as soon as possible.

Yours truly,

Ben Trovato (Mr)

Mr Andries Viljoen
CEO: South African Airways
Private Bag X13
Johannesburg Int. Airport
1627

Mr Ben Trovato
PO Box 1117
Sea Point
8060

7 August, 2002

Dear Mr Viljoen,

I have not heard from you in connection with my query dated 17th July. However, I am sure your response has gone astray in the mail since SAA can hardly afford to alienate loyal customers like Brenda and I.

If you recall, I was seeking assurances that it is safe to fly with one of your darker-skinned pilots. Since then, my fears have been exacerbated by the news that one of your Previously Disadvantaged Pilots was caught with a mound of Bolivian cocaine in his underwear. I appreciate that he may well be telling the truth when he says he does not know how it got there. Do you know how it got there? Are you planning to introduce random testing for staff?

The idea that your pilots indulge in sex-soaked drug orgies the moment they reach cruising altitude does not inspire confidence in the airline.

Once again, I ask for your assurance that it is safe to fly with SAA pilots who might be other than white, whether they be drugged or not.

Thank you.

Yours truly,

....
Ben Trovato (Mr)

SOUTH AFRICAN AIRWAYS

07 August 2002

Dear Mr Trovato

André Viljoen, President and CEO of South African Airways, has shared your letter, dated 17 July 2002, and has requested that I respond on his behalf.

Mr Trovato, it seems to us that you have been misled through wrong information which could cause a serious adverse effect upon South African Airways. I just happen to have a copy of our Wings edition where we announced the first appointment of our very qualified black Captain, Mpho Mamashela. I am enclosing a copy of this report. You will see that Captain Mamashela is a fully qualified pilot and through his commitment to aviation and personal success he managed to become one of our best pilots through skill, enthusiasm and passion.

Mr Trovato, you and your wife can rest assured that South African Airways have some of the best pilots in the world on our team. The safety of our passengers, crew and aircraft is never compromised. You also have our assurance that although the air traffic may at times be busy, that it is nothing similar and cannot be compared to the rush hour traffic or manner in which our taxis operate on the roads.

Thank you for taking the time to write to us. Mr Trovato, in this day and age the colour of a person does not label a man and we hope that you will see things from a different perspective and support our decision to have someone as well credited as Captain Mpho Mamashela, and others like him.

With kind regards

Gillian Watts
EXECUTIVE OFFICE – SOUTH AFRICAN AIRWAYS

SOUTH AFRICAN AIRWAYS

14 August 2002

Dear Mr. Trovato

Thank you for your letter dated 7 August 2002. We so happened to respond to your original concerns on the same date and have pleasure in forwarding a copy of our reply.

The recent incident involving one of our pilots was an unfortunate one indeed and will be dealt with the seriousness it deserves. Safety at South African Airways is of paramount importance and will not be compromised at any cost. You have my emphatic assurance that all precautions humanly possible are taken to ensure the safety of you, our valued customer, our crew and equipment at all times. For obvious reasons we cannot elaborate on what measures we take to prevent an occurrence such as the one under correspondence.

We at South African Airways sincerely value your custom and trust that we can look forward to your continued support.

Kind regards

Michael van Niekerk
Senior Manager
CUSTOMER RELATIONS

The Director
SA Brain Research Institute
6 Campbell Street
Waverley
Johannesburg

Mr Ben Trovato
PO Box 1117
Sea Point
8060

17 July, 2002

Dear Sir,

I am sure you are a very busy man, so I will get straight to the point.

I would like to donate my brain. Not immediately, of course. But once I die, it is all yours. I imagine that you do not get many offers like this, so you must be very excited.

It is a fine brain, I assure you. Many of my friends have grown dimwitted with age and alcohol abuse. As a man of moderation, I am proud to say that mine remains in perfect working order. And I take good care of it, too. Whenever my wife and I have an argument, I am quick to strap on a kevlar cycling helmet to ensure that the cranium remains in one piece. There are many, many men out there who have clearly suffered one too many blows to the head. Some are in prison, some are in parliament. I need not tell you, of all people, that science has little use for addled brains.

Naturally, my brain is no longer the Porsche that it once was. These days it is more like a station wagon – a family brain that is slightly worn from years of trying to squeeze in too many people and a wet dog at the same time. But the synapses still crackle like a log fire on a winter's night in Cape Town.

In return for my brain, all I ask is that you help resolve an issue that has been troubling me. A friend of mine in America (he is a Harvard graduate currently spending some time in a state facility in Colorado) referred me to an MIT man by the name of Marvin Minsky on this same issue. Here it is. How long will it take before scientists are able to download human consciousness into a machine? Minsky says it will happen.

On my demise, would you like someone to courier my brain to you? If so, would it be acceptable to send the entire head? I doubt that any of my friends would be prepared to perform the retrieval procedure. Alternatively, you may wish to collect it personally, in which case I will give you my home address. Mind you, there is no guarantee that this is where I will shuffle off the mortal coil. It could be down the road at the post office. But if Brenda has her way, you are more than likely to find my body at home. For your sake, I hope she uses poison and not a blunt instrument. Bludgeoning could ruin everything.

I look forward to hearing from you.

Yours truly,

....
Ben Trovato (Mr)

The Director
SA Brain Research Institute
6 Campbell Street
Waverley
Johannesburg

Mr Ben Trovato
PO Box 1117
Sea Point
8060

7 August, 2002

Dear Sir,

I have not yet received a reply to my letter of 17th July. I assume it has gone astray in the mail, since I find it unlikely that you would ignore a man who is prepared to donate his brain in the name of science.

Did you manage to come up with an answer to the Minsky prediction?

You may be pleased to know that I am cutting back on the whisky so that my brain is not too damaged by the time you harvest it. If you are not interested in my offer, please let me know so that I can resume my regular intake. There is no point in depriving oneself needlessly.

Hope to hear from you soon.

Yours truly,

....
Ben Trovato (Mr)

PS. I am including a stamp in case you have run out.

The Director   Mr Ben Trovato
SA Brain Research Institute   PO Box 1117
6 Campbell Street   Sea Point
Waverley   8060
Johannesburg

7 August 2002

Dear Sir,

I have not yet received a reply to my letter of 17th July. I assume it has gone
astray in the mail, since I find it unlikely that you would ignore a man who is
prepared to donate his brain in the name of science.

Did you manage to come up with an answer to the Minsky prediction?

You may be pleased to know that I am cutting back on the whisky so that my
brain is not too damaged by the time you harvest it. If you are not interested in
my offer, please let me know so that I can resume my regular intake. There is no
point in depriving oneself needlessly.

Hope to hear from you soon.

Yours truly,

....
Ben Trovato (Mr)

PS. I am including a stamp in case you have run out.

13/08/02

We do not take Brain Donations - you should
donate it rather to the Anatomy dept @ UCT

The Manager
Blakes Hotel
Keizersgracht 384
1016 GB Amsterdam
Netherlands

Mr Ben Trovato
PO Box 1117
Sea Point
8060
Cape Town
South Africa

23 July, 2002

Dear Sir,

My wife and I are planning to be in Europe this summer. We met many years ago at the Running of the Bulls in Pamplona, although she was so drunk that she cannot remember a thing. Even today, she still thinks I should be somebody else.

I am arranging an itinerary to take in several of Europe's most romantic cities. You will probably agree that Amsterdam is not among them. The reason I wish to visit your city has more to do with the Dutch government's attitude towards narcotics. Do not get me wrong. I am not an international drug fiend. However, Brenda has led a sheltered life and I feel that now is the time to introduce her to something a little more on the wild side. Please be assured that I have no intention of holing up in your hotel with piles of heroin and hard-core pornography. Russian tourists are known for this kind of behaviour, but not independently wealthy South Africans from good families.

As it will be our second honeymoon, I was hoping to get Brenda to smoke a little marijuana. You will appreciate that I am not able to do this in my own country. I cannot risk having a platoon of heavily armed police officers bursting into my home and setting their vicious man-eating dogs loose on the family. Unlike in your civilised country, the use of relatively harmless narcotics in South Africa will land you in prison where black men will ravage you with their enormous members. I understand that some men actually pay for this kind of thing, but I can assure you that I am not one of them.

Your hotel has been recommended to me by friends in the government. I did not ask them whether you provided guests with marijuana for recreational purposes, but there was an implication that I would be able to get whatever I wished. Again, let me assure me that I will not be requiring bags of the stuff. One or two rolled cigarettes, what we call zols in our country, will be sufficient to get Brenda to loosen up enough to participate in the occasion.

I plan to be in Amsterdam in the latter half of September. Please let me know if your finest suite would be available around that time. I can include the cost of the marijuana in a deposit, if required. The money can be transferred within an hour.

Looking forward to hearing from you.

Yours truly,

....
Dr Ben Trovato

31 July 2002

Amsterdam,

Dear Dr. Trovato,

Thank you very much for your interest in Blakes Hotel Amsterdam.

In regards to you letter, I would like to inform you that the use of Marijuna is indeed since several years legalized in the Netherlands. However the sale of all soft-drugs is only permitted in the destinated Coffeeshops, well controlled by our government.

As an hotelier I am able to offer you several Suites, which we still have available in the later half of September. My concierge team will be pleased to direct you to the finest coffeeshops in town, but not able to buy you any soft-drugs.

If you would like to make a reservation for one of our finest suites, please call our Reservations department at:
+31-20-5302010 or via e-mail: hotel@blakes.nl

Please feel free to contact me if you have any questions regarding the above.

Kind regards,

Richard van Batenburg
General Manager

The Manager
Athenee Palace Hilton
Str, Episcopei 1-3
Bucharest
Romania

Mr Ben Trovato
PO Box 1117
Sea Point
8060
Cape Town
South Africa

23 July, 2002

Dear Sir,

I am interested in reserving your finest suite or a week in the latter half of
September. It will be a special occasion since my wife and I are travelling around
the world on our second honeymoon. I thought I would include Romania on our
itinerary since it has such a violent and romantic history. Much like my marriage,
actually.

Your hotel was recommended by a good friend who serves in my government.
Normally, I would take his advice without a moment's hesitation. However, he is
also a high-ranking member of the South African Communist Party. And given
Romania's past, I am not altogether sure if I should trust his judgement in this
case.

It seems just the other day that President Nicolae Ceausescu unleashed the
troops on unsuspecting tourists in the middle of Bucharest. My neighbour
tells me that Ceausescu's execution was faked, and that he is hiding out in
the Carpathian Mountains waiting to make his move. He could even be hiding
somewhere in your hotel. Have you checked the basement? I am capable
of taking care of myself, but I know Brenda would object to having our stay
disrupted by mobs of drug-crazed socialists hell-bent on revenge.

And what about King Michael? Unless I am mistaken, he has a score or two of
his own to settle. I do not want to be sitting down to breakfast when the hotel is
overrun by vicious crypto-communists and embittered royalists. It would spoil the
mood.

I read in the paper the other day that a charming fellow by the name of Nicole
Mischie, head of the Party of Social Democracy, was threatening to chop the legs
off any journalist who dared report that there was corruption in the ruling party.
I do not have a problem with this. If your journalists are anything like ours, they
deserve to be dismembered. But Mischie should simply offer them free lunches
twice a week. It is easier to clean up afterwards and just as effective.

Please let me know if you are expecting an uprising of any kind before
September. If not, keep a week open at the end of the month. As I said, nothing
but the finest suite will do.

Yours truly,

....
Dr Ben Trovato

Athénée Palace Hilton
Bucharest

6 August 2002

Bucharest

Dear Dr. Trovato,

Many thanks for your letter dated 23 July. We would be very happy to welcome you and Mrs. Trovato to the Athénée Palace Hilton Bucharest in late September. We have a variety of suites for you to decide upon should your travel plans firm up.

While I can not answer your letter point for point in an official letter from us, suffice it to say you certainly brightened my day, and put a smile on my face as well as on the face of our PA, Mariana Eremia. We would be happy to assist you with your plans in September, you just need to be a bit more specific with dates and requirements. While no uprisings or coups are planned, one never knows, and should one begin, the Athénée Palace would certainly be the place to be.

Looking forward to hearing from you again in the near future, we all remain at you disposal for any assistance you
may require.

Sincerely,

Robert G. Krygsman
Director of Operations
DO_Bucharest@hilton.com

SA Hunters and Game
Conservation Assoc.
PO Box 18108
Pretoria North
0116

Mr Ben Trovato
PO Box 1117
Sea Point
8060

28 July, 2002

Dear Sir,

I am relatively new to the hunting game. Since purchasing my 12-gauge shotgun, all I have managed to bag are two chacma baboons that were scavenging in garbage bins near Scarborough. They look magnificent on my study wall. The taxidermist managed to change their startled expressions into something more akin to the snarling, savage brutes that they really are. Visitors are astounded that I managed to escape with my life.

However, I need something more challenging. There is not much point in messing about with kudu and gemsbok. All they do is stand there with grass hanging out of their mouths, waiting to be shot through the head like some dumb animal. I am quite keen on keeping my eye in by shooting vermin like jackal, hyena and zebra. But the real prize is one of the Big Five.

I am having some trouble finding an elephant gun. Not even my contacts on the Cape Flats have been able to help. Perhaps you could point me in the right direction. You will agree that if I am going to work my way through the Big Five, I will need a Big Gun. Anything that can drop an elephant is my kind of weapon. A black rhino in full charge would be child's play with hardware this powerful. Even a lion would be no match for me. As for the other two members of the Big Five, the cheetah and the hippo, I could probably beat them to death with the butt of the rifle.

I understand that canned hunting is gaining in popularity. This sounds like the one for me. I am not one of those hunters who likes to spend his day endlessly tracking spoor and sniffing dung to see how fresh it is. Give me a comfortable chair, an air-conditioned hide and a clear shot at anything that comes down to the waterhole. My neighbour tells me that as a member of the SA Hunters Association, I will get special rates at game farms that provide canned hunting. Will my membership include one of those waistcoats with pockets for your bullets and grenades? If not, I hope that I will at least get to learn a funny handshake so that I can identify fellow members out on the hunt.

Please let me know what it costs to become a lifetime member. And whether I can purchase an elephant gun through your organisation. Enclosed is a ten rand deposit.

Yours truly,

....
Ben Trovato (Mr)

CASH GIVEN
R10

S.A. Jagters- en Wildbewaringsvereniging
S.A. Hunters' and Game Conservation Association

Kamdeboweg 626 Kamdebo Rd
Florauna
0182

Tel: (012) 565-4856
Tel: (012) 546-2622
Tel: (012) 546-1636
Fax: (012) 565-4910
E-Mail: sahunt@mweb.co.za

Posbus/P.O. Box 18108
Pretoria-Noord/North
0116

Dear Mr Trovato

Your letter dated 28 July 2002 refers.

The information you have been given by your neighbour is totally incorrect, and
the S.A. Hunters' and Game Conservation Association does not support your
views on hunting.

We are unable to help you in any of your requests and therefore return the R10
deposit which accompanied your letter.

Yours faithfully

André van Dyk
Communication Manager

The Manager
Londolozi Game Reserve
Private Bag X27
Benmore 2010
Mpumalanga

Mr Ben Trovato
PO Box 1117
Sea Point
8060
Cape Town
South Africa

1 August, 2002

Dear Sir,

My wife and I are planning a second honeymoon and we have always wanted to visit Londolozi. We have heard so much about the place, especially from our friends in the government.

We are hoping to spend two weeks at the lodge, and would need your finest suite towards the end of October.

I understand the weather is pleasant at that time of year. Let us know what we can expect, since I need to know what clothing to pack. My wife, on the other hand, will not be packing much. She is a nudist, you see. For years we used to go on outings and strip off together. But the harsh African sun took its toll on my poor willy, and the doctor advised that I cover up. So whenever Brenda wants to go au naturel, I slip into a skimpy pair of leopard skin briefs and my Johnson lives to fight another day.

Brenda is something of a purist in that her decisions on where and when to wear clothes are guided by the weather and not by social considerations. This means that on a balmy evening, Brenda may well choose to dine in the buff. We would not want to alarm the other guests, so you may want to allocate us a table in a discreet corner of the room.

Game drives could prove to be a little more awkward, but I assume that most of your guests will be more interested in trying to spot the Big Five than catch a glimpse of my Brenda's hamster. Unless they are German, of course. In which case I shall deploy my 250-volt Tazer. You need not worry about fatalities. Even a Pacemaker can withstand the shock. Most of the time. It is vital that a woman's dignity is protected, not so?

If I do not hear from you, please expect our arrival around the 15th of October.

Yours truly,

....
Ben Trovato (Mr)

PS. We are also practicing gymnosophists and will be performing our rituals in the privacy of our room. Unless, of course, our visit coincides with the full moon.

184

CC AFRICA
CONSERVATION CORPORATION AFRICA

2 September 2002

Dear Mr. Ben Trovato

We are in receipt of your letters to Ngala Private Reserve as well as Londolozi.

Unfortunately we do not believe that our operation is suitable for your specific needs.

Thank you
Yours Truly,
YVONNE SHORT
DIRECTOR SA LODGES

The Manager
Meikles Hotel
Cnr 3rd Street / Jason Moyo Avenue
Harare
Zimbabwe

Mr Ben Trovato
PO Box 1117
Sea Point
8060
South Africa

2 August, 2002

Dear Sir,

My wife and I are planning one last trip to Zimbabwe before the country goes up in flames. Our friends in the government tell us there is only one place in which to stay in Harare, and that is the Meikles. However, none of them have been there since President Mugabe lost his marbles and I was wondering if you had the same high standards of three or four years ago.

I would not wish to arrive at the Meikles only to find that the porters had been replaced by 14-year-old machete-wielding war veterans. I am a trained Signalman, so I know how to defend myself. But Brenda would not react terribly well to being rounded up at dawn and marched to breakfast at gunpoint.

I understand that most of the country has run out of food. Would you suggest that we bring along a hamper or have you got the Red Cross on your side? This is our second honeymoon and we would not want to sacrifice the Beluga, Moet and other essentials.

My neighbour tells me that tourists now have to check in with the Central Intelligence Organisation. Do you have a representative at the hotel, or would we have to go to their offices? Perhaps this applies only to homosexuals from Britain.

Unless you expect civil war to break out soon, please let me know if your finest suite will be available for two weeks towards the end of September.

Thank you.

Yours truly,

....
Ben Trovato (Mr)

MEIKLES

Zimbabwe's Premier Hotel

8 August 2002

Dear Mr Trovato

Thank you for your letter, your sense of humour has lightened an otherwise miserable Thursday morning.

I have booked the Imperial suite for the period 15th – 30th September 2002 and trust that you will find comfort in this little haven away from the anarchy that exists at the moment.

I would like to believe that despite the prevailing situation, you will find the Hotel standards intact and up to previously acceptable standards.

Please can you provide me with your flight details and exact dates so I can organize a military escort to collect you from the Harare "International" Airport.

We look forward to accommodating you at the Meikles Hotel and trust you will have a relaxing and "peaceful" stay.

Yours sincerely

KARL SNATER
GENERAL MANAGER

The General Manager   Mr Ben Trovato
Kentucky Fried Chicken   PO Box 1117
PO Box 4870   Sea Point
Rivonia   8060
2128

6 August, 2002

Dear Sir,

You are a difficult organisation to reach. I called your Customer Care Line to get your postal address and a woman told me that they are not allowed to give out this kind of information. What are you people afraid of? Complaints? Before you set the police on to me to find out how I got your address, let me just say that I picked up the telephone directory and there it was under Kentucky Fried Chicken.

The point of my letter is to inform you that someone who claims to be a former high-ranking member of your team has been in touch with me. He is offering to sell me the Colonel's secret recipe. At quite a price, I might add.

I run my own crunchy chicken outlet from a caravan outside my home. It may not sound like much competition to KFC, but I get an extraordinary amount of passing trade. There is no doubt in my mind that if I do purchase the secret recipe, it will only be a matter of time before I set up caravans around the country.

At the moment, my prices are lower than yours. In fact, my slogan is: "The Chicken That Goes Cheep". And when I open up franchises using the Colonel's formula, I expect most of your customers will be quick to switch allegiances.

I assume you would want to avoid a situation that could well lead to KFC going out of business. If so, I am prepared to make a very generous offer. I am willing to sell the recipe back to you at double the price.

If you are interested, please let me know as soon as possible and we can talk numbers. If not, expect to see a red and white Bentrovato Fried Chicken™ caravan appearing on a street corner near you.

You have been warned.

Yours truly,

Ben Trovato (Mr)

Tricon
Restaurants International

26 August 2002

Dear Mr Trovato

USE OF KFC SECRET RECIPE

Your letter dated 6 August 2002 refers.

We note the contents of the above-mentioned letter and we hereby reserve all rights we may have at law. We further wish to advise you that we will fiercely oppose any attempted emulation of any of our products and will defend any infringement of our rights.

We are certain that you will take note of the above and will not act in any way that may be detrimental to you or your business.

Kind regards

LUIS BARRETO
LEGAL & FRANCHISING
TEL: (011) 540-1093
FAX: (011) 463-2160

CC: W Pretorius, B de Villiers

Mr Luis Barreto
Legal & Franchising
Tricon Restaurants International
PO Box 71105
Bryanston 2021

Mr Ben Trovato
PO Box 1117
Sea Point
8060

3 September, 2002

Dear Mr Barreto,

That is an Italian name, is it not? You may have noticed that I, too, am of the blood. My roots are in Sicily. And yours? Naples, probably, judging by the tone of your letter dated 26th August. You may have heard of Guido Trovato. If not, I am sure your relatives back home will recognise the name. Please be assured that this is not a threat. I am simply pointing out that I have friends in the family.

You say in your letter that you are certain I will not act in any way that may be detrimental to me or my business. Perhaps you are from Sicily, after all. These are tactics born in Palermo. However, a true Sicilian would have included my wife and children. And my elderly parents. And all my friends. And their friends. Neapolitans have never quite understood that retribution cannot be threatened in half measures.

Mr Barreto, I have good news for you. The recipe in my possession is not what I thought it was. My contact swore it was a copy of an extremely valuable document that was in the possession of no more than three of Kentucky Fried Chicken's most trusted managers. But when I got my wife to make up the secret concoction, it turned out to be nothing more than the glop used in the production of koeksusters. I was bitterly disappointed. And yet, at the same time, strangely relieved. To be honest, I was not looking forward to having you fiercely opposing me in court. We both know what happens when Italians begin hurling recriminations at one another in a confined space.

If you have already put your boys on me, please call them off immediately. It would be a terrible tragedy if I were to meet with an unfortunate "accident" when the issue has already been resolved.

I will not be going into competition against KFC and the Colonel's secret is safe. The crispy chicken market is all yours.

Omerta!

....
Ben Trovato

The Production Manager
Clover SA
PO Box 6161
Weltevreden Park·
Johannesburg

Mr Ben Trovato
PO Box 1117
Sea Point
8060
Cape Town

`6 August, 2002

Dear Sir,

As an expert in these matters, I am sure you will be able to assist me.

I am having problems with my dairy cow, Manto. I bought her fairly recently and she stays out on a plot of land I have near Betty's Bay. I visit her most weekends with a view to obtaining a few litres of milk. However, Manto refuses to give me anything. I tug and tug at her udders but not a drop comes out.

Clover has been producing milk ever since I was a little boy. What are you doing that I am not? Am I pulling incorrectly? Does Manto need to have the company of a bull before she makes milk? Is it possible that Manto is, in fact, a bull?

I am desperate. Every time I go to the plot, my wife hands me two plastic canisters to fill up. And every time I have to stop at a 7-11 on the way home, buy four litres of milk and empty them into the containers. Brenda is amazed at the quality of Manto's milk, and I dare not tell her the truth.

I would deeply appreciate any suggestions you may have.

Thank you.

Yours truly,

....
Ben Trovato (Mr)

The Production Manager
Clover SA
PO Box 6161
Weltevreden Park
Johannesburg

Mr Ben Trovato
PO Box 1117
Sea Point
8060
Cape Town

29 August, 2002

Dear Sir,

I wrote you on the 6th of August but have not yet had a reply.

If you recall, I was asking for a little advice on how to get milk from my cow. You may have gathered that I am not much of a farmer. However, Manto has large udders and it seems such a waste not to tap this rich resource. But as I mentioned, I have had no luck in getting her to part with even a single drop.

As someone who is an expert in the milk business, I was sure you would be able to assist me. I can only assume that your failure to respond is linked to my failure to provide the necessary incentive. Nothing, not even information, comes free these days. Enclosed please find ten rand to cover your costs.

I hope to hear from you very soon. Manto looks like she is about to burst.

Yours truly,

....
Ben Trovato (Mr)

OPERATIONAL OFFICE / BEDRYFSKANTOOR

MILK PROCUREMENT/MELKWINNING
Vry Street/straat, Heilbron 9650
PO Box/Posbus 750, Heilbron 9650
Tel: (058) 853-3341
Fax/Faks: (058) 853-3323
E-mail/E-pos: anduples@clover.co.za

NATIONAL CO-OPERATIVE DAIRIES LIMITED
NASIONALE SUIWELKOÖPERASIE BEPERK

Dear Ben,

Thank you for your letter stating the problem that you had with Manto. I tried to get hold of your telephone number to save time but apparently it is not listed. We apologise for the late response. Something must have happened to the first letter as we have no record of receiving it.

I assume that your problem with Manto started immediately after calving because this is common that lactating cows do not release milk after calving. Milk release in the udder is a physiological process controlled by the hormone oxitosine. After calving the cow is normally under stress and if circumstances in and around the parlour is such that the cow does not relax sufficiently the brain does not release enough of the hormone into the blood stream for the alveoli mussels in the udder to release the milk. If she does not release milk after the first two milkings you need to advise a vet. Normal treatment will be to inject the cow with oxitisine for two or three days. Usually the cow responds very rapidly to the treatment and should not have much of a problem thereafter. I am however concerned that in Manto's case it is very late to apply this kind of treatment and I presume that some complication to the udder might have stepped in. Please consult your vet immediately.

A few practical tips:

1. If the cow had a difficult calving she will be under stress. Give her an injection of oxitosine.

2. Make sure that the calf had the opportunity for the first three days to suck from the udder. This will relax the cow and give the calf the opportunity to drink the colostrum that it needs.

3. Make sure that the milking process is relaxing to the cow. Do not hit or shout at her.

4. Give her something to eat while you milk her.

I do hope that this will solve your problem. Please find enclosed you R10 sent to us.

Kind regards

Marius Nel.

MARIUS NEL
Managing Director: Agri Services and Transport

Mr Marius Nel
Agri Services and Transport
National Co-operative Dairies
PO Box 750
Heilbron 9650

Mr Ben Trovato
PO Box 1117
Sea Point
8060
Cape Town

9 September, 2002

Dear Mr Nel,

Thank you so much for replying to my enquiries regarding my cow, Manto.

I shall certainly take your advice and inject her with oxitosine. It sounds like just the stuff she needs to begin giving us buckets of milk.

The only problem is that my wife is recovering from a rather nasty drug addiction and it is probably not a good idea for me to leave syringes lying around the house. Knowing Brenda, she will inject herself as soon as I turn my back. I will certainly take every precaution to make sure this does not happen. But if I am distracted, by something good on the telly, for example, and she manages to get a few cubic centimetres of oxitosine into her system, I need to know if she will also begin producing milk. If this is the case, would you recommend that I refrain from hitting or shouting at her as well? How long would it be before our relationship could return to normal? I will make sure Brenda gets something to eat, but I cannot promise that I will be able to milk her. I may have to bring in a specialist for that.

Do not worry if you are unable to set my mind at rest on this score. It is probably best that I consult a doctor.

Or maybe a vet.

Thank you again for all your help.

Ben Trovato (Mr)

Mr Theo Grimbeek
Institute of Traffic &
Municipal Police Officers
Private Bag X1258
Potchefstroom 2520

Mr Ben Trovato
PO Box 1117
Sea Point
8060

13 August, 2001

Dear Mr Grimbeek,

I understand the Institute is planning to hold a Road Rage and Aggressive
Driving Symposium in Bloemfontein on October 15, and I would like to register
as a delegate.

I have come close to death on many occasions while taking my car for a spin.
They seem to lie in wait for me, then come lunging out of each driveway and side
road that I pass. They box me in and cut me off at every opportunity. I get sworn
at, spat on and vilified by everyone from truck drivers to little old ladies.

I now realise that the problem lies with me. I am a passive driver and I appear
to incite people whenever I get behind the wheel. It has become clear that I
must change if I hope to survive. This is why I was so pleased to hear about your
symposium.

I am confident that the Institute is able to teach even the most placid motorist
basic aggressive driving skills. I wouldn't want to start off with anything too
fancy. Perhaps a little rush-hour lane switching without the use of indicators,
and progressing until I reach the stage where I am comfortable with overtaking
on a blind rise with a cellphone in one hand, a beer in the other and my knees
gripping the steering wheel.

Blinding your opponent is clearly an important strategy that timid drivers like
myself tend to overlook. However, I have invested in a pair of powerful halogen
arc lights and plan on welding them to the roof racks.

On the road rage front, I presume that beginners get to start out with a crash
course in hand signals and facial expressions. But I fear this will not be enough.
I would like to know what you offer in the way of high-speed intimidation
techniques. And it goes without saying that I will need to learn the art of hand-
to-hand combat. I want to become one of those men who can have a driver out of
his seat and face down on the asphalt within three seconds. Five, if the window
is closed.

Enclosed please find ten rand as a deposit towards my registration fee. Looking
forward to seeing you at the symposium!

Yours truly,

....
Ben Trovato (Mr)

INSTITUTE OF TRAFFIC AND MUNICIPAL POLICE
OFFICERS OF SOUTHERN AFRICA

Tel: (018) 297 6388
    (018) 299 5490
Fax: (018) 297 6388

website: www.itmpo.org.za
e-mail: itmposa@xsinet.co.za
info@itmpo.org.za

Private Bag X 1258
POTCHEFSTROOM
2520

16 August 2002

Dear Sir

Could you please supply me with your physical residential address on receipt of which I will contact you.

Yours faithfully

THEO R. GRIMBEEK
HONORARY SECRETARY

TRG/sr

Mr Theo Grimbeek
Institute of Traffic &
Municipal Police Officers
Private Bag X1258
Potchefstroom 2520

Mr Ben Trovato
PO Box 1117
Sea Point
80607

25 August, 2002

Dear Mr Grimbeek,

I received your reply dated 16th August and, to be honest, I am alarmed that you want to find out where I live.

I hope I have not given you the impression that there is something more between us. I was writing to you purely in a professional capacity. If you are looking for company, I suggest you try the classified section of your local paper. Internet chat rooms are another way to meet people. Or so I have heard.

I have gone through both of my letters over and over again, and I am unable to find even a hidden suggestion that you and I get together at my place. This can only mean one thing. That you would like an altogether more serious word with me. Is it because I expressed an interest in brushing up on my aggressive driving tactics? It is unlikely that you wish to give me private lessons. This leaves only one conclusion. That the men from the Institute intend turning up at my front door with batons and electrified cattle prods to teach me how to be a model motorist.

Quite frankly, both scenarios scare me. Right now, all I want is my money back. I wish I had never heard of the ITMPO. The whole business is giving me sleepless nights and when I go out I keep thinking that I am being followed.

I am prepared to meet you, Mr Grimbeek. But on my terms. We must rendezvous at a public place such as a crowded restaurant or a busy shopping mall. My personal preference is the ice rink at Grandwest Casino. It is not important that you need to know how to skate. You can hire boots there. I will meet you in the middle of the rink at midday on the Sunday of your choice. Bring my money.

Yours truly,

Ben Trovato (Mr)

The International Missionary
Association
PO Box 74169
Turffontein
Johannesburg

Mr Ben Trovato
PO Box 1117
Sea Point
8060

13 August, 2002

Dear Sir,

I have reached a stage where I need to do something that will make me feel as if
my life has been worth something. The odds are heavily against cracking the big
one on the Dream Machine at GrandWest, so I thought the next best thing would
be to convert people to Christianity. At least there is a guaranteed return.

Are there any heathen savages left in the world? While I am prepared to travel,
it would be nice to do the Lord's work a little closer to home. I was thinking of
the North Coast, between Umhlanga Rocks and Richards Bay. Have all the Zulus
been done? If not, I am quite prepared to go out there and turn them into God-
fearing, church-going people.

Saving souls must be a very rewarding occupation. I imagine you would need to
be quite fit, too. From what I have heard, pagans can put up quite a fight. And
when they resist the Word, I suppose one has to take action. At times like this,
being a missionary must be physically draining. Heretics are dangerous people.
And even more so if they have a broken bottle or an assegai in their hand.

It is a worthy challenge to turn agnostics into believers. I, myself, am married to
a woman who is a doubter. She rarely believes anything I say. But I have been
practicing my technique on her and I think she is beginning to see the light. Or
she will when the bandages come off, at any rate.

Please let me know what I have to do to qualify as a missionary. I would also
need some sort of handbook that could serve as a guide in tough situations. For
example, Reverend Allan Boesak is a Christian. Then he went to jail for theft and
fraud. And when he came out he was still bleating about being a sacrificial lamb,
so it's my guess that he needs some kind of redemption. What would be the
missionary's position in a case like this?

I need to get started as soon as possible. In fact, I have already turned my
neighbour into a Protestant. He was a Catholic. Are missionaries allowed to
do inter-denominational conversions? No matter. I can stick with the sun
worshippers for now.

I look forward to hearing from you.

Yours in Christ.

Ben Trovato (Mr)

PS. I assume the association provides newcomers with protective clothing and
weapons. If not, I can borrow something from my wife. Let me know. Here's R10
in case.

INTERNATIONAL MISSIONARY SOCIETY
SEVENTH DAY ADVENTIST REFORM MOVEMENT
Southern African Union – Reg. No.: 017-270 NPO

98 BERTHA STREET- TURFFONTEIN 2140- SOUTH AFRICA
P. O. BOX 74169. TURFFONTEIN 2140. SOUTH AFRICA
TELEPHONE (27) 011- 683 5406. FAX (27) 011-683 5406 E-MAIL info@imssdarm-sau.org.za

20 August 2002

Dear Mr Trovato

Re: Qualification of being a missionary

May the peace of God be unto you.

Thank you for your letter dated 13th August 2002. It is very much encouraging to know that the Lord still has many 'who have not bowed the knee to the image of Baal' and are willing to enter the vineyard of the Lord.

Every one has been called to be a co-worker with Christ in the work of soul saving. However Christ has said in Mathew 28:20 "Teaching them to observe all things whatsoever I have commanded you:. Therefore before one could be sent out as a missionary, he has to be instructed in the Biblical truths (not indoctrinated) so that we may all come to the unity of faith. There after he could be sent to the field just like the disciples who were trained by Christ before receiving the commission.

Therefore in your case I would advise and suggest that we first have Bible instructions with you by someone in Cape Town and we take it from there.

I hope my advice will meet your favorable consideration. Any queries please direct them to me. Once again thank you for showing interest to enter into the Lord's vineyard.

Yours in Christ

Elijah Zwane

199

The Managing Director
Santam
PO Box 3881
Tyger Valley

Mr Ben Trovato
PO Box 1117
Sea Point
8060

17 August, 2002

Dear Sir,

I was on the point of approaching Santam to take care of my short-term insurance when I happened to read in the paper that the company has been listed as a gay-bashing organisation run by homophobic bigots.

To be honest, I generally have nothing against normal, red-blooded people who are driven to violence at the sight of men kissing one another. I have often felt the urge myself. To commit violence, I mean, not to kiss another man. In fact, this is one of the reasons I need insurance.

However, I am worried that the company is going to be severely affected as a result of the 'pinklisting' by that unholy bunch of catamites and coprophiliacs who go by the name of the Gay and Lesbian Alliance.

What guarantees are there that Santam will survive this unholy onslaught? I understand these lost souls are everywhere, not just Cape Town. A global uprising of left-handed nancy boys and bull dykes with motorcycle chains could well put you out of business.
The share price would be the first thing to go. Then your offices would be invaded by bands of gilded deviants scaring the staff with Sapphic war chants and engaging in tribadism right there on the boardroom table.

I thought of taking my business to Mutual & Federal until I saw that they, too, had been 'pinklisted'. What are we meant to do? Find a company run by screaming queers flouncing about in spandex bodysuits? Insurance is a tough game run by tough people. Directors are expected to show profits, not swan about in togas having shiatsu massages and burning rose scented incense in color-coded, feng shui aligned offices.

Please let me know if you think it is safe to invest in Santam.

Keep the faith.

Yours truly,

....
Ben Trovato (Mr)

PS. I see that if you admit guilt, apologise to the gay community and pay R20 000, your name will be taken off the pinklist. Enclosed please find R10 towards the fine.

21 August 2002

Dear Mr Trovato

Thank you for your letter that we received this morning.

The recent publicity that followed the actions taken by the Gay end Lesbian Alliance could possibly have created misconception and incorrect perceptions about Santam. I want to emphasise that we at Santam oppose any form of discrimination. We have responded to the GLA's accusations with a statement published on our website and in a general media release. I include a copy for your attention.

I can assure you that you do not have to worry in the least about entrusting us with you insurance matters. In the past eight decades we have proved over and again our ability to weather storms – of both the real kind and those brewing in teacups.

Thank you also for your kind contribution towards the imposed fine. We accept it with grace and have paid it over to the Santam Child Art Trust, an initiative enabling children in marginalized and previously disadvantaged communities to experience the joys of art classes.

Please feel free to contact our call centre on 0800 123 747 to discuss your insurance needs.

Yours sincerely

Steve Zietsman
Executive Head: Marketing

Mr Marthinus van Schalkwyk
Premier of the Western Cape
Private Bag 9043
Cape Town
8000

Mr Ben Trovato
PO Box 1117
Sea Point
8060

17 August, 2002

Dear Mr van Schalkwyk,

I was appaled to hear that you have been 'pinklisted' by the Gay and Lesbian Alliance as an intolerant, homophobic bigot. This certainly does not sound like the most powerful man in the country's best-run province!

What have you done to make the moffies so angry? I have not heard you make any statements that could remotely be construed as homophobic. I can only imagine that you were approached by one of them and rebuffed his advances. These people are very sensitive to rejection. But I have found that you cannot be gentle when turning them away. They are quick to sense weakness and they will bring you down like a pack of hyenas bring down a young springbok. I would suggest that you stay away from public urinals and move with a crowd. If you are isolated they will pick you off.

I suspect that they are aligning you with the National Party of old. In their minds, you still represent a regime that made sodomy illegal. They do not care that the same regime made it illegal to be black. All they care about is their right to fondle each other's buttocks. But it goes beyond that. They also want the right to fondle any buttocks that happen to come along. They believe that buttock fondling is a basic human right. Turn them down and they are quick to flounce off to the Constitution Court to claim in shrill voices that it is their bottoms they want violated, not their rights.

I find it ironic that they are targeting politicians who live in Cape Town, a city that has more tailgunners per square metre than the bathhouses of San Francisco. In Cape Town, it is easier to find a woman who has had a strapadicktomy than it is to find one who has had a hysterectomy.

They are hardly persecuted. In fact, they have their own bars, clubs, clothing stores and genetically modified vegetables. If anyone is oppressed, it is people like you and me. We are the minority here. Not them.

I understand that if you admit guilt, apologise to the bandits and hand over R5 000 to the Gay and Lesbian Alliance, your name will be removed from the pinklist. It seems that we either arm ourselves and go to war, or pay up. My weapon is oiled and ready. However, should you choose to take the soft option, I enclose ten rand towards your fine.

Keep up the good work and watch your backside!

Yours truly,

....
Ben Trovato (Mr)

Kantoor van die Premier
Office of the Premier
I-ofisi yeNkulumbuso

26 August 2002

Dear Mr Trovato

By direction of Mr MCJ van Schalkwyk, Premier of the Western Cape, I acknowledge receipt of your letter dated 17 August 2002, the contents of which have been noted.

Your R10.00 is hereby returned because it cannot be accepted.

Yours faithfully

CI NASSON
ADMINISTRATIVE SECRETARY

Mr David Baxter
Gay and Lesbian Alliance
Postnet Suite 800
Private Bag X9
Benmore 2010

Mr Ben Trovato
PO Box 1117
Sea Point
8060

18 August, 2002

Dear Mr Baxter,

I understand you are in the process of 'naming and shaming' people and organisations that you consider to be homophobic. And that you charge R100 to have them blacklisted, or, as you put it, "pinklisted". I see your list already includes Mutual & Federal, Santam, the Dutch Reformed Church, the Apostolic Faith Mission, PW Botha, FW de Klerk, Marthinus van Schalkwyk and Peter Marais. You are even calling for a global tourism boycott of countries like Namibia and Zimbabwe.

I am deeply concerned that someone is going to give you my name. I am ashamed to admit that I used to live in Namibia. I also voted for FW de Klerk on two separate occasions and several years ago I attended a wedding in a Dutch Reformed Church. And I have an insurance policy with Mutual & Federal. To make matters even worse, I once called a woman a poisonous bull dyke because she refused to give up the pool table. However, I paid the price almost immediately when I was set upon by a mob of depraved cue-wielding faggots representing at least three genders.

I bitterly regret my actions and offer my wholehearted apologies. Please do not put me on your pinklist as I have a family and a reputation to protect.

However, my neighbour, Ted Goodfellow, is an appalling homophobe. When he goes out he thinks every second man is giving him the eye. By the end of the evening, he is convinced that absolutely everyone who is not a woman is trying to get at his bum. He has even taken to wearing a cricket box in case a gentleman brushes up against him at the bar and "accidentally" fondles his willy. I have tried telling him he is being paranoid. Then again, this is Cape Town we are talking about. Anything is possible.

I think Ted should be pinklisted for his own good. Nobody in their right mind would want their name linked to Peter Marais. I have no doubt he will come to his senses. I am unable to pay the full R100 to get him on to the list. Ten rand is all I can afford right now.

I understand that individuals must first admit guilt, publicly apologise to the gay community and pay R5 000 to get their names removed. I can assure you that Ted will cough up. So even though I am R90 short, you certainly gain in the long run.

Yours truly,

....
Ben Trovato (Mr)

PS. Any chance of a commission if I give you more names?

GAY & LESBIAN ALLIANCE
Lesbigay political voice of South Africa

26 August 2002

Sir,

The GAY & LESBIAN ALLIANCE (GLA), political voice of lesbigay South Africa acknowledges your letter dated 2002-08-18, regarding a homophobic individual in Cape Town.

We further acknowledge the amount of R10 as administration fee, thus we need the balance of R90 to ensure effective investigation and pinklisting.

Please forward or deposit the R90 balance, together with any form of contact details of the accused. Your identity will never be revealed to anyone. We also keep you inform through out our investigation. The period of investigation is a maximum of fourteen (14) days.

We hope to receive the above as a matter of urgency, to enable us to launch such a investigation.

Your Sincerely,

On behalf of the National Executive Board, GLA
Spokesperson DISCRIMINATION, RACISM & HOMOPHOBIC affairs.
Apuis Mokamedi

Mr Raymond Ackerman
Chairman: Pick 'n Pay
PO Box 23087
Claremont
7735

Mr Ben Trovato
PO Box 1117
Sea Point
8060

22 August, 2002

Dear Mr Ackerman,

Congratulations on writing such a fine book. It has inspired me to write to you with an idea that is bound to make you even more money.

The other day I overheard snippets of a radio discussion about hunting, I think it was, and someone said something about canned lions. What a splendid idea, I thought. I am not much of a chef, but I suspect that chunks of lion in a rich gravy would be delicious with a serving of Spanish rice and a small French salad.

Is it possible that you are already aware of this new product? If so, when can I expect to see it on your shelves? I am sure Proudly South Africa would like to be associated with a local product that is bound to be highly nutritious and full of protein. And tins of canned lion have more of an African flavour than tins of canned asparagus, for example.

Your advertising could say that it "Roars With Flavour". No, hang on. I think Simba has that slogan. But even if they do, I am fairly certain that their product contains synthetic lion. What about something like "The Beef with Teeth"? Just don't try saying it quickly over and over again. Or maybe "King of the Stews". Mind you, this is bound to incite the religious fundamentalists. What about giving your kids "The Lion's Share". And why not make lunch your "Mane" meal? You get the picture.

I have a lion suit which I wore during my honeymoon, and you might want to give some thought to the idea of hiring me to promote the new product at some of your stores in the Western Cape. The suit took a bit of a hammering but I think most of the stains will come out in the wash. It has also developed a patch of mange on the rump.

In the event that others have had the same idea, I am enclosing ten rand to help your secretary slip my name to the top of the list.

Yours truly,

....
Ben Trovato (Mr)

STORES LIMITED

28 August 2002

Dear Mr Trovato

Thank you for your letter and kind comments concerning my book – I am pleased you enjoyed it.

I appreciate your sense of humour, Mr Trovato ! and not only will the R10.00 you sent me, put you on "top of the list" as you say, but it will also help to swell the coffers of the "House for AIDS Orphans" charity.

With kind regards.

Yours sincerely

RAYMOND ACKERMAN

Dr Isak Burger
President: Apostolic Faith
Mission of South Africa
PO Box 890197
Lyndhurst 2106

Mr Ben Trovato
PO Box 1117
Sea Point
8060
Cape Town

5 August, 2002

Dear Dr Burger,

As a fellow Christian, I am sure you will agree with me when I say that advertising has become the Devil's trade. I am not talking about a housewife selling Skip, although some of these certainly do push the limits. I am talking about the amount of sex that is being used to sell certain products. Not only sex, but drugs too. Did you know that Sasol has an advert that encourages youngsters to get high with a little help from their friends?

But the adverts that really get my blood boiling are those for Magnum ice cream. I am not sure if you have seen them, but they border on the pornographic. I have done a little research and discovered that Unilever makes this particular product. I was appaled to learn that the company publicly, and proudly, admits that this is the "first ice cream developed especially for adults".

This obviously accounts for the lurid advertisements, one of which has a young woman moaning as if in the throes of sexual pleasure. Another caresses the ice cream with her tongue, implying that if you buy this product you will be surrounded by beautiful women wanting to lick your "ice cream" too.

What kind of degenerate perverts are these people? I would not be surprised to hear that advertising executives meet secretly in covens where they drink the blood of junior copywriters and carve pentagrams into one another's naked buttocks.

Encouraging young people to indulge in adult ice creams is where it all begins. The next thing you know, they are having unprotected sex in our restaurants and on our beaches. We live in an age of unbridled licentiousness and it is up to people like you and I to put a stop to it.

Please let me know what I can do to fight not only Unilever, but also every company that exploits men, women and animals as sexual objects to sell their products.

I enclose ten rand towards the war on smut.

Yours in Jesus Christ.

....
Ben Trovato (Mr)

CASH GIVEN
R10

The Apostolic Faith Mission
Of South Africa

P.O. Box 890197, Lyndhurst, 2106
Tel: (011) 786-8550

Die Apostoliese Geloof Sending
van Suid-Afrika

Posbus 890197, Lyndhurst, 2106
Tel: (011) 786-8550

From the desk of the President...
Van die lessenaar van die President...

9 September 2002

Dear Mr Trovato

Warm Christian greetings!

Thank you for your letter. I did receive your first letter as well as the ten rand.
Thank you for the donation.

Magnum announced that they are withdrawing their planned advertisement due
to the many objections. They are indeed planning a new ad which they say would
exclude the words "seven deadly sins". As the new format is still a secret, I
cannot comment on it. I've warned them that we will continue with our action if
it is still offensive. Keep your eye on the press for more details.

Thank you for your support. I sincerely appreciate it!

Yours sincerely

DR ISAK BURGER

The Managing Director
Kentucky Fried Chicken
12th Avenue
Rivonia 2128

Mr Ben Trovato
PO Box 1117
Sea Point
8060

22 August, 2002

Dear Sir,

I have seen your latest advertising campaign. I am talking about the one where you use a little deaf girl to sell your product.

After giving it some thought, I came up with an idea for your next campaign. A little blind boy is walking along the pavement when he is suddenly hit in the face by a flying chicken. It might be best to use a rubber chicken since a real one could cause some damage with its claws and beak. This would get a huge laugh, I assure you. Here are some suggestions for the payoff line:

• "KFC - for people who would rather eat chicken than duck."
• "You might be blind – but our chicken isn't."
• "KFC - You don't have to see it to like it."
• "KFC...the low-frying chicken."
• "Nando's is for people who haven't heard about KFC."

I have more ideas using mute orphans and even amputees.

I am enclosing ten rand as a deposit on securing the advertising contract.

Let's make money!

Yours truly,

....
Ben Trovato (Mr)

BRIBE GIVEN
R10

 **Yum!** *Restaurants International*

Restaurant Support Centre - Southern Africa
Yum! Restaurants International (Pty) Limited
Charlton House, Hampton Park
20 Georgian Cresent
Bryanston
P.O. Box 71105,
Bryanston 2021
South Africa
Tel: +27 (011) 540-1000
Fax: +27 (011) 463-2735

11 September 2002

Dear Mr Trovato

SUGGESTED MARKETING CAMPAIGN

Your letter dated 22 August 2002 refers, the contents thereof having been noted.

Our marketing strategies are formulated at a national and international level, utilizing the services of internal expert employees and external consultants. The services of these experts are used in conjunction with national and international market trends and market research information, and together serve to dictate current and future marketing and sales strategies.

Although your suggestions make for interesting reading, we do not believe that they are relevant to our current and future marketing strategies. However, should similar marketing mechanisms be implemented in the future, this will be as a result of an actual need in the market and not as a result of your suggestions. We record that we will not be forwarding your letter to our national and international marketing and sales departments, nor are we prepared to offer you any payment, now or in the future with regard to the suggestion set out in your letter.

We return herewith you R10,00 as received with your letter.

Kind regards

LUIS BARRETO
LEGAL & FRANCHISING
TEL: (011) 540-1093
FAX: (011) 463-2160

CC: W Pretorius, B de Villiers, M Willows

Governor Tito Mboweni
South African Reserve Bank
PO Box 427
Pretoria
0001

Mr Ben Trovato
PO Box 1117
Sea Point
8060

8 August, 2002

Dear Mr Mboweni,

Congratulations on the fine job that you are doing. It is not your fault that none of us can afford to go abroad on holiday. In the bad old days of apartheid the rand was a lot stronger, which meant we could travel overseas. On the down side, no country with any real integrity would have us. Now that we are a democracy we can go anywhere we want, but can't afford it. Ironic, isn't it? It is almost as if the Illuminati are punishing us for achieving self-determination and nationhood.

I have a suggestion you may be interested in. Have you ever thought of getting the Mint to produce a 99 cent coin? You probably have someone to do your shopping for you, but you must have noticed that most things cost however many rand and 99 cents. Everything from ice creams to new cars end with 99 cents.

Some of us have amassed enromous quantities of one cent coins and we do not know what to do any more. Beggars won't take them and the banks are less than enthusiastic. A 99 cent coin will at least ensure that nobody will ever again be given one cent in change.

Obviously I understand the psychology behind pricing strategies. Manufacturers, entrepreneurs and other assorted free marketeers believe that consumers will be tricked into thinking they are getting a good deal on a new BMW that costs only R249 999,99. Make that same car R250 000 and he will immediately shy away. That's a quarter of a million rand! Far too expensive, he will say. And while he is thinking about his next move, he will buy a hamburger from a street vendor for R9,99 after threatening to sue a restaurant owner for extortion for daring to sell burgers at the exorbitant price of R10.

It follows that when you do introduce the 99 cent coin, the capitalists will end all their prices with 98 cents. And that is when you flood the market with 98 cent coins. They are then forced to drop to 97 cents, and you counter their move with a 97 cent coin. Do you see where this is going? Of course you do. You would not be the Governor of the Reserve Bank otherwise. The natural progression is that prices will keep plummeting as fast as the Mint can keep the coins coming.

This is the most revolutionary inflation-busting strategy ever devised. And to think I came up with it just a few minutes ago!

The inevitable outcome, of course, is that everything will eventually be free. Other governments will adopt the strategy and within a certain period of time (I tried to do the maths but my head began hurting) there will be no such thing as money anywhere in the world.

I am prepared to let you claim the idea as your own, and I am enclosing R10 towards the awareness campaign. Let me know what else you need.

Yours truly,

....
Ben Trovato (Mr)

Governor Tito Mboweni
South African Reserve Bank
PO Box 427
Pretoria
0001

Mr Ben Trovato
PO Box 1117
Sea Point
8060

29 August, 2002

Dear Mr Mboweni,

I have not yet heard from you since I wrote on the 8th of August. I expect that your reply has gone missing in the mail.

You may recall that I provided you with a revolutionary inflation-busting idea that would simultaneously ensure that nobody would ever again be given one cent in change.

I also provided you with ten rand towards the cost of implementing this brilliant scheme. If you never received it, you might want to have a word with your secretary. Staff with sticky fingers should not be encouraged to work for the Reserve Bank.

I plan on being in Pretoria in the near future. If I do not hear from you within a couple of weeks, I will assume that you are interested in hearing more about my idea and shall stop by your office to brief you on the details.

Keep up the good work.

Yours truly,

....
Ben Trovato (Mr)

SOUTH AFRICAN RESERVE BANK
OFFICE OF THE GOVERNOR

18 September 2002

Dear Mr Trovato

Thank you very much for your letter of 8th August 2002. The contents thereof have been noted.

I think your idea of a 99 cent coin is worth looking at. I will ask the relevant people in the Bank to examine it.

Best wishes

TT MBOWENI
GOVERNER

The Manager
Amathus Beach Hotel
Amathus Avenue
PO Box 513
Limassol
Cyprus

Dr Ben Trovato
PO Box 1117
Sea Point 8060
Cape Town
South Africa

23 July, 2002

Dear Sir,

I am planning a surprise second honeymoon for my wife. Naturally, I will be accompanying her. I have friends in the government who recommend your hotel. Needless to say, these friends are not Turkish sympathisers.

I am very interested in occupying your finest suite for a week in the latter half of September. However, there are a few concerns which I hope you can address.

To be honest, I am worried about the Turks. These are dangerous and unpredictable people, and they remain in military occupation of a third of your country. The African solution would be to poison their water supply and drive the survivors into the sea. But you seem to have your own way of dealing with these things.

I am concerned that Brenda and I will wake up in your hotel one morning to find that the Turkish Republic of Northern Cyprus has been extended across the entire island. Brenda has blonde hair and I need not remind you of what Turkish men are capable of when they come across fair-skinned women with long, flaxen hair.

I understand that Greek Cyprus is likely to join the European Union in 2004, and that this prospect is unsettling the invasion army's political masters in Ankara. As you know, Turkey has 30 000 armed men in the north. Does your hotel have enough security to keep them out should they march on Limassol? Would you recommend that I bring some sort of weapon to help keep the hordes at bay? International air travel is not what it used to be, and it might be difficult to bring along the heavy stuff. It would make more sense for the hotel to issue guests with sidearms when they check in. If you agree with this idea, please could you reserve me a Walther PPK? My father owned one and he used to take me hunting, although I could hardly hit a wall at ten paces. But rest assured, when the Turks come swarming over your front gate I will perform like a trained marksman.

Turkey also seems to be cosying up to Iraq, and if America invades Baghdad then Cyprus could well find itself drawn into a war that could end with the entire region being consumed by a nuclear holocaust. And what kind of second honeymoon would that be?

If you can assure me that my fears are unwarranted, please keep the fourth week of September open for Brenda and I. As I said, your finest suite will be required.

Yours truly

....
Dr Ben Trovato

DD/RC/A2A

August 9th, 2002

Dr Ben Trovato
P O Box 1117
Sea Point 8060
Cape Town
South Africa

Dear Dr Trovato

I acknowledge receipt of your letter dated 23rd July 2002 and thank you for your interest in visiting the Paphos Amathus Beach Hotel.

With regards to the political situation, coming from a country that is continuously troubled by military upheaval, I understand your concern with Cyprus. I would like to assure you that for the last 28 years no military incident has taken place in Cyprus and despite our differences between the Republic of Cyprus and the Turkish Cypriot Community, we are trying to resolve our differences through the political route.

Bringing arms in Cyprus, unlike perhaps South Africa, is illegal. Should you decide to do so, you run the risk of being caught at the airport and immediately being imprisoned.

The scenario you mention with regards to nuclear holocaust, I can only consider as amusing. Even though I am not a nuclear warfare specialist, I am sure that there are many other areas on the globe, which impose a much higher risk rather than the Iraq-Turkey region.

If you feel that the above explanation given, put your fears at ease, please advise us on the dates you intend to visit Cyprus in order to forward you our rates and conditions.

Assuring you of our best attention at all times.

Yours sincerely
PAPHOS AMATHUS BEACH HOTEL

Demetris Demetriou
General Manager

Reservation/De-de-letter-Au-02

Poseidon Avenue, P.O.Box 62381, 8098 Paphos, Cyprus
Telephone 00357-26964300, Fax 00357-26964222
Our Internet Site: http://www.pamathus.com
Direct E-mail:pamathus@pamathus.com.cy

The Manager
Hyatt Regency Manila Hotel
2702 Roxas Boulevard
Manila
Philippines

Mr Ben Trovato
PO Box 1117
Sea Point 8060
Cape Town
South Africa

30 July, 2002

Dear Sir,

My wife, Brenda, and I would like to take up snorkelling and we understand that your country offers some of the best diving in the world. We also realise there are certain dangers attached to diving in the Philippines. Not from sharks, but from Muslim rebels.

As you may know, our very own Callie and Monique Strydom had their romantic diving holiday rudely interrupted by those Abu Sayyaf thugs. And now we hear that another group of tourists has been abducted. Among them are two American missionaries. Well, they only have themselves to blame. They should have been in the Sudan converting the natives to Christianity, not lolling about on a tropical island sucking on purple cocktails and ordering the servants to bring them more caviar.

Brenda is concerned that our idyllic two-week vacation will turn into a four-month ordeal of eating grasshoppers, defecating in the bush and dodging bullets fired by crazy-eyed youngsters with an eye on spending all eternity with seventeen virgins and a golden calf.

I am less concerned, since I was in the Signal Corps when I was younger and I know how to take care of myself. But I will not be able to defend the others when the fundamentalists arrive armed with machetes and machine guns.

Please let us know what the Philippine government plans on doing about this sad state of affairs. You could always ring the resorts with electrified blade wire and unleash attack dogs to patrol the beaches. For some of us, it would feel just like home.

I am interested in reserving a week or two in your finest suite in late September or early October. But I need assurances that your hotel is safe. Not only from the rebels, but from the alarming number of American troops that appear to have invaded the Philippines.

I have also heard reports that Osama bin Laden is hiding out in Manila. Brenda's heart is not strong enough to survive an accidental encounter with this gentleman in the Hyatt Regency's elevator. Please keep an eye on the register. And let me know if it is safe to make a reservation. As I said, only the finest suite will do. Money is no object.

Yours truly

....
Ben Trovato (Mr)

19 August 2002

Mr. Ben Trovato
P O Box 1117
Sea Point 8060
South Africa

Dear Mr. Trovato,

Warm greetings from Shangri-La's Mactan Island Resort!

Thank you for your letter dated 30 July which we received on the 17th of August.

We are delighted to note of your plans to visit Cebu and to stay at the resort. You can be assured that Cebu is a safe place for tourists who want to come and enjoy the beauty of the place. The diving spots in the area are definitely one of the best in the country. The hotel has in place strict security measures for the protection of its guests and patrons.

Should you decide to visit and stay with us, we are pleased to offer a Panorama Suite at US$336++ per night under the Shangri-La Summer Rate break promotion which is valid until the 30th of September or Value Rate at US$560++ after 1st October.

We do hope that we would have the opportunity to welcome you the beautiful island of Mactan.

Yours sincerely,

JEREMY E. AMBLER
Director of Rooms

Punta Engaño Road, P.O. Box 86, Lapu-Lapu City 6015, Cebu, Philippines
Tel (63-32) 231 0288 Fax (63-32) 231 1688 E-mail: mac@shangri-la.com Internet: www.shangri-la.com

The Manager
Port Elizabeth Rifle and Pistol Club
PO Box 2771
Port Elizabeth 6056

Mr Ben Trovato
PO Box 1117
Sea Point
8060

28 July, 2002

Dear Sir,

My family and I plan on moving to the Port Elizabeth area in the near future and I was hoping you could assist me.

I understand there are several fine game farms in the Eastern Cape, and it is my intention to take up hunting. I have shot a little game in and around Cape Town, so I am not a complete newcomer to the sport. I do, however, need to brush up on my technique. Shooting from the hip with a 12-gauge shotgun might work in the movies, but it is not necessarily the best method to use while chasing a fully-grown Chacma baboon over busy roads and neighbourhood fences.

Since big game hunting is on the agenda, I am upgrading my equipment. Right now, I am negotiating the purchase of an elephant gun. Once I have this fine piece of hardware, I will need to learn how to shoot it. And this is where I hope your club can help.

I need to know if any of your instructors are familiar with the elephant gun. If I am to be the owner of a high-powered, heavy-calibre weapon equipped with a hair-trigger and telescopic sights, it might be a good idea to put me under expert supervision.

Does your club come equipped with targets in the shape of animals? It is all very well learning to shoot at a conventional target, but it is very unlikely that brightly coloured red and yellow circles are going to leap out at you when you are in the bush. Since my focus will be on the Big Five, I would want to practise on targets that are shaped like elephants, lions, hippos and so on. This would also sharpen my ability to instantly identify a particular animal. The last thing I would want to do is shoot a protected species or even a bakkie full of German tourists.

Kindly inform me as soon as possible about your membership rates and whether you can assist me with the training.

Keep your gun cocked!

Yours truly,

....
Ben Trovato (Mr)

P.E. RIFLE & PISTOL CLUB

P. O. BOX 2771
PORT ELIZABETH
6056

9th August, 2002

Mr Ben Trovato
PO Box 1117
Sea Point
8060

Dear Ben,

Received your letter yesterday, and I will do my best to set you on the right path! This club is primarily a Pistol club with regard to formalised competition shooting. Although we do have at least 100 rifle owners as members , they tend to do their own thing on a casual basis, and do not attend any formal shoots, with the result that we hardly know them.

Another factor is that most of the hunters I have signed up to this club, are venison hunters, going after all species of buck, with the biggest being eland or kudu.

However, we have a most knowledgable gun-shop owner in NEIL SEADY of Seady Guns in Port Elizabeth. Neil is a National Springbok shottist in various disciplines, especially Clay Pigeon, and has an indoor training range on his premises. He has also to my knowledge, hunted the Big Five, and would be able to advise you and train you to handle an elephant gun.

We also have an organisation called the "East Cape Game Management Board", and several of our members belong to them as well as the club. One member was in fact their Chairman at one time, and if you phone Mr ROB MARRIOTT at Cell No 0836547691 or Work No 041-4841710 he will advise you further.

In the meantime, contact Neil Seady on Cell No 0832284800 or Work No 041-4872670 We are supposed to be a friendly crowd here in PE, and if one of these guys cant help you, I'd be very surprised !!

Incidentally, I don't even own a rifle…I'm a pistol man myself . If you need any more information , you can contact me LEW WILLIAMS at Work 041-4631183 or Home 041-3602063. Hope you come right, and welcome in advance to PE, we'll be pleased to have you as a new member !

Yours truly,

L.G.WILLIAMS
SECRETARY/TREASURER/CHIEF RANGE OFFICER & INSTRUCTOR

Makadi Safaris
PO Box 9818
Windhoek
Namibia

Mr Ben Trovato
PO Box 1117
Sea Point
8060

28 July, 2002

Dear Sir,

I need to get away for a while. If you are a married man, you will know what I am talking about. That's right. I am looking for a few days away from the incessant nagging. Away from the interrogation sessions and the mindless threats. Namibia is far enough away to get some peace of mind.

During the last few days, I have felt a growing urge to shoot something. Naturally, Brenda was the first thing that came to mind. But she is a moving target and I fear that the furniture would be the only casualty. Besides, I intend having a trophy on the wall in my study. The idea of Brenda stuffed and mounted has its own appeal, but the thought of having her up there watching me with disapproving glass eyes is too horrible to contemplate.

This is why I am interested in spending a few days at your ranch. My trophy of choice would be a lion, but I am a little concerned about hunting anything that is covered in teeth and claws. I was thinking of bagging something a little smaller. Like a warthog. These little fellows bear an uncanny resemblance to my Brenda when her blood is up. Shooting one of them would be good for me in a cathartic sense.

I would be looking for a big bugger with fierce tusks. However, I am not interested in crawling through the bush on my hands and knees trying to pick up the spoor. I have seen these things run in the bush, and there is no way I would be able to keep up. The only way to bring the animal down would be to lob mortars at it. Do you do that kind of thing? If not, I presume you at least offer canned hunting. It is probably not very sporting, but we are talking about a pig, not a Bengal tiger. Although if you are prepared to throw in a lion, we could talk business. In fact, the lion could bring down the warthog for me and while he is eating I could sneak up and shoot him in the back of the head. That means I could be back at the lapa guzzling cold beer before the heat of the day sets in.

Well, do we have a deal or not? Please could you quote me a price for three nights at the ranch, plus the going rate for a warthog and maybe a lion. Do you have a taxidermist at your place? I would not want to risk running into a roadblock with a bloody corpse in my boot.

Hope to hear from you soon.

Yours truly,

Ben Trovato (Mr)

Ben Trovato
P.O.Box 1117
Sea Point 8-60
Cape Town

15. August, 2002

Dear Mr. Trovato,

Thank you for your enquiry! We do have Kudu and Warthog available on our
hunting farm amongst others. But unfortunately we do not offer canned hunts nor
Lion. For more information attached please find our brochure and price list.
If you are hunting on your own we are looking at 6 nights x U$ 350.00 = U$
2100.00 plus the trophy fees as well as packing and dipping at U$ 330.00, the
transfer fee of U$ 165.00 and the hunting licence of U$ 30.00.
To sum it up, six nights with Makadi Safaris will cost you U$ 2625.00 plus the
trophy fees.
We would accept the equivalent of this amount in N$ if necessary.
What would be the preferred dates for such a hunting trip?
Awaiting your reply I remain with best regards,

Yours faithfully,

Katja Metzger

KAMAB

GUEST FARM
SIMBRA STUD

and

MAKADI

SAFARIS

P. O. BOX 9818

WINDHOEK

NAMIBIA

TEL: +264-62-503732

FAX: +264-62-504024

E-MAIL:

kamab@iafrica.com.n

MAKADI SAFARIS:

WEBPAGE:

www.makadisafaris.co

The White Shark Society
PO Box 50775
V&A Waterfront
Cape Town 8001

Mr Ben Trovato
PO Box 1117
Sea Point
8060

5 August, 2002

Dear Sir,

I was relieved to hear that there is an organisation working towards ridding the ocean of Great White Sharks. As you know, they can leave a nasty bite and prevent many of us from swimming in the sea.

I want to be able to enjoy a day at the beach and know that at the end of it I will be returning home with all my limbs still attached. This is my right as a Human Being. Who gave sharks the right to rule the ocean? Imagine if Great Whites wanted to get out of the water and have a picnic in the park across my road. I wouldn't rush out without provocation and start taking enormous bites out of them. I would not chew on the heads of their children. No, I would leave them in peace. I might even greet them as I walked by, although I would not want to sit down and share their lunch. Not because I would be afraid, but because they are a different species and they should know their place.

I need to know if you have managed to develop any weapons that can successfully keep these predators at bay. I am in the process of adapting a speargun to fire submersible explosive devices similar to handgrenades but lighter. These will detonate on impact and are likely to deter the most aggressive of Great Whites. However, water resistance means they only work at close quarters. I need something that can pick off these vicious brutes from a distance of a hundred metres. Another idea is to strap incendiary bombs onto live animals and force them to swim around the area in which one would like to take a dip. Patrolling sharks would come across an easy lunch and seconds later they would be torn apart. Let's see how they like it. I was thinking that chickens and even stray dogs would be perfectly suited. Do you have access to Semtex?
Keep up the good work and please let me know if you have anything else on the drawing board.

Death to the Great White!

Yours truly,

....
Ben Trovato (Mr)

WHITE SHARK PROJECTS

WHITE SHARK PROJECTS

**Phone: +27 (0) 21 4054537 -Fax:021(0) 21 5529795-Address: Clock Tower Precinct, shop 107
South Arm Road V&A Waterfront Cape Town. email:
sharks@tourcapetown.com/whitesharkprojects@tourcapetown.com
wsp@iafrica.com www.whitesharkprojects.co.za**

04 September 2002

Dear Ben

I received your letter of 5 August 2002. The tone of your letter leads me to believe that it is a hoax, and if it is, I am not sure as to your motives.

If however, you are serious in what you write, it is a shame that you feel this negative towards an animal, which is essentially innocent, as it does not have the capacity to determine between good, and evil.

I could go into an entire lecture on the many things in daily life which are far more dangerous than sharks, however, I feel that the best way to show you the white shark, is for us to take you out on our boat where you can come face to face with the animal and make your own judgments based on what you see and what we can translate to you.

We would be more than happy to introduce you to the with sharks in the wild, where I am quite certain, you will change your perception of these highly complex animals with a vital role.

Please feel free to contact me on my mobile phone and we will take you on a trip. 082 375 3472

Yours Sincerely

Craig Ferreira

Commission on Gender Equality
PO Box 32175
Braamfontein
2017

Mr Ben Trovato
PO Box 1117
Sea Point
8060

7 August, 2002

To Whom It May Concern:

May I compliment you on the fine work that the Commission is doing. Everywhere I go, I see that respect is once again being shown towards men. Whether they are construction workers or physicians, women are realising that men also have feelings.

The golden age of men came to a swift and terrible end when the feminist movement emerged with shrill cries of "Burn them! Burn them!" Nobody was told that the big-boned women were talking about brassieres and not the actual men themselves.

The result was that men everywhere were forced into hiding. They hid out in pool halls, bars, clubs and brothels. Anywhere they thought might be safe. And only now are they beginning to emerge, blinking in the sunlight and recoiling from loud noises.

It will still be a while before they regain enough confidence to take charge of the remote control, order the wine at a restaurant or invade a small, neighbouring country.

Thanks to the Commission on Gender Equality, men will soon be able to proudly take their place among all the citizens of this great nation. Naturally this does not include men who believe they are trapped in a woman's body. I am sure you will agree that they should form their own commission. There is enough confusion between conventional males and females, as it is. The last thing we need is for the waters to be muddied even further by flouncing mobs of limp-wristed she-men lisping threats of violence unless the state pays for them to get a new set of genitals.

Women are once again wearing makeup and undergarments. They no longer want to fly jet planes and be kick-boxers. They want to stay home and nurture things. When a woman puts her hand out, men no longer automatically flinch. No more is lingering eye contact followed by a prolonged burst of pepper spray.

I would like to become a member of your commission. Enclosed is ten rand to secure me a place. Do you have a Cape Town chapter? I will get Brenda to bake a cake for my first meeting.

Yours truly,

Ben Trovato (Mr)

225

Commission on Gender Equality

10th Floor ● Braamfontein Centre ●
23 Jorissen Street ● Braamfontein ● Johannesburg ● South Africa

PO Box 32175 ● Braamfontein ● 2017 ● South Africa
email: cgeinfo@cge.org.za ● website: http://www.cge.org.za
Tel: +27 (0)11 403-7182 ● Fax: +27 (0)11 403-7188

October 29th, 2002

Mr. Ben Trovato
P. O. Box 1117
SEA POINT
8060

Dear Mr. Trovato,

On behalf of the Commission on Gender Equality I acknowledge receipt of your letter dated August 07th, 2002 whose contents have been noted. I must apologise that it is only now that I am able to respond. The CGE's Legal Department has been snowed under with projects, that resulted in delays in responding to most of the letters.

The Commission on Gender Equality ("the CGE") is an independent statutory body, established under Chapter 9 of the Constitution, with a mandate to monitor, promote and protect gender equality. As one of six Chapter 9 institutions supporting democracy, it has been given a pre-eminent role in assisting the transformation of South African society. The CGE is subject only to the Constitution and the law, and it must exercise its powers and perform its functions "without fear, favour or prejudice".

The CGE is established to promote the protection, development and attainment of gender equality. To this end, the Commission on Gender Equality Act No.39 of1996 gives the Commission the power to investigate complaints concerning gender related issues. The Act also provides the Commission with the power to refer complaints to other bodies.

I have carefully considered the contents of your letter and I am of the view that these concerns do not really constitute a complaint. I therefore will address them as follows.

In paragraphs three and four of your letter, you have mentioned that men were confused about alleged utterances by people from a certain sector in the past. Gender inequality and discrimination is still a major concern of the society. In the sixth paragraph of your letter you mention that "women … no longer want to fly jet planes and be kick-boxers. They want to stay at home and nurture things" I am uncertain as to which women you are talking about here. This allegation is demeaning to women and stereotyping on the basis of gender. The CGE does tolerate such insinuations at it untrue.

The constitutional democracy that has been attained and been in existence for the past eight years actually encourages women to get involved and to become professionals in spheres that previously excluded them. There are laws in place at the moment that essentially assist women and those that were previously unlawfully discriminated against to have access to, and to participate in activities that were reserved for a few beforehand.

It is disturbing and worrying that you sound to be confusing the struggles of activist to attain gender equality and what you termed "feminist movement". In the last sentence in the second paragraph of your letter you also refer to the "..... lingering eye contact followed by a prolonged burst of pepper spray". The CGE has noted that there is an increasing number of sexual harassment where women are victims. What you have described may be construed to be sexual harassment depending on your relationship with the person who may lodge such a complaint. It does not make sense why a man does not expect such reaction for a conduct that is regarded by the woman to be uncomfortable and offensive to her. If men are also subjected to the same conduct, the reaction may be different and may be followed by deafening silence.

In the last paragraph you also demean and degrade Brenda, whatever the relationship, may be with you. Why does "Brenda have to bake a cake" is it a further disrespect that you show to gender equality and promotion of rights of women?

In conclusion the CGE would like to return your money as there is no such thing as securing membership of the CGE. Please call our Cape Town Office at 021 426 4080 for a detailed briefing session on what exactly does the CGE stand for and what roles and tasks different members play at the CGE.

Please contact me if you have any further problems related to this matter.

Yours sincerely

Ms. Mmathari Mashao
Head of Legal Department

Mr Joof Lamprecht
Rooikraal Game Ranch
PO Box 1443
Windhoek
Namibia

Mr Ben Trovato
PO Box 1117
Sea Point 8060
Cape Town

26 August, 2002

Dear Mr Lamprecht,

You come highly recommended by a friend who served in the old government.

I am an amateur hunter and I want to build up my trophy collection on my lounge wall. I do most of my hunting at my cottage near Kommetjie. There is not much big game left in the area. In fact, baboons and tortoises are all I have seen in years. I do not hunt the tortoises. They make terrible trophies, as you can imagine. If they had square shells it would be a lot easier to fix them to the wall. And if you remove the shell there is not that much left to work with. Certainly not enough to take to a taxidermist. Instead, I have found that a fully-grown chacma baboon with fangs bared makes a far more impressive conversation piece.

I was wondering if you offered warthogs. I know that these animals are referred to as the poor man's rhino, but I think they would make wonderful trophies. With their speed and agility, I imagine that they are also tremendous fun to hunt. But I am really after monkeys. They would be perfect to fill in the gaps between the baboons.

I normally hunt with a 12-gauge shotgun because my aim is not as good as it once was. When I was in the army many years ago, I wanted to be a sniper deep in the Angolan bush. But it all went terribly wrong and I ended up in Signals learning how to type 45 words a minute.

I realise that trophy hunting with a shotgun has its own set of problems. Especially if the target is as small as a monkey. I don't want something on my wall that looks like it stepped on a landmine. The face needs to be in good condition. Do you offer bow hunting? A clean shot with an arrow could be the solution. However, since I need to bag around a dozen of the little fellows, it may take some time. I know monkeys. They are hyperactive and I expect that hitting one of them with an arrow might be more difficult than it sounds. Would it be possible to slip some kind of narcotic into their food? Nothing that is going to kill them or make them hallucinate, of course. That would be cruel. But just enough to make them drowsy. Even a novice archer like myself would be able to hit a sleeping monkey. Unless it is 500 metres away. Perhaps you could herd a bunch of them into a small enclosure so I need not spend the whole day on my feet.

Let me know as soon as possible what a week in your best room would cost. And give me a quote on the monkeys and the warthogs.

Yours truly,

Ben Trovato (Mr)

TROPHY HUNTING and PHOTOGRAPHIC SAFARIS
ROOIKRAAL GAME RANCH, OMITARA

September 16, 2002.

Mr. Ben Trovato
P.O.Box 1117
Sea Point 8060
Cape Town

Mr. Trovato

Your letter dated August 26, 2002 refers.

As an ethical hunter I find your letter disturbing and insulting. Are there still people out there that think like you when it comes to hunting ? This kind of view and attitude about hunting is what gives hunting a bad name and press. I suggest you buy some books on hunting and see if what you read about real hunting makes sense to you.

Yours sincerely

Joof Lamprecht.

Owners & Professional Hunter Joof & Marina Lamprecht
P.O. Box 1443 • Windhoek • Namibia • Tel: (Intl.) 264 - 62 - 560238 • Fax: (Intl.) 264 - 62 - 560266
Joof's e-mail: huntersn@mweb.com.na • Marina's e-mail: hunters@iafrica.com.na
Website: http://www.icon.co.za/~trophyhunt

Dr Tim Noakes
Sports Science Institute
Private bag X5
Newlands 7725

Mr Ben Trovato
PO Box 1117
Sea Point
8060

19 August, 2002

Dear Dr Noakes,

I would be very interested to hear what you think of Pieter van Zyl's strategy during the recent test against New Zealand. Looking at the television pictures, it seemed to me that he should rather have made his break from the stands at the northern end of the field. That way he would have been able to blindside the entire scrum and bring the ref down with a clean tackle. Do you agree?

To me, van Zyl's game plan also lacked subtlety. For a start, referee David McHugh is Irish (with Scottish roots, I should imagine). The Irish are easily bamboozled but hard to bring down. The British know this more than most. And since van Zyl's forefathers fought the British, he should have known this too. The Irish are all too accustomed to brute force. They react well to it. But a cunning attack always leaves them baffled.

Had van Zyl managed to employ diversionary tactics, he would have been able to not only bring McHugh to the turf, but also take out two or three of the All Blacks.

What do you think of the suggestion that supporters should also undergo fitness training sessions? It certainly would have helped things if van Zyl had been in better shape. He has the right attitude for the game, but if he wants future interventions to be more successful he needs to lose the stomach and build up his legs. Cut back on the starch and get his 100 metre dash down to around fifteen seconds. What kind of diet and workout plan would you suggest for a man like van Zyl? How important is mental preparation for those who want to turn rugby into a true spectator sport?

There may also come a time when van Zyl decides to play the ball and not the man. For this to work he will need to have his wits about him. Disabling the ref and then still going for a try will not be easy, not even for someone of van Zyl's obvious talents. One has to bear in mind that he would probably have all thirty players and the linesmen chasing him. And the police. I suspect he would need the help of a second party, or do you think he could get by on sheer speed and agility alone?

I would greatly appreciate your expert opinion on van Zyl's strategy and how you think it could be improved on in the future.

Yours truly

....
Ben Trovato (Mr)

Dr Tim Noakes
Sports Science Institute
Private bag X5
Newlands 7725

Mr Ben Trovato
PO Box 1117
Sea Point
8060

7 September, 2002

Dear Dr Noakes,

I have not yet received a reply to my letter dated 19th August.

If you recall, I was asking your professional opinion of Pieter van Zyl's strategy during the recent test against New Zealand. My neighbour believes that supporter participation in blood sports like rugby is going to be the next big thing. Do you agree?

I realised after sending my first letter that I had failed to enclose payment for your opinions. Nothing is for free these days. I apologise for this lapse of judgement and enclose ten rand in this correspondence.

I hope to hear from you soon.

Yours truly,

....
Ben Trovato (Mr)

CASH GIVEN
R10

Department of Human Biology

UCT/MRC RESEARCH UNIT FOR EXERCISE SCIENCE & SPORTS MEDICINE
Faculty of Health Sciences, University of Cape Town
Private Bag, Rondebosch 7700, South Africa
Tel: + 27 21 650 4557
Fax: + 27 21 686 7530
Director: Professor T D Noakes

Monday, October 21, 2002

Mr Ben Trovato
P O Box 1117
Sea Point
8060

Dear Mr Ben,

Thank you so much for your letter of the 19th of August and more especially for the letter of the 7th September, which included a financial contribution for my services. I might add that my usual hourly rate is $450 (R4725) (0.76 rand per second) for a detailed medical opinion of a complexed legal issue. Thus your R10.00 purchases you precisely 13 seconds of my time.

Unfortunately it has already taken me more than 13 seconds to dictate this letter and I have not yet been able to provide you with my opinion. Accordingly it seems only right and appropriate that I should return your contribution on the basis that hopefully next time you will include the remuneration appropriate to the complexity of the topic on which you require a medical opinion.

I trust you will not be offended by my directness in this matter.

I have however managed to acquire the opinion of a first year student in this department and his expert opinion offered for free, is enclosed as a separate page.

With kindest regards and hoping that this will not deter you from continuing to write for the Cape Times Newspaper.

Yours sincerely,

Timothy Noakes

Professor T. D. Noakes

The University of cape Town is committed to policies of equal opportunity and affirmative action which are essential to its mission of promoting critical inquiry and scholarship

Expert Opinion on Mr. Ben Trovato's letter of the 19th of August 2002 to Professor Tim Noakes.

Dear Mr. Trovato,

Your detailed analysis of Mr. Peter van Zyl's strategy during the recent test against New Zealand has been referred to me by Professor Noakes for my expert opinion. My knowledge of this topic is vast having myself been present at at least 3 rugby matches where a pitch invasion occurred. Indeed on Professor Noakes' suggestion I have reviewed the video information on those 3 cases and have had an opportunity to compare the techniques used on those occasions with that of Mr. Peter Van Zyl.

1. In your first question you wonder whether Mr. van Zyl would have been better advised to attack from the North-end of the field rather than of the West-end, and would have been able to bring the referee down with a clean tackle.

   Having considered this strategy and having compared the video evidence including another series of famous cases from New Zealand and Australia, the clear evidence is the following:

   Attacks from the north-end of the field: 2. Success rate 0%
   Attacks from the south side of the rugby field 3: Success rate 0%
   Attacks from the east side of the rugby field: 5. Success rate 0%
   Attacks rates from the West side: 1. Success rates 100%. Referee hospitalized.

   Accordingly the statistics of analysis clearly reveal that Mr van Zyl with his classic approach from the west side of the field is the only one to have a 100% success rate in removing the referee from the field.

   Accordingly our analysis is that attacks on the referee should always come from the west side of the field.

2. Your second question is whether van Zyl's game plan lack subtlety and that a cunning attack lacking in brute force would have left the Irish referee David McHugh baffled so that van Zyl would have been able to take out not only McHugh but also 2 or 3 All Blacks.

   Of course this is entirely possible but it assumes that the All Blacks are also Irish. My understanding is that the current All Black team is dominated by players from Christchurch, which was established by the Scots. I also expect that there are many Polynesian players in the team. Thus an appropriate approach would have been one, which would bamboozle both Irish, Scottish and Polynesians. Although it is unlikely that a South African from the Hinterland would be able to develop a strategy sufficiently clever to

1

bamboozle persons from such diverse backgrounds, this would have been less of a problem for a Cape Town supporter given the greater probability that persons with combined Irish, Scottish and Polynesian backgrounds are present in the Cape Town community.

3. With regards to your suggestion that supporters should undergo fitness-training sessions, we find your observations on Mr. van Zyl accurate but perhaps a little too personal. Our analysis is that Mr. van Zyl would benefit by being taller so that his weight was more evenly distributed. What many perceive as a protruding abdomen is in fact really a common South African disorder of the too short spinal column. Much research of this syndrome has been done including the novel suggestion of spinal column elongation as a cure for the condition. This research has been enthusiastically endorsed by the sponsors of the South African rugby team, Castle Lager, who believe they have been unfairly targeted as the cause of this stunted spinal column syndrome (SSCS) in the majority of male South African rugby supporters.

Thus we suggest that Mr van Zyl will need to undergo intensive investigation to determine whether or not he suffers from the SSCS and whether a surgical solution can be offered to him. You are quite correct of course that persons suffering from the SSCS do have significant mental disturbances so that mental preparation is crucially important for them.

4. Your fourth question was whether van Zyl decides to play the ball and not the man would he still be able to go for the try with all thirty players and the linesmen chasing him.

It is interesting that you should make this observation. I am led to believe that new research is soon to be released showing that persons with SSCS who undergo corrective surgery have been shown to increase their 100m running speed by more than 20km per hour and, surprisingly, their intellectual capacity by over 100%. That even if Mr van Zyl started from a low physical and intellectual base, it seems that these modern techniques should allow him to achieve even greater heights of performance in the future.

I do hope these simple thoughts will be of assistance to your client. In keeping with modern medical practices, we would be happy to refer Mr. Van Zyl to the appropriate expert SSCS surgeon with, of course, appropriate remuneration to your good self for your contribution to good ethical medical practice. By so much will this referral reduce Mr. Van Zyl's future medical costs that in future he will be able to buy season tickets for all the major rugby venues in South Africa for the next fifty years.

We do hope this information will be of value to you and look forward to providing more services to you in the future.

2

The Chairman
National Council on Tunnelling
PO Box 93480
Yeoville 2143

Mr Ben Trovato
PO Box 1117
Sea Point
8060

20 August, 2002

Dear Sir,

You seem to be the right organisation to give me a little advice.

My wife, Brenda, has put a temporary ban on me nipping out for a beer with the lads. It has something to do with her garden gnome, but the details are unimportant. What is important is that I find a way to sneak out of the house without setting off the alarm.

A tunnel seems to be my best hope.

As experts in the field, I was hoping you could give me a little advice. I have already lifted the tiles beneath a large flowerpot in the bathroom. I expect that if I go straight down for about a metre then take a sharp right and continue for about 20 metres I should be on the other side of the fence. Then it's just a matter of popping up, dusting myself off and heading for the pub. Brenda, of course, will be at home asleep.

I need to know if my tunnel needs some kind of internal support structure. I have researched the subject by watching a copy of *The Great Escape*. Steve McQueen seemed to know what he was doing. Their tunnel was shored up with pieces of wood. But my tunnel will be much smaller so it might not be necessary to get quite so technical.

What about air quality? Would you suggest I send a canary down there first? It's only 20 metres so I reckon that unless I accidentally do a particularly harsh trouser cough, I should be able to breathe quite freely.

Most importantly, I need to know if a metre down is deep enough. I would not want my neighbour staggering drunkenly about my lawn (he does this sometimes) only to have him collapse my tunnel to freedom. My greatest fear is that I would be directly underneath him at that very moment. Brenda's heart is not strong enough for the sight of Ted and I emerging like giant moles from the front lawn in the middle of the night.

I am enclosing a diagram to give you a better idea of what I have in mind. Since advice is rarely given freely, I am also sending you ten rand.

Please hurry. I am beginning to suffer from Cabin Fever.

Yours truly,

....
Ben Trovato (Mr)

CA$H GIVEN
R10

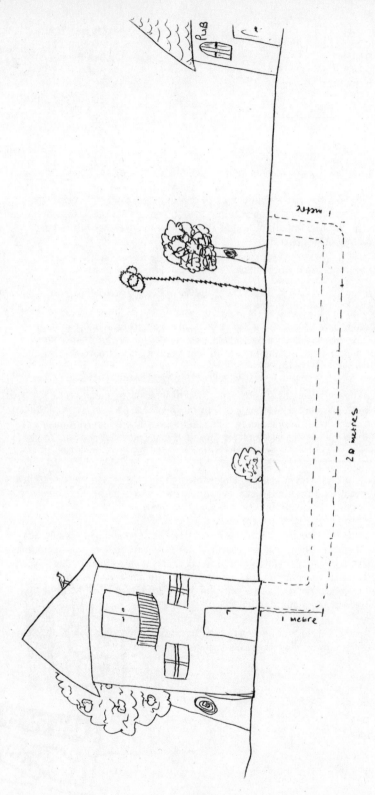

Pub

1 metre

20 metres

1 metre

SOUTH AFRICAN NATIONAL COUNCIL ON TUNNELLING

18A Gill Street
Observatory
Johannesburg 2198
South Africa
Tel/Fax: xx27 (0) 11 487 1556

PO Box 93480
Yeoville
2143
South Africa

Mr Ben Travato
P O Box 1117
Sea Point 8060

21.10 2002

Dear Sir,
Please let me apologise for the delay in returning your correspondence. Our Council only meet each quarter this is when they were able to discuss your dilemma.

After much discussion and empathy for your situation they all agreed that the best solution was to come clean with your wife.

Should you however still wish to pursue your plan. You would need to carefully think how deep you should go. One meter is not sufficient as you would require at least a full head clearance. The downward shaft requires a structure to hold the soil in place, suggest old dustbins with bottoms cut out placed one on top of the other. Three should do the job. You can then dig the tunnel to a height according to whether you wish to crawl or walk. Here again you would have to support the ground above your head. The dustbins can be useful should you decide to crawl. To ensure a good supply of air we suggest that at various sections you place a long pipe from the tunnel to the surface. It is definitely a good idea to take a canary with you. It would indicate very quickly should your air supply be reduced. However it was pointed out that you would have to take the canary with you to the pub…this may present a problem should you forget it on your return.

When you reach the exit side you will have to do the same as the entrance and camouflage this well to avoid discovery.

We are returning your ten rand and trust you will use it wisely.

Good Luck!

The Secretary on behalf of the
The Committee
SA National Council on Tunnelling

Member of International Tunnelling Association - Printed on re-cycled paper

The Managing Director
Tiger Brands Ltd.
PO Box 78056
Sandton 2146

Mr Ben Trovato
PO Box 1117
Sea Point
8060

2 September, 2002

Dear Sir,

I am sure you are a busy man so I will come straight to the point.

A few months ago, my wife began giving our teenage son Tiger Oats for breakfast. Clive always used to eat those disgusting chocolate-coated puffy things that masquerade as health food. He began to get more and more sickly until one day a stranger stopped us in the street and told us that our son was suffering from urticaria. We were stricken with grief and that night, when Clive was asleep, we even discussed the possibility of euthanasia. The next day we found out that urticaria is just a fancy name for hives.

Anyway, the point is that Clive's condition was a result of the muck he was eating for breakfast. So Brenda switched to Tiger Oats. Everything was fine for a few weeks. The boy seemed alert and relatively cheerful. He was even starting to pass some of the class tests. Then, almost overnight, he became sullen and withdrawn. When we tried to engage him in conversation he would snarl at us and back away. And the incidents began. First it was the bicycle shed, then the gymnasium burned down. Mr Dubrovnik's boy went to hospital with a broken collarbone and two days later Mrs Snitcher who teaches Religious Education reported that she was being stalked by a boy who looked very much like Clive.

The other night we had the neighbours over for a few drinks and we got to discussing this bizarre change in Clive's behaviour. The ladies put it down to adolescence (he recently turned thirteen). But Ted said it had to do with diet. After a process of elimination, we narrowed it down to the Tiger Oats. I was not convinced, particularly since people have been eating this for years without turning into malevolent creatures hell-bent on wreaking havoc. However, I may be wrong. Perhaps people like Eugene Terreblanche and Eugene de Kock are nothing more than innocent victims of a breakfast cereal. Or it might simply be because their mothers gave them such girly names. I was tempted to make a joke about cereal killers but I won't because this is a serious matter.

Ted suspects that the change in Clive's nature is because your company has begun using genuine tiger products in the cereal and the boy is allergic to the stuff. I find this unlikely since tigers are a protected species and it would not be easy to catch fully-grown Bengals and grind them up for use in an oat-based breakfast food without somebody noticing.

It is imperative that you let me know if Ted is right. I swear not to divulge your secret to anyone. I just want to know if I should put Clive back on the chocpuffs.

Yours truly,

....
Ben Trovato (Mr)

Tiger Brands

Cnr Bute Lane and Fredman Drive, Sanlam Park, West Block, 2nd Floor, Sandown, Sandton
Tel: +27(11) 305-2300 Fax: +27(11) 305-2323

P O Box 78056. Sandton 2146, Republic of South Africa

Thursday, September 26, 2002

PO Box 1117
Sea Point
8060

Dear Mr. Trovato

Your letter dated 2 September 2002 regarding the ingredients used to manufacture Tiger Oats refers.

I can assure you that only high quality oats, which are sourced from various countries, is used in the manufacture of Tiger Oats. No other ingredients are added. This healthy product can be safely consumed by people of all ages without any side effects.

I trust that this information answers your question and provides you with peace of mind regarding the consumption of our products.

Yours sincerely,

Luke Horsten
Category Director

TIGER BRANDS LIMITED Registration No. 1944/017881/06

Directors

R A Williams (Chairman), N Dennis (Managing Director) (British), B H Adams, D D B Band, B P Connellan, D E Cooper, M H Franklin, U P T Johnson, J H McBain (British),
A C Nissan, M C Norris, G N Padayachee, I B Skosana, R V Smither, J L van den Berg, C F H Vaux,

Company Secretary: I W M Isdale

The Royal Norwegian Embassy
PO Box 5620
Cape Town
8000

Mr Ben Trovato
PO Box 1117
Sea Point
8060

6 September, 2002

To Whom It May Concern:

This is an urgent appeal to Norwegians not to kill Keiko.

I took my boy to see all four 'Free Willy' movies when they came on circuit in South Africa and we both cried through every one of them. I felt as if Keiko had become a part of our family. At the end of two of the films I had to physically drag Clive from the cinema because he did not want to be parted from his friend. We were both traumatised for some time afterwards. To this day, Clive refuses to eat fish.

As you know, Keiko was released into the Icelandic wilds six weeks ago. I always thought this was one smart orca. But it turns out that he is not too bright after all. The moment Willy is genuinely free, he puts his head down and swims for fifteen hundred kilometres until he reaches the only country in the world that hunts whales commercially. Under normal circumstances, this kind of stupidity would be punishable by death. But we are not dealing with a normal killer whale. He has been exposed to the excesses of Hollywood. God only knows what those people were feeding him. "Hey Keiko! Get the rescue scene in one take and you can have a whole bucket of cocaine-coated pilchards!" It is no wonder that his little brain is fried.

I read that Keiko is lolling about in the Skaalvik fjord, attracting a lot of attention from people who want to touch him and ride on him and get his autograph. I need not remind you of what can happen when crowds of admirers gather around a famous personality. Remember JFK? Martin Luther King? Let us not add Keiko to the long list of assassinations that have left this world a poorer place. Norway is a whaling nation and it is only a matter of time before someone comes to see Keiko with a harpoon concealed beneath his coat. And this time nobody will be able to blame the Cubans.

Once again, I urge the Norwegian government not to do anything that could jeopardise Keiko's life. Allow him safe passage out of Norway. I am enclosing ten rand towards the repatriation of this fine, if slightly retarded, animal.

If anything happens to Keiko, a group called the Friends Of Killer Whales (FOK-Whales) will be mobilised to mount violent protests outside your offices.

Long live Willy!

....
Ben Trovato (Mr)

CA$H GIVEN
R10

Pretoria 13/9-02

Dear Ben Trovato

With the Compliments
of
the Royal Norwegian Embassy
Pretoria

We return the 2 × R 10
you sent to the Embassy
in connection with your
concern for Keiko. Ret. our
e-mail, Norway will take care
of Keiko. Regards Inger Naess

From :
Næss Inger G. <inger.nass@norad.no>

Reply-To :
Næss Inger G. <IGN@NORAD.NO>

To :
ben_trovato@hotmail.com

CC :
"Cape Town office (E-mail)" <embctn@

Subject :
Keiko and Norwegian policy on whaling

Date :
Fri, 13 Sep 2002 14:46:51 +0200

Dear Ben Trovato

Thank you for your letter where you express your concern for the killer
whale Keiko, alias Willy, which has been in Norwegian waters for some weeks.

The Norwegian Embassy is happy to inform you that we will not do anything
that can harm Keiko, as he (as a killer whale) is a threatened species.
Norwegian only hunt minke whales, as the population of that species is
large enough to be sustainable harvested. These days researchers from Norway
and abroad are doing there very best to save Keiko and make sure he is not
suffering a painful death in a Norwegian fjord, as he has not been eating
for the last weeks.

If you want to know more about the Norwegian policy on whaling, please visit
the web-site: www.odin.dep.no/odin/engelsk/norway/environment

Also - please tell your son that he should eat fish as whales are mammals
and not fish, and to eat fish is very healthy.

Best regards

Inger Naess
First Secretary

Norwegian Embassy Pretoria
Tel.:   + 27 12 342 6100
Direct: + 27 12 431 2865
Cell.: + 27 82 901 8133
Fax.:   + 27 12 342 6099

The Chief Executive Officer
Pfizer Laboratories
PO Box 783720
Sandton
2146

Mr Ben Trovato
PO Box 1117
Sea Point
8060

17 September, 2002

Dear Sir,

Allow me to congratulate you on your company's breakthrough in the field of erectile dysfunction. The discovery of Viagra has changed lives around the world. However, I am looking for an antidote to this particular drug.

My wife, Brenda, has frozen up on me. Her passion plug has tripped. Frigid as a polar bear's testicles, she is. Getting ready for bed is like preparing for an Arctic expedition. You will appreciate that Viagra is about the last thing I need.

This is why I am looking for something that has the opposite effect to your wonder drug. Something that will anaesthetise my ardour. I need a soporific for my snub-nosed pistolero. A pharmaceutical to flummox the flagpole. A narcotic to numb the knobkierie. A tranquilliser for the troglodyte. You get the idea.

I was hoping that Brenda would thaw out in the warmer weather, but this has not happened. I tried to improve her circulation with a rigorous slapping, but she woke up immediately and repaid my efforts with an alarm clock to the side of the head.

To minimise casualties, it would be best if I also opted for a life of celibacy. Please let me know if you have anything that might help ease my passage into this strange place.

Thank you.

Yours truly,

....
Ben Trovato (Mr)

Pfizer Laboratories (Pty) Ltd
PO Box 783720
Sandton 2146
South Africa
Tel: +27 11 320 6000   Fax: +27 11 783 0912

Pfizer Pharmaceuticals Group

02 October 2002

Mr Ben Trovato
PO Box 1117
Sea Point
8060

Dear Mr. Trovato,

Thank you for your letter dated 17 September 2002. I apologise for any delay in our response to your request for information from Pfizer. Unfortunately Pfizer has no drug either marketed or in development, designed to reduce libido.

Kind regards,

Dr Damian Largier
Medical Director

Pfizer Laboratories (Pty) Ltd Reg No 1954/000781/07
Directors: B.H. Buck, J.P. Kearney (British) (Chairman), N. Magan (Managing), I. Piccione, K.G. Randell

Adrian Gore
Discovery Health
Private Bag X19
Milnerton

Mr Ben Trovato
PO Box 1117
Sea Point
8060

7 March, 2003

Dear Mr Gore

I am freshly divorced, but this is not your problem and I shall not burden you with the details.

I am writing to you to seek clarity on a matter of great importance to me. I am considering a sex change operation and I urgently need to know if Discovery Health is prepared to pay for the procedure. I am not currently a member, but would certainly sign up if my request meets with a favourable reply.

The experts say that divorce is the most traumatic thing that a person can experience. Well, let me tell you that the experts are wrong. Marriage is far more traumatic. In my case, anyway. And I will never again be able to put my trust in a woman. Having said that, please be assured that I do not intend becoming a transvestite or a homosexual. I could not imagine anything worse than having my bottom ravaged by a gimp in a rubber hood. It is simply that I have been betrayed one time too many by the "fairer sex" and I will no longer be able to share my life with one of them.

Since I have made up my mind to spend the rest of my days alone, I wish to have a sex change operation so that I can still enjoy what a woman has to offer without having to argue with her or buy her flowers.

Please let me know as soon as possible which hospital I should report to. I would prefer to be allocated a woman surgeon. They know so much more about female genitalia. The last thing I need is someone like Dr Wouter Basson carving his idea of a vagina into my body.

I would appreciate a speedy reply.

Thank you and best regards.

Ben Trovato (Mr)

Discovery ❤ Health

26 March 2003

Mr Ben Trovato
P.O.Box 1117
Sea Point
8060

Dear Mr Trovato

Thank you for your recent letter to Adrian Gore, our Chief Executive.

I have heard speak that marriage is a bribe to make a housekeeper think she's a householder. Mrs Trovato we take it has been relegated to that of housekeeper again – hope that she is coping with her loss of status. The experts are quite right, a divorce is one of the most traumatic things a person can experience. It has often been said that divorce is the psychological equivalent of a triple coronary bypass, so I really empathise with your recent change of marital status.

That said, I must advise that should you have written wanting confirmation on whether we would cover your bypass procedure, we would have gladly accomodated your request. The sex change unfortunately is not a covered benefit.

Thank you for the R10 incentive, we will be donating it in your name to the Red Cross Children's Fund of which we are sponsors.

Regards

Barry Swartzberg
Managing Director

p.s. Do you think that you would look good in a dress ?

155 West Street, Sandton, P. O. Box 786722, Sandton 2146, Tel 0860 99 88 77 (Client Services), (011) 529 2888 (Switchboard), Fax (011) 529 2958,www.discovery.co.za

Directors: L L Dippenaar (Chairman), A Gore* (CEO), B Swartzberg* (Managing), R B Gouws, M I Hilkowitz (Israel), N S Koopowitz*, S R Maharaj, H P Mayers*, J M Robertson*, S D Whyte*, (*Executive). Secretary: A Cimring.

Discovery Health (Pty) Ltd. Registration Number: 1997/013480/07

The Chairman
England and Wales Cricket Board
Lords Cricket Ground
London NW8 8QZ
England

Mr Ben Trovato
PO Box 1117
Sea Point 8060
Cape Town
South Africa

5 March, 2003

Dear Sir,

Allow me to offer my condolences on your early exit from the cricket World Cup. We, too, suffered a similar fate, although our demise was largely the result of the Bantu education system. Our players are sportsmen in the true sense of the word. To a man, they are functionally illiterate. If you had to ask our batsmen what pi means, they would want to know if it was mutton or curried vegetable.

Your team got off to a flying start by crushing the Netherlands and Namibia. Although neither country are particularly feared when it comes to cricket, or anything else for that matter, they are hardy little buggers who don't give up easily. Then you went on to give Pakistan a damn good whipping, a trend that was set long ago by the National Front on the fields of Bradford.

This leaves one question unanswered. How on earth can you beat the Boers and the Zulus and lose against the Indians and the Australians? My neighbour, Ted, says you should be suspended from the Commonwealth. At first I was outraged by his remark. But later on, after a few beers, he began making sense. Your captain is called Nasser Hussain. Has the Home Office ever checked his papers? Unlike Smith or Jones, Hussain is hardly typically British. Is it a mere coincidence that Saddam and Nasser share the same name? I think not. Donald Bradman and Dennis Compton were Englishmen. And you never lost a match. Does this not tell you something? I am not a racist. I love black people. Not in that way, of course. But I have a feeling that when war breaks out, Nasser will suddenly disappear only to emerge as a real captain. In the Iraqi army.

Even though your government has the most liberal immigration policies in the civilised world, I urge you to take this man's equipment away from him. Arabs are able to make weapons of mass destruction from almost anything. He has already destroyed your chances of winning the world cup. Don't let him destroy your way of life, too.

Yours truly,

....
Ben Trovato (Mr)

246

Ms Joan Edwards
Coordinator: Women's Cricket Assoc. of
South Africa
PO Box 55009
Northlands
2116

Mr Ben Trovato
PO Box 1117
Sea Point
8060

8 March, 2003

Dear Ms Edwards,

Certain startling information has come to light. I will get straight to the point since you have probably been expecting this moment for some time. Do you deny that the captain of the Proteas is secretly a member of your association? Impeccable sources tell me that Shaun Pollock is, in fact, a woman. His real name is Shawnee. Do you dispute this?

My suspicions were first aroused when he was run out in the game against Sri Lanka. A real man would have dived for the crease. Had Pollock done so, South Africa would still be in the World Cup. The only possible reason for her reluctance to hit the deck was because she was afraid of injuring her tightly wrapped breasts.

I assure you that your secret is safe. I do not want anything in return for withholding this information. Well, maybe one small favour. I have a teenage son, Clive, who is going through an experimental phase at the moment. He would probably be killed if he joined a boy's cricket team. And all I ask is that he be allowed to try out with the girls. Do you have a team in Cape Town?

Please let me know if you are able to help Clive regain his self-respect and become a real man like his father. And the next time you see Shawnee, please tell her not to worry. There will be more matches. One day she will want to breastfeed, and damaging the equipment because of a silly game is just not worth it.

Looking forward to hearing from you.

Yours truly,

....
Ben Trovato (Mr)

Wanderers Club

North St. Illovo 2196

PO Box 55009

Northlands 2116

Tel: (011) 880 2810

Fax: (011) 880 6578

ucbsa@cricket.co.za

Ben Trovato
P O Box 1117
Sea Point
8060

17 March 2003

Dear Mr Trovato,

Further to your letter dated 8th March 2003, addressed to our Women's Cricket Department:

You may recall that you have previously written to the UCB with regards to your "son" Clive, the cat batterer! Imagine my surprise when I saw my reply published in the Ben Trovato Files!!

So, what can I say this time other than HA HA HA...

Thank you for your ongoing interest in South African cricket!

Regards,

ROSALYNNE GOLDIN
Marketing Director
United Cricket Board

Cc Joan Edwards, Women's Cricket

General Council: P Sonn (President), R Kurz (Vice-President), J Blair (Treasurer), P Bacela, A Bloch, B Foot, M Gordon,

M Jajbhay, A Jinnah, T Khumalo, R Mall, Dr L Naidoo, G Nkagisang, H Paulse, C Robinson, C Sullman, R Tseladimitlwa

Chief Executive Officer: G Majola

cricket•co•za

Mr Gerhard Aigner
UEFA Chief Executive
Route de Geneve 46
Case Postale
CH-1260 Nyon 2
Switzerland

Mr Ben Trovato
PO Box 1117
Sea Point 8060
Cape Town
South Africa
Switzerland

8 March, 2003

Dear Mr Aigner,

Congratulations on taking a stand on racism in sport. It is high time that everyone stopped tiptoeing around the issue and said what was really on their minds. I never heard the report myself, but my neighbour tells me that you stood up at a conference in London on March 5th and called for more racism in sport. Well done! Some of us have always said that racism was a healthy and integral component of sport.

South Africa has achieved much since it broke free from British colonial domination. Apart from things like biltong and Mrs Ball's chutney, we also invented racism. Well, we might not have invented it (I suppose the Americans will want to take credit for that!) but we certainly perfected the art. Even the darkies have caught on and are now using it to steal our jobs and take our women. That's only fair, I suppose.

I am sure you will agree that for racism to have a positive effect on sport, it should not be confined to the colour of a person's skin. Times have changed and today it is quite acceptable to discriminate on the grounds of religious prejudice, homophobia, sexism, and even xenophobia. In the proper hands, these tools can be used to liven up even the most boring sports like golf, snooker and that stupid game played by the French.

With your permission, I would like to start a movement in South Africa campaigning for the full return of racism in sport. I firmly believe in giving credit where it is due, so you will obviously be our patron.

Please let me know if this meets with your approval since I want to get the letterheads and T-shirts printed as soon as possible.

Freedom of hate speech is an essential component to any well-balanced bill of rights.

Down with the pakis, wogs, queers, chicks, dykes and spics!

Looking forward to hearing from you at your earliest convenience.

Yours truly,

....
Ben Trovato (Mr)

Mr Gerhard Aigner
UEFA Chief Executive
Route de Geneve 46
Case Postale
CH-1260 Nyon 2
Switzerland

Mr Ben Trovato
PO Box 1117
Sea Point 8060
Cape Town
South Africa

14 May, 2003

Dear Mr Aigner,

I wrote to you on the 8th of March but have not yet received a reply. I appreciate that you are a very busy man, but I doubt that even the Pope takes nine weeks to answer his mail. And he is a lot older than you are.

If you recall, I wrote to you asking if you would be the patron of our movement (ARS) focusing on racism in sport. The letterheads are ready to be printed with your name at the top of the page.

It is urgent that you give us an indication of where you stand on the issue. Are you with us or against us? Can we use your name or not? Maintaining radio silence will ultimately be construed as permission on your part.

Yours truly,

Ben Trovato (Mr)
President: Aigner for Racism in Sport

WE CARE ABOUT FOOTBALL

Union des associations européennes de football

Mr Ben Trovato
P.O. Box 1117
Sea Point 8060
Cape Town
South Africa

Your reference	Your correspondence of	Our reference	Date
	14.05.2003	LDIR/stu/col	12.06.2003

Dear Sir,

We refer to your letter of 14 May 2003 addressed to Mr Aigner.

With regard to your request to use Mr Aigner's name at the top of the letterheads which you intend to print for the movement ARS, please note that UEFA does not give you any permission to do so. In case of infringements, we reserve all our rights to act accordingly.

Thank you for taking note of the above.

Yours sincerely,

U E F A

Markus Studer
Director
Legal Services and Assistance Programmes

Route de Genève 46
CH-1260 Nyon 2
Tel. +41 22 994 44 44
Fax +41 22 994 44 88
uefa.com

Rt. Hon. Geoff Hoon
Secretary of State for Defence
Room 222
Old War Office
Whitehall
London SW1A 2EU
UK

Colonel Ben Trovato
PO Box 1117
Sea Point
8060
Cape Town
South Africa

9 March 2003

Dear Mr Goon,

Some of us out here in the old colony are terribly excited by all this talk of war!
I only wish we lived a little closer to the action. I don't think the Iraqis will
present much of a problem. You chaps are good in the sand. Remember Dunkirk?

But let me get to the point. Last Friday a few of us got together for drinks and
by the end of the evening we had formed a small fighting unit. We wish to put
ourselves at your disposal. My neighbour, Ted, said he heard that if we joined
forces, we would all be given British passports. I said that sounds very unlikely
and it wasn't long before we were rolling about on the floor practising our hand-
to-hand combat techniques. We are not in this for citizenship. There is nothing
wrong with the South African passport. Well, actually there is. But I need not
go into that now. Suffice it to say that we want to be with your boys when they
storm Baghdad.

I am a trained signalman, and while my Morse Code is a little rusty I am still
damn good when it comes to Semaphore. I don't need to remind you that people
like me are vital to the success of any military operation. Ted is the only one of
us who has his own gun, so he will probably do most of the shooting when we
encounter the enemy. Old Gert is the finest mechanic you will find anywhere. He
works mainly on Korean cars like Hyundais, but he says the engine is similar to
that found in a British tank. He also has his own tools.

With our combined skills, you don't really need anyone else to make up an
effective unit.

We have been studying an old Atlas that Ted found in his basement, and we
reckon that to achieve the element of surprise it would be best for us to hug
the east coast of Africa until we reach Somalia. We will take a fast boat from
Djibouti across the Gulf of Aden and make land at Al Mukalla in Yemen. From
there we will move inland and head east through Oman, possibly spending a
night in Muscat to catch our breath. From there, it's a short hop across the Gulf
of Oman and into Iran. Old Gert says he will be able to take us through the
Zagros Mountains to a small town called Bakhtaran. And from there it's just 250
kilometres to Baghdad. Ted feels we should rather make for Basra and take a
dugout up the Euphrates River. I think he has watched one too many Vietnam
movies. The beauty of our plan is its simplicity. Saddam Hussein will not see us
coming, I assure you.

I am enclosing a small cash donation (rands, I'm afraid) to help towards our equipment. All we are waiting for are your instructions. If we do not hear from you, I will take it that you wish to maintain "radio silence". In which case, we shall meet at your offices.

Yours in the struggle for democracy.

....
Colonel Ben Trovato

From: Grant Fettis, Directorate of Reserve Forces and Cadets

MINISTRY OF DEFENCE

Room 715 St Giles Court, London, WC2H 8LD
Email: drfc-sec3@defence.mod.uk

Telephone	(Direct dial)	020 7218 5293
	(Switchboard)	020 7218 9000
	(Fax)	020 7218 5612
	(GTN)	

Colonel Ben Trovato
PO Box 1117
Sea Point
8060
Cape Town
South Africa

Your Reference

Our Reference
D/DRFC/125/1/4
Date
2 April 2003

Dear Colonel Trovato,

Thank you for your letter of 9 March 2003 to Geoff Hoon, the Secretary of State for Defence, where you and your friends offer to invade Iraq via the Zagros Mountains and eliminate Saddam Hussein. I have been asked to reply on his behalf.

As you may be aware from announcements made by the Secretary of State for Defence, members of the Reserves from all three Services are being called-out for permanent service in support operations in the Gulf. As part of the contingency planning for such operations it has been necessary to ensure that all Reserves called-out for permanent service meet minimum training and medical standards. All personnel being considered must be trained soldiers and qualified in the trade or appointment to be held on mobilisation. As you state that you are trained in Morse Code and semaphore, I assume that your military service was some time ago. You cannot, therefore, be considered as suitably trained. In addition, your friends appear to have had no military training at all. We regret, therefore, that none of you can be considered for service in the Gulf.

As we cannot use your services, I am returning the ten Rand note you enclosed towards your military equipment.

I am sorry for what must be a disappointing reply.

Yours sincerely

254

Lord Bach of Lutterworth
Minister for Defence Procurement
Room 222
Old War Office
Whitehall
London SW1A 2EU
UK

Colonel Ben Trovato
PO Box 1117
Sea Point
8060
Cape Town
South Africa

9 March, 2003

Dear Lord,

Gosh, for one brief moment it felt like I was writing a letter to You Know Who!

I will be brief, since I am sure you are run off your feet making sure that your boys have everything they need to whip Saddam Hussein into submission.

Please allow me to apologise for my government's appalling lack of support for a war against Iraq. I cannot imagine what they are thinking. Perhaps Saddam has promised them cheaper fuel. God knows we could do with it.

I am writing to you to find out if you would be interested in a new weapon that I have designed. For obvious reasons I cannot go into explicit detail here, but let me just tell you that I have come up with a device that can fly, bounce and even travel underwater. The beauty is that it can be programmed to explode at any given time. So even if you are unable to get near Baghdad, you could drop the device in neighbouring Kuwait and time it to detonate once it reached the Iraqi capital. It has a self-guiding system which means you could even put it into the Euphrates River at Basra on the Iranian border and be pretty damn sure that it's going to go off when it reaches Baghdad.

I have no doubt that you get all manner of crackpots writing to you with outrageous ideas on how best to destroy Iraq. My advice is to ignore these mercenaries. My credentials are impeccable. Please let me know as soon as possible if you are interested in doing business. I can assure you that my device will kill large numbers of people as painlessly as possible. My neighbour calls it a humanitarian bomb that will one day win me the Nobel Peace Prize.

Time is short so send word soon.

Your brother in arms

....
Colonel Ben Trovato

Connecting Business to Technology

Sir Frank Whittle Building Cody Technology Park
Ively Road Farnborough Hampshire GU14 0LX
f : 01252 392119
e : inventions@dda.gov.uk
www.dda.gov.uk

Colonel Ben Trovato
PO Box 1117
Sea Point
8060
Cape Town
South Africa

Ref D/Inv.U/1/5/01   Wednesday, 30 April 2003

Dear Harry

Thank you for your letter of 9th of March, concerning your new weapon, The Defence Diversification Agency (DDA) has responsibility within the MOD for handling inventions and technical suggestions sent in by members of the public.

The MOD has a set of arrangements under which assessments of such submissions are assessed. These take care to ensure that the interests of all parties are taken into account. I enclose a copy of the latest Arrangements for the Assessment of Inventions and Technical Suggestions by the United Kingdom Ministry of Defence for your information. If you are happy to accept these conditions, please would you fill in the enclosed form and return it to the above address, together with any documentation, as appropriate.

You are of course under no obligation to proceed. Should we not hear back from you, we shall take the matter no further.

Thank you taking the trouble to contact the MOD.

Yours sincerely,

For and on behalf of
MOD Inventions Unit

synnova®
Intellectual Asset Management

The Mysterious Squiggle
Code Technology Park
Ively Road Farnborough
Hampshire GU14 0LX
UK

Colonel Ben Trovato
PO Box 1117
Sea Point
8060
Cape Town
South Africa

2 June, 2003

Dear For and on behalf of MOD Inventions Unit,

Who the hell is Harry?

I remain,

....
Ben Trovato (Mr)

Rt. Hon. Baroness Blackstone
Minister for the Arts
Department for Culture, Media and Sport
2-4 Cockspur Street
London SW1Y 5DH
UK

Mr Ben Trovato
PO Box 1117
Sea Point 8060
Cape Town
South Africa

9 March, 2003

Dear Baroness Blackstone,

As a relative newcomer to the Internet, I frequently find myself in places I had no intention of going to. So when your face popped up I was half-expecting to be asked for my credit card number to see the rest of you. And I mean no offence when I say that I would have happily paid up! Not that I have ever done this kind of thing, of course. It is just that I was absolutely smitten by you. There is something in your eyes, something about your smile, that set my heart racing.

My wife, Brenda, took the cat and left me recently. And while there are times that I miss our bickering and stony silences, I think my quality of life has improved overall. I was planning on having nothing at all to do with the opposite sex for some time. But that was until I saw your picture.

When I told my neighbour that I had developed a crush on a Baroness, he laughed rather rudely and said that a woman of your calibre was way out of my league. He also accused me of merely wanting a title. While I admit that the name Baron Ben Trovato has a splendid ring to it, my feelings have nothing to do with you being a peer of the realm. Those eyes would give me butterflies even if they were in the head of a washerwoman.

Before we pursue this relationship any further, I do need to know one thing. Is there a Baron Blackstone? If he does exist, the last thing I would want to do is come between the two of you. Besides, he is probably a far better shot than me, what with a lifetime of hunting grouses and foxes.

This is probably not a good time for you. I am sure you are busy making arrangements to protect the government's art collection in case Iraq wins the war. Greece learnt a painful lesson when they lost their Marbles. Don't let Saddam take the paintings, whatever happens.

I was unable to find out your first name. For some reason, Tessa comes to mind. Perhaps that can be my pet name for you. Please let me know if you would be interested in seeing a photograph of me. If you are not interested in pursuing this relationship, I urge you not to inform Interpol. I am not a stalker.

Well, Tess. I look forward to hearing from you.

Fondest regards,

....
"Baron" Ben Trovato

Department for Culture, Media and Sport
Baroness Blackstone's Office

2-4 Cockspur Street
London SW1Y 5DH
www.culture.gov.uk

C02/09761/pa

Ben Trovato
PO Box 1117
Sea Point 8060
Cape Town
SOUTH AFRICA

2 5 March 2003

Dear Mr Trovato,

Baroness Blackstone has asked me to thank you for your letter of 9 March.

I attach a photograph of the Minister which I hope you enjoy.

I regret that the Minister is not looking for a husband but would like to send you her very best wishes.

Yours sincerely

DAVID McLAREN
Private Secretary

Mr Derek The Bandit
5fm Music Radio
PO Box 91555
Auckland Park
2006

Mr Ben Trovato
PO Box 1117
Sea Point
8060

11 March, 2003

Dear Mr Bandit,

I have been having an argument with my teenage son, Clive. He thinks you are
the greatest DJ that has ever lived. To be honest, this accolade means little to
me. In my day, disc jockeys did nothing more than play records so that we could
dance and smash the place up. They had the equipment and the LPs and we
didn't. Once a disc jockey refused to play some of our old favourites, like Nelson
the Seagull and Who Killed Bambi?

Well, Big Bob went up to him and threatened to break his legs unless he played
exactly what we told him to play. Does this ever happen to you? Probably not.
Youngsters these days take drugs that make them want to hug and kiss anything
that isn't bolted to the floor. I still maintain that there is nothing wrong with
good old-fashioned alcohol. It gets your blood flowing. Sometimes it even gets
other people's blood flowing. But it is that kind of thing that makes a great night
out.

But back to the argument I was having with Clive. He has just turned 14 and
keeps nagging me to buy your compilation. My point to him is that you are not a
musician and the music that you have compiled is not yours. The ungrateful little
bastard says I don't know what I am talking about.

To be honest, Derek, and I haven't brought this up with Clive, I am more
concerned about your sexual orientation than your lack of musical abilities. I am
sure you are aware that these days the word "bandit" has certain connotations.
In my day, if you called someone a "bandit" it would mean that he or she
was a brigand, a desperado, a rogue, a ruffian or a Rolex seller from Durban
beachfront. However, times have changed. And I am sorry to say that your nom
de plume suggests that you are, in fact, a "Bottie Bandit". Don't get me wrong. I
am as liberal as the next man. I don't hate homosexuals. None of my best friends
are gay. But that doesn't mean I don't embrace diversity. So long as it doesn't
try to embrace me first, and certainly not when my back is turned. It's just that
Clive is confused enough as it is. He was wearing skirts until a few months ago.
Now that I have taught him to hunt and fish, I don't want him to start idolising
men who cannot appreciate the worth of a woman's body. It's nothing personal, I
assure you. I just want him to grow up with the right values.

However, I may have misinterpreted the entire affair. If you adopted the
nickname to imply that you are a freebooting buccaneer with no regard for
convention, please accept my apologies. But if you are queer, I think you need
to come out and say so. The last thing the world needs is more degenerates
clogging up the closet. Especially now, with war looming. We all need to be on
top of our game.

Poofters are notoriously unreliable when it comes to taking up arms and defending their countries. A bitch slap is not going to save democracy from falling to the barbarians.

Given this country's liberal constitution, you may feel that I am infringing upon your civil rights when I ask you to reveal your sexual preferences in order that I make an informed choice when it comes to purchasing music for Clive. I hope you do not feel this way.

Thank you for your understanding.

I look forward to hearing from you in the near future.

Yours truly,

....
Ben Trovato (Mr)

Mr Derek The Bandit
5fm Music Radio
PO Box 91555
Auckland Park
2006

Mr Ben Trovato
PO Box 1117
Sea Point
8060

14 May, 2003

Dear Mr Bandit,

I wrote to you on the 11th of March but have not yet had a reply. I am sure you are kept very busy playing all those records, but that is no excuse. After all, we are the people who pay your salary.

If you recall, I was enquiring about the origins of your name. My son, Clive, and I have a serious difference of opinion as to why you call yourself The Bandit. My wife, Brenda, says your sexual orientation is your own business. But I feel that if you set yourself up as a role model for the youth, there is a certain amount of responsibility that goes with it. For the sake of domestic harmony, please could you shed a little light on this issue?

Thank you.

Yours truly,

....
Ben Trovato (Mr)

SOUNDREPUBLIC

"IT's WHAT WEEKENDS WERE MADE FOR"

SOUND REPUBLIC CC
CK99/37253/23
VAT NO: 4610184303

POSTNET SUITE # 220
PRIVATE BAG X 11
CRAIGHALL
REPUBLIC OF SOUTH AFRICA
2024
TELFAX: (011) 3264043
E-MAIL: info@soundrepublic.co.za

DATE: 5 June 2003

Dear Mr Ben Trovato

Thank you for your letters.

Please find enclosed 2 copies of my cd's for your son Clive.

My radio name Bandit comes from when I was at school. I lived in Boksburg and was nicknamed
The Boksburg Bandit, for obvious reasons I dropped the Boksburg part.

As for my sexual persuasion I see no reason to come out of the closet, as I am not gay!

I hope Clive enjoys the CD's!

Kind Regards
Derek Richardson

The Headmistress
Springfield Convent Senior School
St John's Road
Wynberg
7800

Mr Ben Trovato
PO Box 1117
Sea Point
8060

23 April, 2003

Dear Madam,

I have not seen the advertisement myself, but my neighbour tells me that your fine school is looking for a biology teacher. Well, look no further. I am your man.

To be honest, I would prefer to teach the older girls. I have found that lasses in their late teens are far more open when it comes to discussing the finer points of what goes where and why. Although I have a very good grasp of women's bodies, I often bring my wife, Brenda, along to classes to help illustrate a point.

Being a Catholic school, I will naturally eliminate the subject of birth control from my course notes. By the time I have finished with the girls, they will know precisely when it is safe to copulate without conceiving simply by looking at the moon.

During the fourth term I prefer to focus almost exclusively on the biology of the male. I think this is especially important for the matric students since they are poised to cross that sweeping divide that separates the girls from the women. I have known schools where the girls stampeded across that divide the moment they discovered the effect mascara and lipstick had on the local lads. However, I am sure that your girls are well-behaved and not at all like the sluts I have had the misfortune to teach in the past. I have no doubt that the older students at Springfield Convent need to be equipped with knowledge enabling them to unlock the secrets of the male body. Most marriages fail because women do not understand the biological makeup of men. This is my area of specialisation and I can assure you that once I have finished with your girls, they will go on to experience healthy, satisfying relationships with men of all race, creed and colour.

I am sure that you will receive several applications for the post, so I am enclosing a small cash donation to ensure that my name is slipped to the top of the list. There is more where this comes from.

If I do not hear from you by early May, I will assume that my application has been successful and I shall report for duty on the 1st of June, 2003.

Looking forward to teaching the girls a lesson they will never forget!

Yours truly,

....
Ben Trovato (Mr)

CA$H GIVEN
R10

SPRINGFIELD CONVENT SCHOOL

St John's Road Wynberg 7800

Tel: Senior School 797-6169 Junior School 797-9637 Bursar 797-5459
Fax: Senior School 762-7930 Junior School 797-8200 Bursar 797-8776

May 23, 2003

Mr Ben Trovato
P O Box 1117
SEA POINT
8060

Dear Mr Trovato

Re SENIOR BIOLOGY / SCIENCE / MATHEMATICS POST

I hereby acknowledge receipt of your application for the above position which has now been
suitably filled.   I therefore wish to advise that your application has not been successful.

Yours sincerely

M A BRUCE (Mrs)
Principal

The Headmaster
SACS Junior School
Private Bag
Newlands
7725

Mr Ben Trovato
PO Box 1117
Sea Point
8060

1 June, 2003

Dear Sir,

My neighbour tells me that you have a vacancy for a Grade 1 teacher. Well, look no further. I am your man. To be honest, and I have always felt it wise to tell the truth to academics like yourself, I do not possess a string of qualifications in the field of teaching. But I am sure you will agree that one need not have attended Harvard in order to impart a little knowledge to a room full of six-year-olds.

I have always found that children work best when they are not called upon to concentrate on too many things at once. This is why I intend breaking the year down into three segments. In the first, I intend focusing on sex. Some may think that Grade 1 pupils are too young to learn about such things. I disagree. The six-year-olds of today are way ahead of their years and evolution is proceeding at such a pace that most of them will begin dating before they reach double figures. It is vital that they are told the truth. They must know that the human body is not some beautiful temple as the Buddhists would have us believe. It is a tangled knot of blood-soaked organs, a breeding ground for disease. Children must be told that sex is not a beautiful experience to be shared between married couples as the Christians would have us believe. It is a sweaty, messy affair that can lead to death or, at best, another mouth to feed. As an educated man, I am sure you will agree with me when I say it is never too early to get the message across.

In the second segment, I intend focusing on drugs. Statistics show that narcotics will play an important role in the life of every third child. And they have to learn that not all drugs are harmful and not all addicts are unreconstructed demons as the police would have us believe. I will teach my pupils the difference between good and bad drugs, and they will learn when to choose between moderation and excess. The mathematics component of this segment entails the pupils learning about the economics of supply and demand.

And in the final segment, my charges will be instructed in the art of self-defence. Together with sex and drugs, this forms the third pillar of wisdom around which the children can build their lives. As a person who believes in the inalienable right to bear arms, I will be teaching them that gun control means gripping the butt with both hands. And, like the school motto, I will urge them to aim high.

I am enclosing a small donation which should go some way towards slipping my name on to the shortlist. If I do not hear from you, I will assume that everything is in order and I shall report for duty on 1st August.

Yours truly,

....
Ben Trovato (Mr)

266

NEWLANDS
21 July 2003

Dear Sir

Thank you for your letter of application and kind donation.
Unfortunately you did not pass. Educators are not allowed to use the
word "fail' anymore. Incidentally you used the word "teacher" in your
application. Again, within the new O.B.E. system, we call teachers
"educators", and pupils are now known as "learners". Teachers no
longer teach, educators rather facilitate – if you know what I mean.

The reason for the delay in contacting you is that there was a string of
applications for the position. We definitely did consider you although I
was a bit concerned whether you would fit in to our leafy suburb, coming
from Sea Point. I mean that environmentally of course.

Your thinking on sex, drugs and self-defence for six-year-olds was
intriguing. I do have the greatest empathy for you in this regard.
Living in such a varied society must play havoc on the mind. All I can
say is, "Three cheers for shrinks"!

An aside, in my first term of teaching, I was approached by a good-
looking mother, and asked "Do I like Secs?"

I do, however, agree whole-heartedly with you on your ideas about
teaching self-defence at schools. It surely would lead in the years to
come, to more gutsy performances from our lily-livered Springboks!

To prove that we are law-abiding citizens at the S.A. College, I return
your donation. Please notice that the serial number on the note is
exactly the same one on the note that you sent me. As we always say,
"Honesty is the best policy."

Yours in Outcomes Based Education.

S. ANDERSON

The Ambassador
The Norwegian Embassy
PO Box 11612
Hatfield
0028

Mr Ben Trovato
PO Box 1117
Sea Point
8060

25 May, 2003

Dear Ambassador,

I was hoping that you could clear something up for me. My wife and I are planning a trip to Oslo in July. However, we are having second thoughts after learning that al-Qaeda has put Norway on its hit-list. This is not good news.

We were under the impression that Norway was one of the safest places left on earth. What have you done to the Muslims? I know that the bunny-huggers don't like you because you people kill whales. But while I am prepared to push my way through a bunch of bearded Greenpeace types wielding placards, suicide bombers are quite another matter altogether.

My neighbour tells me he read somewhere that a man on Danish television said al-Qaeda must have threatened Norway by mistake, and that he really meant Denmark. Is this true? That would be very magnanimous of the Danes, to say the least. Has al-Qaeda apologised for getting the two of you mixed up?

Please let me know if you think al-Qaeda's threat is simply a geographical error. I would not want to change my travel plans and arrive in Stockholm only to find that the terrorists had actually meant Sweden.

Thank you

....
Ben Trovato (Mr)

ROYAL NORWEGIAN EMBASSY
PRETORIA

Our Date	Our Reference
30.05.03	
Your Date	Your Reference

Mr. Ben Trovato
P.O. Box 1117
Sea Point
8060

Dear Mr. Trovato,

I have received your letter of 25 May concerning the question of safety in Norway.

Despite our Viking roots, the Norwegians have always considered themselves peaceful and their country safe. Participation in various peace processes, including the Middle East, does not only produce friends and admirers, however. We must also accept that Norway, despite its geographical position, is part of the world community and like any other countries threatened by international terrorism.

The threat made by al-Qaeda seems to be real and has been taken seriously by the Norwegian authorities. The fact that Norway, together with the US, United Kingdom and Australia has been named as possible targets for terrorist attacks has confused many Norwegians, who believe this is a geographical error or a question of mistaken national identity.

I can assure you that the authorities in Norway are taking the necessary steps to ensure that acts of terrorism does not take place in Norway or that international terrorists are allowed to enter the country. I am personally going to Norway in Mid-June and does not consider the threat of terrorism warranting the visit to be postponed. I therefore hope that both you and your wife will have a nice stay in Norway.

Regards

Jon Bech
Ambassador

Postal Address:	Office Address:	Telephone:	Telefax:	Email / WEB:
P.O.Box 11612	iParioli Building A2	+27 12 342 6100	+27 12 342 6099	embpta@noramb.co.za
Hatfield 0028	1166 Park Street			
SOUTH AFRICA	Hatfield 0083			www.pretoria.mfa.no

Ms Ingrid Newkirk
President: People for the Ethical Treatment
of Animals (Peta)
501 Front Street
Norfolk, VA 23510
USA

Mr Ben Trovato
PO Box 1117
Sea Point 8060
Cape Town
South Africa

28 April, 2003

Dear Ms Newkirk,

My wife and I were overjoyed to hear that you had drawn up a will directing that your flesh be barbecued and your skin used to make handbags and shoes. This is one protest that is unlikely to go unnoticed by those who insist on terrorising our friends who cannot speak for themselves.

Brenda and I feel very strongly about cruelty to any of God's creatures, even people. Out here in Africa we have leaders who struggle to differentiate between humans and animals when new policies are drawn up. To them, there is very little difference between a canned lion hunt and a crippled old lady standing in the blazing sun for eight hours to get her pittance of a pension.

I, too, am rewriting my will. When I die, I want my head to go to your organisation. Please have it stuffed and mounted like so many of the zebra and kudu heads that adorn the walls of hunting lodges and homes around this country. What you do with the trophy after that is your business, but I am sure you will put it to good use in the campaign to stop the slaughter. My teeth and bones should be carved into trinkets and curios.

Brenda would also like to donate her feet to be turned into umbrella stands. While she doesn't quite match up to an elephant, she certainly has enough around the ankles to make a point. I suggested that she allows her liver to be turned into foie gras but it turns out that she's not as brave as you are. Nobody would want my liver, believe me.

I will also be donating my testicles to your organisation. It should be made clear that these are destined for the Japanese aphrodisiac market. I have no idea how I compare to a bull seal, but hopefully they will be sufficient to make some sort of impression.

I am enclosing a small cash donation to help with administrative costs. I would appreciate it if you could acknowledge this letter. Please let us know what else we can do to protest the ill treatment of animals.

Yours truly,

....
Ben Trovato (Mr)

CASH GIVEN
R10

PEMA

**PEOPLE FOR THE ETHICAL
TREATMENT OF ANIMALS**

501 FRONT STREET
NORFOLK, VA 23510
TEL 757-622-PETA
FAX 757-622-0457

www.peta-online.org
info@peta-online.org

May 23, 2003

Ben and Brenda Trovato
PO Box 1117
Sea Point 8060
Cape Town
South Africa

Dear Mr. and Mrs. Trovato,

Thank you very much for your donation and for supporting animal rights. We are thrilled to hear that you are looking for more ways to get involved.

I'm enclosing some information about ways to get active helping animals where you are. Also included are our vegetarian starter kit and the current issue of PETA's *Animal Times*. We look forward to hearing of your successes!

Thanks again for your support and for your compassion for animals.

Sincerely,

Jennifer Venegas
Correspondent

The Managing Director
Irvin & Johnson
PO Box 1628
Cape Town
8000

Mr Ben Trovato
PO Box 1117
Sea Point
8060

9 May, 2003

Dear Sir,

You are undoubtedly aware of a recent study by the Roslin Institute proving that fish do, in fact, feel pain. As South Africa's biggest producer of fish products, I would like to know if you plan on continuing the carnage now that the secret is out. Surely there has been enough suffering already?

For years we have been happily eating fish on the assumption that they feel nothing at all when they have their tails hacked off and their guts ripped out. Now, I cannot walk past the fish section in my local supermarket without seeing their little lips frozen in a silent scream.

The study showed that the rainbow trout has 58 nociceptors, or nerve receptors, on its head. As you know all too well, it is the head that is first to go. Fishermen are notorious for bludgeoning their catches around the occipital region. Does I&J subscribe to the bludgeoning method or do you use other means to kill your fish?

It is people like you who have perpetuated the myth that fish feel no pain. You, sir, are no better than the cigarette manufacturers who claim to be unaware that smoking is harmful to your health. Shame on you.

Many of my friends have placed a moratorium on eating fish until you tell us where you stand on this issue. Let us hear from you soon.

Fish have feelings, too!

....
Ben Trovato (Mr)

A MEMBER OF THE ANGLOVAAL INDUSTRIES GROUP

IRVIN & JOHNSON LIMITED
Reg. No. 1952/001693/06

RCG\JUN03\BEN TROVATO
12 June 2003

Mr Ben Trovato
P O Box 1117
SEA POINT
8060

Dear Mr Trovato

We thank you for your letter and your shared concern with I&J about the welfare of our finned friends.

Rest assured we are fully familiar with the latest research and have done everything possible to reduce the suffering of the fish, whom we consider to be partners in our business. This partnership is one of shared responsibilities, where the I&J staff are involved and the fish are committed.

We are aware that fish feel pain and have alleviated their suffering as far as is practical. We do not bludgeon the fish, but instead allow them to expire gently via asphyxiation. This is similar to gently falling asleep. The fish are left out of water on the deck of our vessels, lying in the sunlight where their last moments can be spent in calm reflection as they drift away.

Even after death the fish are treated with due respect by being laid gently on a bed of ice and carefully lowered into the hold of the vessel.

We hope this knowledge will allow you and your friends to again enjoy a healthy, guilt-free meal of fish.

Yours in fond memory of Henry Root,

Tony Gordon

The Managing Director
British Airways
PO Box 5619
Sudbury
Suffolk CO10 2PG
UK

Mr Ben Trovato
PO Box 1117
Sea Point 8060
Cape Town
South Africa

24 May, 2003

Dear Sir,

Actually, given recent developments at your airline, it is more likely that you are a Madam.

I have been a regular passenger on British Airways for as long as I can remember. The only complaint I ever lodged was in 1974 when a stewardess high on drugs tried to grope me in the kitchen area. In retrospect, complaining was the wrong thing to do. I am older and wiser now, but, sadly, there have been no more groping incidents.

My complaint this time is of a far more serious nature. It concerns a British Airways Boeing 737-200 which took off from Johannesburg recently. Let me point out that I was not on the flight. But other people were, and my concern is for their wellbeing.

British Airways has been operating for 56 years in Africa. A proud record tarnished by that fateful flight from Johannesburg. Why? Because for the first time in 56 years, a BA flight took off with an all-female crew. Yes, you heard correctly. Not a man to be seen on the flight deck. To make matters worse, the first officer was a mere slip of a girl. Anyone in their right mind knows that 25-year-old girls cannot even remember to take their birth control pills let alone remember all the complexities of keeping a jet liner in the air. Their brains are still unformed and they are good for little more than experimenting with hard liquor and lesbian sex. What on earth gives you people the idea that these youngsters can be trusted with a couple of hundred lives? Have you seen how girls this age drive? Most of them have just got their first car and God knows it shows on the road. At least the pilot was a bit older at 36, but there must have still been a fair bit of swerving about in the air. I cannot even imagine what the landing must have been like.

At least BA had the good sense to try this experiment on the Johannesburg to Lusaka route. In the event of a terrible accident, which would no doubt be caused by the pilot checking her lipstick instead of the rearview mirror, the odds are that there would have been nobody of any real importance on board. Zambia is the unwashed foot of Southern Africa, and its capital, Lusaka, is an athlete's foot infection. BA clearly understood that the passengers on that flight were expendable. At least you have some foresight left.

I anxiously await your assurance that BA does not intend stocking all its planes with giggling fillies.

Yours truly,

Ben Trovato (Mr)

Customer Relations
PO Box 5619 (S506)
Sudbury Suffolk CO10 2PG UK
Tel 0845 779 9977 (UK Local Call Rate) +44 (0)191 490 7901
Fax +44 (0)20 8759 4314

29 May 2003

Mr Ben Trovato
P.o Box 1117
Sea Point
Cape Town
8060
SOUTH AFRICA

Our Ref: 001725713
Your Ref:

Dear Mr Trovato

Thank you for your letter. At the moment we have quite a high volume of customer feedback, but please be assured we will respond as soon as we can.

Yours sincerely

Mrs Bhupinder Chummer
Administrative Assistant

British Airways Plc
Registered Office: Waterside PO Box 365 Harmondsworth UB7 0GB
Registered in England No. 1777777

www.britishairways.com

BA15027-1st

one world member

The Chairman
Pharmaceutical Society of South Africa
PO Box 375
Cape Town
8000

Mr Ben Trovato
PO Box 1117
Sea Point
8060

15 May, 2003

Dear Sir,

My neighbour tells me that a new law has been passed making it possible for ordinary people to open up pharmacies. This is great news as I have always been interested in the drug trade. However, I need some information and I was hoping you could help me.

I am sure you will agree that location is everything. Do you have any suggestions regarding a good place for me to set up shop? Like anyone who runs a pharmacy, my plan is to get very rich as quickly as possible. As you probably know, there is a huge market for pharmaceutical products on the Cape Flats. But there is also the risk of being robbed by armed bandits every day. Camps Bay is also a possibility since the suburb is full of women for whom money is no object when it comes to investing in products designed to make them look younger. My wife will deal with this side of the business, since I am more familiar with the Schedule 5 substances listed with the International Psychotropic Convention.

I expect that your organisation is able to offer a substantial discount on stock, so I am enclosing ten rand towards my membership fee.

Once I receive confirmation that we are in business, I shall forward you a detailed list of my requirements. In the meantime, I hope you will give some thought to where I should open up my new store.

Looking forward to hearing from you soon.

Yours truly,

....
Ben Trovato (Mr)

CA$H GIVEN
R10

The Chairman
Pharmaceutical Society of South Africa
PO Box 375
Cape Town
8000

Mr Ben Trovato
PO Box 1117
Sea Point
8060

14 June, 2003

Dear Sir,

I am a little disappointed that you have chosen to ignore me.

If you recall, I wrote to you on the 15th of May requesting advice on setting up my pharmacy. As you know, the government has now made it possible for ordinary people to open up drug stores.

I find your decision not to reply to my letter even more disconcerting given the fact that I enclosed R10 towards my membership of the PSSA.

Please let me know if you are waiting for more money before responding. I shall send it forthwith. It is important that we remain on good terms.

Yours truly,

....
Ben Trovato (Mr)

Aptekersvereniging van Suid-Afrika
· Nasionale Kantoor ·

Vir die gesondheid en welvaart van die mense

Pharmaceutical Society of South Africa
· National Office ·

For the health and welfare of the people

23/06/2003

Director General
Department of Health
Private Bag X399
PRETORIA
0001

Attention: Dr H Zokufa

Dear Dr Zokufa

APPLICATION FOR A PHARMACY LICENCE

Attached please find a letter received from a Mr Ben Trovato requesting assistance in order to establish a pharmacy.

We initially thought that this was a joke but a follow-up letter, also attached, indicates that this person is serious.

We will return his R10-00 as well as a copy of this letter, as we do not intend to further communicate with Mr Trovato.

Your attention to this matter will be appreciated.

Yours faithfully

I Kotzé
EXECUTIVE DIRECTOR

P O Box 26039, Arcadia, 0007 - Pharmacy House, 6 de Veer Lane, Arcadia - Tel: +27 (012) 301-0820,
Fax: +27 (012) 301-0828 (Admin), +27 (012) 301-0836 (Professional), Website: www.pharmnet.co.za; E-mail: pssa@pharmail.co.za
Posbus 26039, Arcadia, 0007 - Farmasiehuis, De Veersteeg 6, Arcadia - Tel: +27 (012) 301-0820,

Mr I Kotzé
Executive Director
Pharmaceutical Association of South Africa
PO Box 26039
Arcadia
0007

Mr Ben Trovato
PO Box 1117
Sea Point
8060

27 June, 2003

Dear Mr Kotzé,

I received your letter addressed to Dr Zokufa which referred to me in the third person, and quite frankly it scared me.

Why have you reported me to the government?

All I ever wanted to do was sell drugs legally. But quite frankly, you have put me off the idea altogether. Whatever happened to the free market system? Are you a Communist sympathiser? May I remind you that this country is run by President Thabo Mbeki and not Daniel Noriega. This is not Uruguay, for heaven's sake!

I find it ironic that your association's motto reads: "For the health and welfare of the people." I am a people, too. And yet you show scant regard for my personal wellbeing. Knowing that the mysterious Dr Zokufa and his posse are on my tail has had a terrible effect on my health. I am writing this from a secret location where I live in constant fear of a visit from jackbooted thugs wearing the insignia of the Department of Health. You have set in motion a chain of events that will inevitably end in my demise. Your people have access to drugs and I don't. This is not fair. I barely have access to food.

I beg you, call off the dogs and you will never hear from me again.

I no longer want a pharmacy licence. All I want is to be left alone to grow my vegetables in peace.

Thank you for returning my money, but I am sending it back to you because my neighbour warned me that you have probably impregnated it with a microtransmitter that will give my position away. Please do not send the money back to me. Perhaps you could keep it in trust. I will need it for a phone call when the stormtroopers finally run me down and take me in on charges of being serious in the first degree.

May Gob be with you.

....
Ben Trovato (Mr)

The Director
Cape Mental Health Society
22 Ivy Street
Observatory
7935

Mr Ben Trovato
PO Box 1117
Sea Point
8060

27 June, 2003

Dear Sir I hope I am not being presumptuous in assuming that you are a Sir because if it turns out that you are in fact a Madam and not a Sir then please accept my apologies I do not mean to discriminate God knows I have my faults but judging a person by their gender is not one of them my neighbour is a sexist not me I only talk to him because he is the only real friend I have my wife Brenda used to be my friend but now she has become a bit of a sexist herself that's probably the wrong word to use because when a woman becomes a sexist she is often labelled a lesbian but I know that is wrong because some women simply want to be respected and have car doors opened for them but not my Brenda because when I tried to open the door for her the other day she slammed my fingers in it and then started to apologise but while I was bent over with pain I looked up and saw that she was busy with one of those cruel silent sniggers which doesn't make her a lesbian at all but I think it does suggest that she is becoming one of these New Women who want men to share power with them when what they really want is all the power for themselves which I am sure you will have experienced yourself if you are a Sir but even if you are a Madam I am sure you are not one of those who make a habit of deceiving men into thinking that they are trying to help a formerly disadvantaged group when all along they are being used as unwitting pawns in a secret operation that will eventually topple men from all positions of power in governments and corporations around the world and don't for one minute think that the women who work in these governments and corporations are going to be handed the reigns because they won't because these positions are reserved for the agents of Operation Bridal Council which you might not think exists but believe me it does and we need to warn as many men as possible before it is too late which it might already be but if we give up now then we might as well start growing our nails because they will be the only weapons left for us to defend ourselves let alone our country's borders which will no longer even be our responsibility anyway because the face of global terrorism as we know it will quickly come to an end and be replaced by something far more frightening I am not exactly sure what it is yet but I have a mole who is feeding me information although she refuses to meet me or even tell me what her name is which is understandable because you can imagine what would happen to an operative who confides in the enemy especially at this critical stage of the mission and in case you have forgotten the enemy is us the men and again I hasten to say that if you are not a man then I am sure you are one of us anyway because no woman who lusts for complete domination over others would choose to work with mad people so I am sending you some money as a deposit on a room because when they come for us I want to be among folk I can trust thank you and if you are a Sir keep strong and watch your back because they are a duplicitous people who will not hestitate to take away your power when you are at your weakest yours truly Ben Trovato

280

06 June 2003

Mr Ben Trovato
PO Box 1117
Sea Point
8060

Dear Mr Trovato

Your letter dated 21 May 2003 refers.

Thank you for the trust you have in our organisation. We have no rooms for the purpose required and as a result I am unable to accept your generous deposit. I have therefore returned the R10.00 that you have sent to us.

I would like to recommend that you make an appointment with our intake social worker, Rabia Canfield to discuss some of the feelings and concerns expressed in the letter. The telephone number is listed below.

Wishing you all of the best.

Yours sincerely

Ingrid Daniels
Director

Cape Mental Health Society Reg No 003-264 NPO Private Bag X7 Observatory 7935 22 Ivy Street Observatory 7925
Tel 021 447 9040 Fax 021 448 8475 Email info@cmhs.co.za Website www.capementalhealth.co.za

MEMBER OF COMMUNITY CHEST • CONSTITUENT BODY OF THE S.A. FEDERATION FOR MENTAL HEALTH

The Director   Mr Ben Trovato
Valkenberg Mental Hospital   PO Box 1117
PO Box 61   Sea Point
Observatory   8060
7935

                                                  21 May, 2003

Dear Sir,

I urgently need to know how I go about having my wife committed. When I
married her, she struck me as being a little batty, but in a rather delightful way.
Today, however, she is barking mad. There is nothing at all delightful about being
chased around the house by an angry naked woman well past her prime.

Brenda's refusal to clean the house or fulfil her other connubial responsibilities
are further signs that her brain is diseased. Naturally I do not want her
incarcerated for life. That would be cruel. But I do think that a year or so of
electroconvulsive therapy would do wonders for her attitude.

To be honest, I am a little concerned that shock treatment might not have the
desired effect. She is a hardheaded woman and it would not surprise me if a
powerful electrical current were unable to penetrate her cranium. I do not want
her returned to me in the same damaged condition. If all else fails, I would be
interested in Brenda being fitted with the brain of a fresh young thing instilled
with an education and a sense of duty. Given the fact that those Satanists at
the "Embryo Centre" in Brits are cloning all manner of cloven-hoofed beasts, I
expect that you chaps are sufficiently advanced to perform a transplant of this
nature. I must emphasise that I do not want an old brain that cannot be taught
new tricks. At risk of stating the obvious, I would expect you to find me a brain
that has the capacity to grasp concepts like "cooking", "laundry" and "sex".
Brenda's brain is sadly lacking in these departments.

If I do not hear from you by the first week of June, I will assume that everything
is in order for me to deliver my wife into your care. I had Uncle Rodney's old
straitjacket lying in the attic for years, but I think Brenda threw it out. She must
have subconsciously known that this day would arrive. Would you advise that
I fashion something out of my sports coat? Brenda is likely to resist violently.
Please let me know what weapons you use on your patients when they lose
control. If it is something simple like mace or a cattle prod, I could probably
pick it up from my local hardware.

Money is no object. I am enclosing a small deposit towards the treatment.
Obviously there is much more where this comes from.

Please respond soon. The situation is becoming desperate.

Yours truly,

Ben Trovato (Mr)

The Director
Valkenberg Mental Hospital
PO Box 61
Observatory
7935

Mr Ben Trovato
PO Box 1117
Sea Point
8060

14 June, 2003

Dear Sir,
Is it the institution's policy to ignore people desperately in need of advice? If so, you are well on track.

I wrote to you on the 21st of May enquiring about the possibility of having my wife committed.

Even worse than your silence is your avaricious retention of the R10 deposit I sent you towards my wife's treatment.

The way I see it, you have two choices. Either you give me advice or you give my money back. There is a third alternative, but it is too horrible to contemplate.

Yours truly,

....
Ben Trovato (Mr)

Reference:

Enquiries: Dr B. Eick

Telephone: (021) 4403-260

Facsimile:

Email:

Date: 18 June 2003

PROVINCIAL ADMINISTRATION: WESTERN CAPE
Department of Health

PROVINSIALE ADMINISTRASIE: WES-KAAP
Departement van Gesondheid

ULAWULO LWEPHONDO: INTSHONA KOLONI
Isebe LezeMpilo

Mr Ben Trovato
P.O.Box 1117
Sea Point
8060

Dear Sir

Receipt of you letter dated 14 June 2003 is herewith acknowledged.

Please accept our apologies for not replying to your first letter, but seemingly we do not have any record of such.

If your wife requires any kind of medical assistance she should be seen by her GP, or a Medical Officer at the Community Health Centre, who would in turn refer her to the appropriate Specialist if so required.

In general terms according to the new Mental Health Act 2 (two) Mental Health Care practitioners are required for certifications.

Kind regards

SENIOR MEDICAL SUPERINTENDENT

VALKENBERG HOSPITAL
PRIVATE BAG X1
OBSERVATORY, 7935
TEL: 021 – 440 3111
FAX: 021 – 447 6041

Mr Brian Loyd
Manager: Parks & Bathing Amenities
Services
PO Box 1694
Cape Town
8000

Mr Ben Trovato
PO Box 1117
Sea Point
8060

18 May, 2003

Dear Mr Loyd,

I read in the paper that the City Council is soliciting objections to its plans to demolish the wall surrounding Graaff's Pool in Sea Point. Well, I object. Strongly.

You cite "safety and security" as your reasons for wanting to tear down a perfectly good wall that affords us a modicum of privacy. I can assure you, Mr Loyd, that those of us who pursue an alternative lifestyle pose no threat whatsoever to the safety and security of you and your kind. What is it with you breeders that you feel so threatened by us?

Graaff's Pool holds many special memories for me. I met my first love there while skinny-dipping in the sea. He was a young Korean sailor covered in tattoos. Even his you-know-what had a snake coiled around it. I won't mention his name because you will probably alert Interpol and have him assassinated.

I agree that a lower class of pederast has begun frequenting the pool in recent months. However, this simply reflects the evolution of the culture. Besides, they add a little colour to the environment and make a refreshing change from the usual boring Jewish accountants and furtive Catholic priests.

I advise you not to attempt to bring in the bulldozers before you have provided us with an alternative place of recreation. There are enough of us who are prepared to lay down our lives in the defence of our darling pool. I am sure the mayor does not want a West Bank situation developing on his doorstep.

Apart from that delightful lesbian who runs the tourism show, this city is dominated by wall-breakers and gay-bashers. Graaff's Pool is our Berlin Wall. We do not want to end up like the East Germans.

I await your assurance that the white-collar homophobes will not win this battle.

Yours truly,

....
Ben Trovato (Mr)

PS. I am enclosing R10 to help swing the decision our way. There is more where this comes from.

Community Services	liNkonzo zoLuntu	Gemeenskapsdienste
Civic Centre	Iziko loLuntu	Burgersentrum
12 Hertzog Boulevard	12 Hertzog Boulevard	Hertzog-boulevard 12
P O Box 1694, Cape Town 8000	P O Box 1694, Cape Town 8000	Posbus 1694, Kaapstad, 8000
Ask For : Mr Lloyd	Cela: Mr Lloyd	Vra vir: Mnr Lloyd
Tel : 400-3829	Umnxeba: 400-3829	Tel: 400-3829
Fax: + 21 425-2685	Umnxeba: +21 425-2685	Fax: +21 425-2685
E-Mail: Blloyd@cct.org.za	l-E-mail: Blloyd@cct.org.za	E-pos: Blloyd@cct.org.za

CITY OF CAPE TOWN
ISIXEKO SASEKAPA
STAD KAAPSTAD

File Ref No: PB 37/2/2/1/3/12

COMMUNITY DEVELOPMENT

2003.05.27

BEN TROVATO
P.O BOX 1117
SEA POINT

8060

Dear Sir / Madam

DEMOLISHING OF THE WALL AROUND GRAAFF'S POOL

Receipt is hereby acknowledged of your correspondence dated 2003.05.18

The correspondence has been registered as Letter No. 1713 and the contents thereof have
been brought to the attention of the relevant officials for the necessary investigation and / or action.

You can expect a further response from our offices in due course.

Yours faithfully

B. Lloyd.

for ACTING MANAGER
PARKS AND BATHING AMENITIES SERVICES
for CITY MANAGER

* P.S.
Your R10 note returned
ferewith.

B. Lloyd.

Cape Town - the City that works for all

CASH RETURNED

Mr Mabela Satekge
Head: Procurement Dept.
Cape Town Unicity
Private Bag X9181
Cape Town
8000

Mr Ben Trovato
PO Box 1117
Sea Point
8060

25 May, 2003

Dear Mr Satekge,

I wish I had been at GrandWest Casino to hear you speak at the black empowerment conference the other day. By all accounts, you were magnificent. I would have been on my chair applauding when you called on the government to urgently review the definition of historically disadvantaged individuals to exclude white women. Congratulations!

I am married to a white woman and you are so right. These people have had it their own way for far too long. White women get away with murder. Literally, in some cases.

I have come to the conclusion that white women are basically evil. You will not come across a more malcontent, duplicitous bunch of muttering grumps. In fact, getting them struck off a list of people who deserve preferential treatment is not going far enough. If I were in your shoes, I would recommend that every palefaced wench between the ages of 18 and 50 be placed under house arrest. That way they can raise the children, clean the house, cook the dinner and minister to the needs of their hardworking men without wreaking havoc on the roads and sitting at the bar making it impossible for us to order a drink. Please don't misunderstand me. I am neither a sexist nor a misogynist. All I want to do is prevent these white devils from destroying our way of life. I cannot imagine what Finance Minister Trevor Manuel was thinking when he came up with a preferential procurement policy that identified historically disadvantaged individuals as women, the disabled and those who could not vote before 1994. It would not surprise me in the least to hear that Mr Manuel is married to a white woman. What other explanation can there be for this appalling oversight? Granted, there is no ambiguity when it comes to blacks and cripples. But Mr Manuel, of all people, should have known that you cannot simply lump all women into the category of "Women". The very genus itself can be divided and sub-divided into a plethora of classifications. They must be grouped according to class, size, type and name. They must be codified and assigned. Calling them all "women" and leaving it at that has caused a huge amount of trouble. My wife, Brenda, continues to make enormous capital out of being "historically disadvantaged". And while she is busy "rectifying the iniquities of the past", is Mr Manuel going to cook my dinner? Is Mr Manuel going to do my laundry? Is Mr Manuel going to get down on his knees and ... actually, scrap that one.

Mr Satekge, I am enclosing a small donation towards your campaign to get white women declared persona non grata. I wish you the best of luck.

Yours truly,

....
Ben Trovato (Mr).

CA$H GIVEN R10

287

35 Wale Street
Cape Town 8001
P O Box 16548
Vlaeberg 8018
Tel: +27 21 487 2400
Fax: +27 21 487 2188
E-Mail / iE-mail /E-pos:
Ref / Iref / Verw:
Enquiries / Imibuzo / Navrae:
Date / Umhla / Datum:

35 Wale Street
eKapa 8001
Ibhoksi 16548
Vlaeberg 8018
Umnxeba: +27 21 487 2400
Ifeksi: +27 21 487 2188
mabela.satekge@capetown.gov.za

Waalstraat 35
Kaapstad 8001
Posbus 16548
Vlaeberg 8018
Tel: +27 21 487 2400
Faks: +27 21 487 2188

M Satekge
2 June 2003

CITY OF CAPE TOWN
ISIXEKO SASEKAPA
STAD KAAPSTAD

FINANCIAL SERVICES DIRECTORATE:

M Satekge: Director Procurement

Mr Ben Trovato
P O Box 1117
Sea Point
8060

Dear Mr Trovato

Your letter dated 25 May 2003 refers.

Thank you for your comments and interpretation of my speech at the Black Economic Empowerment.

Please find the enclosed donation of R10 which you have offered to me, which regrettable I cannot accept.

Yours Faithfully

M SATEKGE
DIRECTOR: PROCUREMENT

cc: City Manager
        The Mayor
        Mr R McKechnie

C:\Back-up\My Documents\Mabela\Correspondence\Ben Trovato.doc

288

Mrs Louise Joubert
San Wild Wildlife Trust
PO Box 418
Letsitele
0885
Limpopo

Mr Ben Trovato
PO Box 1117
Sea Point
8060

23 May, 2003

Dear Mrs Joubert

Congratulations on acquiring two lions from the Baghdad Zoo! Unfortunately, not everyone is applauding such a noble act. I got into a terrible argument with my neighbour when he said you were nothing but a common looter. Please! If the Americans can confiscate the entire country and get away with it, I cannot imagine how on earth anyone would even notice that a couple of mangy old cats are missing. Besides, anyone with half a brain knows that lions, unlike Iraqis, belong in Africa. Oddly enough, they are like black Americans in that way.

My only concern is that you have Bushmen living on your land. As you know, the San people are renowned for their ability not only to gather but to hunt as well. They can't help it. It is in their blood. From what I have heard, these people can smell a lion from ten kilometres away. Your two newcomers won't stand a chance. For a start, they have spent their whole lives in a cage and will probably walk right up to a San hunting party expecting a handout.

I understand that Bushmen like a drink as much as anyone else and it's my suggestion that you provide the chaps on your land with a regular supply of cane spirits. Prices have come down quite a lot since I was a youngster and I don't think it would cost you very much to keep the community happy. In exchange, the lions get to keep their lives.

I am enclosing R10 for the first bottle of Clipper. Please let me know if you would like me to hold a fundraiser. It shouldn't be too difficult to raise enough for a case or two.

Keep up the good work!

Ben Trovato (Mr).

SAN WILD

WILDLIFE   TRUST
Non profit Organisation Number 011-266

20 June 2003

Mr. Ben Trovato
P.O. Box 1117
<u>SEA POINT</u>
8060

Dear Ben,

I thank you for the R10.00 as well as your concern for the lions. They will be ensured absolute safety from hunters of all walks of life – including that of the San Bushmen. May I point out that the SAN in SanWild by no means indicate that we have San Bushmen in the reserve. SAN is derived from the 1st three letter of SANCTUARY and the WILD is derived from the word WILDLIFE. SanWild therefore bring the term "Sanctuary for Wildlife" together.

I can assure you that from time to time our work might force us to have a drink or two, but all our staff are moderate drinkers and very rarely have the urge to indulge. I have returned herewith you R10.00 in case you might need it for the San in the Kalahari.

Kind and warm regards from SanWild.

Louise

LOUISE JOUBERT

PO Box 418 · Letsitele 0885 · South Africa
Tel & Fax +27 (0) 15 345 1979
sanwild@pixie.co.za
www.sanwild.com.

The Director   Mr Ben Trovato
Men's Clinic International   PO Box 1117
PO Box 784551   Sea Point
Sandton   8060

7 June, 2003

Dear Sir,

I have a problem that I hope you can help me to solve. It is my teenage son.
His voice refuses to break and his mother and I are desperately worried that
he will go through life with a squeaky little voice that is bound to attract the
wrong kind of people. Already he seems to be making more friends who are boys
than are girls. And while this may seem unimportant in an age of licentious
and ambidextrous behaviour, we are deeply concerned that he may never find a
girlfriend while he continues to squeal and shriek.

Most boys blame their mothers for restricting their freedom. But who is Clive
going to blame for limiting the vibration of his vocal chords? Not me, I can tell
you that right now.

I refuse to be blamed for anything. I am not stupid. I have read Freud and Jung.
Well, I haven't, personally. But my neighbour has. And he says that the mother
is always to blame. As a medical man, you know this already. Please don't
misunderstand me. I am not casting aspersions on your mother. You can blame
whoever you want. I don't even know your mother.

But back to my problem. Clive's voice shows no signs of breaking naturally.
And not to put too fine a point on it, we all know that a boy's voice only breaks
once his balls drop. The other day I went into the bathroom while he was taking
a shower and tried to check whether his landing gear was showing signs of
descending. He is a very highly strung lad, so when he caught me looking he
started screaming for his mother and the sound was so disturbing that I had to
leave the house and spend a few hours down at the pub.

I have decided that Clive needs a little manual assistance. I would rather
someone else did the job, but girls avoid him precisely because of his girly
voice. So it is up to his mother or me. When I approached Brenda with the idea
she threatened to call the authorities and have me locked up. So it is up to
me to take matters into my own hands, so to speak. And this is where I need
professional advice. Would you suggest that I wait until he is asleep and then
give the old gonads a good, firm tug?

This should be done as quickly as possible. I do not want to spend years in
therapy. Your advice is essential. If there is a technique of which I am unaware,
please share it with me. But we have to move fast. I can no longer stand the
sound of his voice. I keep thinking I have a daughter. And that is something I
would not wish on my worst enemy.

Please respond with urgency.

Yours truly,

....
Ben Trovato (Mr).

291

MENS CLINIC
INTERNATIONAL
Reg. No.99/15058/07 PR 1547003

HEAD OFFICE
1st Floor
Pentagon House
137 Tenth Street
Parkmore, Sandton
2196
P O Box 784551
Sandton 2146
Tel: (011) 784 2313
Fax: (011) 884 0613
e-mail: mcijb@iafrica.co

4th July 2003

Mr. Ben Trovato
P. O. Box 1117
Sea Point
8060

Dear Sir,

With reference to your letter dated the 7th June 2003 I would like to suggest that you take your son to see your general practitioner as our clinics are not equipped to deal with these kinds of problems. Your general practitioner will be able to examine your son and refer him to a specialist if necessary.

Kind Regards,

Dr. Nevon Ramsunder

The Chief Executive Officer
Durex
SSL International Head Office
Toft Hall
Knutsford WA16 9PD
United Kingdom

Mr Ben Trovato
PO Box 1117
Sea Point 8060
Cape Town
South Africa

7 June, 2003

Dear Sir,

I was putting on one of your condoms on Tuesday night when it broke. Luckily I had a box of them with me. So I put another one on and that one broke too. Then another one broke. And by the time the box was empty my girlfriend had gone to sleep.

Everybody knows that African men are bigger than white people. Actually, I am a white people. But there are parts of me that are very African.

Please, Sir, can I have some more?

Thank you.

....
Ben Trovato (Mr).

SSL International

UK EXPORT

Canute Court
Toft Road
Knutsford
WA16 0NL
Tel: 01565 625000
Fax: 01565 625075

Our ref: RN/MR
18 June 2003

Mr Ben Travato
PO Box 1117
Sea Point
8060
Cape Town
SOUTH AFRICA

Dear Mr Trovato

Thank you for your letter which we found very amusing but at the same time have taken your complaint very seriously. We would be interested to find out what Durex product specifically you used and whether you have kept the packaging. If so please can you return the carton to us so we can report the matter to our factory for investigation.

We are investigating the opportunity to launch a larger Condom for South Africa where even the white people seem to be bigger! We will keep you informed of our plans in this regard.

In the meantime please accept with our compliments a few packs of Durex including a pack of our new Performa Condom which we hope you will enjoy for longer.

Yours sincerely

Rhys Neale

Rhys Neale
Regional Manager – UK Direct Export
Tele 0044 1565 625272

SSL International is a division of
SSL International plc
Registered in England No. 388828.
Registered Office:
Toft Hall, Knutsford, Cheshire England WA16 9PD

The Managing Director
Albex Bleach
PO Box 98
Paardeneiland

Mr Ben Trovato
PO Box 1117
Sea Point
8060

8 June, 2003

Dear Sir,

I was hoping you would be able to sort something out for me. Well, actually, it is more for my gardener than for me.

Sipho has been with me for a long time. But now he says he is tired of being black. He says he is still treated like a second-class citizen and he still lives in a shack in Langa. When I pointed out that democracy had brought with it many other benefits, he asked me to name them. To be honest, I could not think of anything right then. So I had to pretend to get cross with him and storm back into the house shouting about ingratitude and the culture of entitlement that is crippling this once great nation.

Later on he came to me and apologised. But he insists that his life would be much better if he was white. He says he has heard in the township that if you drink a cup of Albex Bleach a day, you will be completely white within six months. I told him that this does not sound right to me. I said it would be far more effective if he bathed in it each day. It makes more sense to bleach the skin from the outside than from the inside. Eventually he began seeing the logic in it and now wants to use my bath for an hour a day because all he has at home is a bucket of cold water. I suggested that he bleach himself in sections, starting with his feet, but he wants to become white all at once. The impetuosity of youth!

What I need to know from you is this. How many cups of Albex Bleach would you recommend he puts in a normal sized bathtub? I doubt that he would want to end up as white as, say, a tourist from Putney. But nor will he want to come out half-done like someone from, say, Manenberg. I know for a fact that he would not want to be mistaken for an NNP supporter. Sipho will be aiming for more of a creamy, off-white colour. But to be honest, I don't know if that takes one cup or ten cups per bath. And how long should he keep up the bathing? I am not a racist, but I would not want everyone to find out that the gardener is using my bath. You know how people talk in this town.

I realise that once Sipho is white he will probably not want to work for me any more. And even if he does, he will be entitled to more money. So either way I lose. But I am not doing this for myself. I am doing this to ensure a brighter future for this land.

I hope to hear from you soon.

....
Ben Trovato (Mr).

From the Desk of Frank Kerbel

78 Short Road, Walmer, Port Elizabeth 6070, South Africa
Tel: +27-(0)41-581 2290 Fax: +27-(0)41-581 4021 cell: +27-(0)83 654 5030
E-mail: frank@kcw.co.za

July 11, 2003

Mr Ben Trovato
P O Box 1117
Sea Point
8060

Dear Mr Trovato

Your previous letter gave me many moments of mirth.   As I have been unable to trace a B Trovato in the Cape Town telephone directory, I am convinced that you are either a friend or family of mine having me on.

So come clean!

Please give me a call on 041 – 4019000

FRANK KERBEL
MANAGING DIRECTOR
ALBION CHEMICAL CO (PTY) LTD

"ALBEX BLEACH IN THE BLACK BOTTLE STAYS STRONGER FOR LONGER"

Advocate Mbuyiseli Madlanga
Amnesty Unit
Private Bag X124
Pretoria
0001

Mr Ben Trovato
PO Box 1117
Sea Point
8060

1 June, 2003

Dear Mr Madlanga,

I understand that an amnesty has been declared for those who contravened exchange controls and income tax laws. If I remember correctly, the amnesty is effective from today. This is great news! In fact, this is the first Sunday in a long time that I have been able to relax with the weekend papers without worrying about an unexpected visit by the boys from the Revenue Service.

I am not sure if this is the correct protocol, but I assume it is acceptable to confess one's crimes and receive absolution via the mail. To be honest, I would rather not have to appear before some or other tribunal. I become very nervous in such situations and often have difficulty in keeping my story straight.

Like many white South Africans, I viewed the 1994 elections with some trepidation. To us, democracy meant losing our houses, jobs and even our lives. Many of us are to this day astounded that nothing of the sort has happened. White South Africans continue to live the lives they have always lived. For this, we thank the black majority. A more compassionate and understanding people you will not come across.

Driven by a fear of the unknown, many of us liquidated our assets and invested the money offshore. My neighbour (who I won't name as he suspects the whole amnesty deal is a trap) made several trips to London with aluminium flight cases stuffed with R100 notes. He managed to get at least five million rand across in less than a year. I, too, was among those who violated South Africa's draconian exchange control laws. But if you don't mind I would rather avoid providing you with numbers. It's a bit embarrassing.

I need to know one or two things from you. If I receive amnesty, can I leave my money where it is? There doesn't seem much point in being let off only to watch your hard-earned dosh lying about in the local bank getting devalued by the hour. Secondly, if I am refused amnesty, can I leave my money where it is?

I am enclosing a small gift as a token of my goodwill and an indication of my willingness to cooperate with the authorities, i.e. you.

I will be watching my postbox anxiously for the next few weeks.

Thanking you in anticipation of amnesty.

Yours truly,

....
Ben Trovato (Mr).

CA$H GIVEN
R10

297

Adv. Mbuyiseli Madlanga
Amnesty Unit
Private Bag X124
Pretoria
0001

Mr Ben Trovato
PO Box 1117
Sea Point
8060

28 June, 2003

Dear Sir,

I have made a terrible mistake.

You may recall receiving a letter from me dated the 1st of June in which I confessed to having salted away enormous sums of money in overseas bank accounts. None of this is true. I suffer from an illness similar to Tourette's Syndrome. The doctors are baffled. I once confessed to being the second gunman on the grassy knoll, but when the authorities investigated they found that I have never even been to America. It also emerged that I was only ten years old at the time of the shooting.

At first I was pleased that you had chosen to ignore my first letter. But then I got very, very scared. My neighbour told me that your men are probably watching the house right now waiting for you to give them the signal to move in. I have not been outside in three weeks and food is running low. The electricity has been cut off and the cat is sick. I beg you, end the siege before it is too late.

I am enclosing another R10 as an act of good faith. I feel so much better knowing that this horrible misunderstanding has been sorted out. There is just one last thing I need to get off my chest. Who can I speak to about the murder of Rick Turner?

Peace be with you.

....
Ben Trovato (Mr).

AMNESTY UNIT
REPUBLIC OF SOUTH AFRICA
Private Bag X124, Pretoria, 0001   Tel: +27 12 315 5420, Fax: +27 12 315 5530

24 July 2003

Mr B Trovato
P.O. Box 1117
Sea Point
8060

Dear Mr Trovato

We cannot keep on corresponding with you if all you are bent on doing is trifling with the unit. Your R10.00 note is returned. Contrary to what you say in your second paragraph I responded to your first letter and returned your first R10.00 note.

Should you continue sending us money, we shall donate it to a charity organization of the unit's choice.

Yours faithfully

MR MADLANGA SC
CHAIPERSON

Other titles by Jacana

New South African Keywords
Nick Shepherd & Steven Robins (editors)

Cyril Ramaphosa
Anthony Butler

The ANC Underground
Raymond Suttner

Stoep Zen
Antony Osler

Till We Can Keep an Animal
Megan Voysey-Braig